THE DAYS

OF THE

DOG STAR

By

Christine Blandford

Dog Star is a nickname for Sirius (from the Greek 'glowing' or 'scorching), the brightest star in the night sky. Its first appearance in late July heralds the 'dog says', a period which lasts throughout August, in other words the hottest part of the year.

SUMMER

Wash your gullet with wine for the Dog-Star returns

with the heat of summer searing a thirsting earth.

Cicadas cry softly under high leaves, and pour down

shrill song incessantly from under their wings.

The artichoke blooms, and women are warm and wanton –

but men lean and limp for the burning Dog-Star

parches their brains and knees.

Alcaeus – Greek poet. Born c. 620 B.C.

Translated by Willis Barnstone (1962)

CONTENTS

Chapter 1

Only when she sat down in the departure lounge past all the check points did the full significance of the decision, taken on the spur of the moment, hit her. From now on she was trapped in a giant conveyor belt, allowing the traffic to move only in the outward direction. 'I've been a fool to give up everything for a holiday,' she thought.

She looked around, relieved to see that the surroundings were reassuring, if somewhat dull. Businessmen in suits shook out their creased newspapers from those characteristic black briefcases every executive had to have if advertisements were to be believed. People drifted slowly in and out of the duty-free shops and the bar. She looked at her immediate neighbour: a swarthy man, an Arab or a Turk perhaps, who was holding a screaming child he had caught after its numerous attempts to upset a tall, cylindrical ashtray. The child now lay rigid in the man's arms, emitting outraged howls, waving his little hands smeared with cigarette ash. Above her wafted a continuous hum of the ventilating system pumping air into the building from which they were all too soon to be catapulted into space. More people were coming in, filling the plastic seats, their colour harmonised tastefully with the carpet and the lounge walls, the result of the expensive efforts of interior designers. She absorbed these comings and goings idly, the images forgotten as soon as they were formed. A woman with lots of packages passed through her field of vision, making her wonder how she managed to get that amount of hand luggage through the control point. Another woman sat opposite, dressed in black. Black jumper, black straight skirt over large hips: a Greek peasant maybe? She was sitting with her knees

1

apart and Joanna couldn't help noticing her stockings only reached slightly above the knees. Another Greek came along, a short, dark man in a hat, carrying a small, cardboard suitcase. No doubt about it, they were to be her companions on her flight to Athens. There was a group of young people who, judging by their cabin luggage tickets, must have booked their flight through the same tour operator. The girls looked bluish-pink and uncomfortable in their summer clothes, as if they were wearing them for the first time this year. Joanna felt equally dowdy, but shrugged her shoulders. It didn't matter any more. It may have mattered in her other life, but not any more. That life had now reached the end of the chapter.

I didn't want it to end, but it happened just the same. From now on, it's just a question of a few formalities to sign, and it will be all over. Forget it? Of course, I'll forget it, I'm forgetting it already, aren't I? How can I ever forget it? I am here to forget. Everybody said a change will do me good, so that's why I am here. I'll forget Alex, forget the divorce, meet new people, have a break. I might even get myself a Greek lover.

She wasn't sure whether having a Greek lover was to be an act of defiance, a luxury item, or a symbol of her liberation.

There was a commotion all around as her flight was called, and a stewardess appeared in the doorway. Joanna repressed a feeling of irrational disappointment because the girl was not particularly pretty. Weren't they supposed to be pretty, chosen for their looks? Following her to the plane, the passengers were met by another stewardess as they walked down the aisle towards their seats. This one had a dazzling smile, fresh and spontaneous but, like a picture on wallpaper, repeated endlessly. Joanna took her place by the window, carefully placed the plastic bag with the duty-free whisky and cigarettes on the shelf above and, having, composed her facial expression to a bored *déjà-vu* which belied the anxiety she always felt when flying, she rummaged in the pocket of the seat in front for the safety instructions.

What was she doing here on this plane, anyway? There was no chance of survival, not the slightest if anything went wrong. In a car or a train, it wouldn't matter, but in an aeroplane! Well, they say the best-selling novels at the airports are all about air disasters. Joanna sat rigid, not letting herself relax, surprised to see that everything around her seemed to be under control. The engines hummed evenly, the captain welcomed the passengers, told them about the sunny weather awaiting at their destination, and a placid queue had already formed outside the toilets.

Having been served a meal, she surprised herself by eating it all. Her feeling of panic slowly gave way to a pleasant anticipation of mild adventure ahead. For someone who was ready to back away and flee, or possibly even die in an air disaster, it wasn't a bad turn-around.

Athens. How long ago was it since she had last visited Athens? She tried to count the years. The first time must have been by car when they had been married for a year.

Their wedding was marred somewhat by the absence of her side of the family. She was the only child of a broken marriage. Her father divorced her mother when she was still a toddler and emigrated to Canada with his new wife. Her mother died unexpectedly, the result of an infection in the hospital ward where she went for some minor procedure. There were no aunts or uncles as her mother, too, had been an only child.

Alex was driving from Patras where the ferry from Italy had deposited them. It was already getting dark as they drove towards Athens, the backdrop of the mountains turning from mauve to dark blue in the setting sun. They had passed little villages where the cafés (which she only later learned to call *taverna*), lit by rows of coloured electric bulbs hanging on poles and trees around them, stood out among the rows of dark houses. In their light, she could see spits and barbecues of rotating pieces of meat, as well as men's faces as they sat at the little tables. Always men, hardly any women. These little oases were quickly swallowed by the ensuing darkness. The lorries they overtook were also lit by a great number of lights. There was none of the restraint of two lights in front and two at the back. These were veritable Christmas tree decorations.

Gradually, the traffic increased as they approached Athens. It wasn't the Athens of Pericles and the grey-eyed goddess Athene that met them in that warm, velvet night, but a bustling, living city of dark, swarthy Greeks. There was music blaring from the loudspeakers, throbbing with strange rhythms played on unfamiliar instruments, and neon signs advertised things in a strange alphabet. They soon found themselves in a whirlpool of street vendors, women in black, bad drivers and congested traffic. Oh, that wasn't the Hellas of the inspired orators or philosophers, of the people who dared to challenge the gods, claiming man to be the measure of all things! Were there still any descendants of those golden-haired heroes of antiquity among those crowds? She slept badly that night, little prepared to accept the ravages of history. Later she tried to sweep aside the modern Greece and look for nymphs and maenads in every field, under every gnarled olive tree, more prepared to meet the god Pan than a shepherd looking after goats.

On their first morning in Athens, they breakfasted in a little café, or rather *taverna*, where a man in a white apron put glasses of water in front of them as soon as they sat down, before taking the order. He came back with little plates on which a pat of butter was smothered in spoonfuls of delicious honey which she mopped up with fresh Greek bread, bread that tasted like no other bread, in other words, heavenly.

Greece surprised her with a variety of colours – a heady mixture of deep red and mauve sunsets, the dazzling white of the villages under a blue sky, the pink and orange of the sunrises. She remembered reading somewhere that the purity of air was something special to Greece, that it had almost a tangible quality. This, to her, was not so much true of light as of shade, which was concrete and smooth like a stone. The pure, crystalline light only made things more real.

She remembered visiting a place with Alex somewhere in the Peloponnese in early autumn. Their fancy took them to search for a medieval castle rather than an ancient monument. Having at last found a gate with a coat of arms embedded in a wall above it, they wandered into the grounds. Not much remained of the original structure, just the gate, some walls, paving stones, a crumbling watch tower. The area within the walls was divided into plots, each surrounding a little holiday home. In one of them, two elderly ladies in soft straw hats were picking almonds from the trees growing by the veranda. As they went past their fence, muttering a perfunctory greeting, one of the ladies looked up and, stretching her hand, gave her a handful of almonds, saying "Welcome". The almonds had soft, greenish outer skins hiding hard shells. Looking back now, those soft, green almonds in the hand of the elderly lady distilled the essence of the serenity of that golden autumn she had had with Alex, now to be consigned to the past. Alex, now a happy father after his "one-night stand". Where did that leave her?

She was woken up from her reverie by the voice of the stewardess telling the passengers to stop smoking and fasten their seatbelts in preparation for landing. This time, the city of Athens did not spread itself before her eyes. From her window, she could only see the blue expanse of the sea, so near she felt she could almost touch the waves. It was her fear of flying again, giving her silly ideas; of course, they couldn't be that low. But, as she was to notice later, it wasn't just her imagination playing tricks – the runway was practically on the sea. The wheels touched down, the engines roared as they sped along the runway, and finally they came to a stop. She was in Greece again! The warm air rushed in through the open doors to welcome her.

After they had parted, Joanna had felt split into two. One part was on the outside, talking, eating, walking, while the inside one shrivelled. When the two merged, she would re-live the final scene when Alex said *à propos* of nothing as they were having an evening glass of wine: "I never told you. I had a one-night stand some time back. She's just told me she's going to have a baby", then added with a smirk "Actually, I'm quite looking forward to being a father. I'll be moving out at the end of the week."

Joanna was sick for days. Eventually, she forced herself to get in touch with a solicitor recommended by a friend. His detached voice and the impression he gave that hers was one of many similar cases he was handling had given her a measure of self-control. That night, she cried for the first time and felt better. At that point she decided to take a break, go away, take a holiday. Flicking idly through a yachting magazine in the solicitor's waiting room, her eyes had fallen on an advertisement. *Cook/girl Friday required for an extended cruise of Eastern Mediterranean. Forty foot yacht berthed in Athens. Experience not essential. Will pay travel and expenses. Write to PO box … etc.* This sounded good! It might suit her. She had sailed a few times before and enjoyed it in spite of the damp, cool English climate. But this was the Mediterranean, a much warmer, sunnier place altogether. Also, an added opportunity to see Greece again. Plus, the terms were good, almost too good – both passage and expenses paid! She answered the advert without much hope. It was bound to be oversubscribed …

It had been a pleasant surprise to find a letter bearing an Athens' postage stamp lying on the doormat almost by return of post. It was signed by Simon Ratcliffe, skipper of the ketch *Zainda*. He and three other persons in his party required a cook and general help, light duties only. The intention was to island-hop around the Greek side of the Aegean, with the possibility of touching the Turkish coast and going on to Istanbul. He needed someone quickly because the party had already assembled, and the cook who was to join them had dropped out at the last moment. As they were anxious to get under way, he would be obliged if she could let them know by the end of the week if she was able to commit.

Joanna had exactly three days to inform her employers and wind up her affairs. Her boss, a small, shy man in his fifties who, whenever Joanna saw him, always scuttled along the corridor as if afraid someone might assail him before he could reach the sanctuary of his office, was surprisingly sympathetic. His bolt hole was sparsely furnished, with stacks of publications piled on the desk providing, or so it seemed, an additional barricade behind which he would look at his "assailants" above his half-moon spectacles. In fact, he had already become worried by her recent diminished performance and listlessness but wasn't sure how to tell her to pull herself together. The news saved him a lot of embarrassment and his face registered relief as he listened. He agreed that Joanna could take an extended, unpaid holiday on the proviso that there might not be a job to come back to if a permanent replacement had been found in the meantime.

There were no regrets on her side, either. After years at a university reading classics, she had taken on the job reluctantly. It seemed nobody was impressed by her qualifications, even the teaching profession had its glut of classical scholars. Finally, a small firm of publishers dealing with technical literature offered her the post of technical writer. However, technology bored her, she simply could not arouse sufficient interest to write about its various aspects. The job was disappointing and so were the people with whom she had to work. Having spent four years at a university, she was used to having intelligent, stimulating people around her. When this turned out not to be the case, at first it had made her impatient, then simply bored. There was only one girl, Marjorie, with whom she had made friends. Marjorie was the boss's secretary, though she liked to call herself "personal assistant to the managing director". They spent their lunch hours together, Joanna listening to Marjorie's endless prattle, mainly revolving round men and clothes. It irked her that Marjorie, who had left school at sixteen, was on a higher salary. Still,

Joanna would not let it stand in the way of their friendship, such as it was, and was glad of her lunchtime company.

The job, unsatisfying as it was, provided the money to pursue the interests in her life – classics and travel. Her love of travel bordered on compulsion. Alex used to laugh at her, saying she was possessed with a pilgrim spirit. Having just turned twenty nine, a feeling of having flitted her youth away had now been made worse by the marriage fiasco. She and Alex had embarked on their marriage as an arrangement in recognition of social conventions, on the proviso of no children to hamper them in pursuing their interests. Well, *that* failed. Where did it go wrong? Was she in some ways to blame? After all, it takes two to make a marriage and two to break it. *Right, now,* she told herself, *let's put it all that behind.* Greece could be the beginning of a new chapter.

Athens. If she'd been asked to paint the city, she'd have covered the canvas with streaks of the dull yellow and marble white of the Parthenon to which she had in the past made a pilgrimage in the spirit of mystical concentration. It was possible to eliminate in one's mind the crowds of milling tourists, filling the gaps in the edifices ravaged by the passage of time in her imagination. She could almost see the presiding statue of the goddess Athene by the celebrated sculptor Phidias, and place the Elgin marbles in the mutilated spaces. The dull yellow was the colour of the streets and the dust of modern life. That had to be ignored, it was a pilgrimage to the past. How would Athens appear to her now?

She followed the patient group of 'her' passengers onto the bus taking them to the airport building, then past passport and customs control. She anxiously scanned the crowd waiting at the barriers. A young man, casually dressed, waving a card marked *Zainda* in big letters detached himself from the crowd and waved. Tall, dark wavy hair, black-rimmed glasses, his sensitive face stretched into a huge grin which made him look very young. He could be not more than twenty.

'Hello. You must be Joanna.'

'How did you know? Oh, of course, the photograph.'

'I'm David,' he said and looked at her sideways, as if absorbing her appearance: the tall, slim figure, the blonde hair brushed back into a pony tail. 'The photograph doesn't do you justice.'

A conquest so soon? No, he's just being polite.

He took the kit bag she'd bought specially for the trip (after considerable trouble finding it in her local shops) and led the way to the taxi. The smell, the bustle and the traffic gave her a sense of light-headedness, enhanced by the transfer from one world to another in a mere three hours. Her body was still in the temperate climate, getting ready for tea, whereas her mind was trying to accept the heat and the traffic, whilst taking in the impression of the busy streets. This young man intruded on her thoughts, though he fell silent as soon as they drove away, with only a side glance from time to time, blushing whenever she caught his eye. *Oh dear, how is this going to work out, confined as we shall be to a relatively small yacht?* Too late for doubts now. Her curiosity about what to expect prompted her to ask him a question.

'Who else is there apart from Mr. Ratcliffe and yourself?'

'Well, Mr. Ratcliffe is Simon and he's my uncle. There's his girlfriend, Brenda, and another chap, Colin, a friend of Simon's. With you on board there'll be five.'

David did not elaborate further, and they continued to sit in silence for the rest of the journey.

By the time they reached the harbour, the sun was sinking behind the horizon, leaving a glowing smudge of pink and orange on the darkening sky. Neon signs were lighting up the city, imparting a carnival air. Smells of spice, barbecued meat and warm city smells said "Welcome". An absurd feeling of elation bubbled inside Joanna as she followed David along the pontoons, while he manfully carried her kit bag.

The yachts in the harbour swayed and squeaked gently on their mooring lines, dazzling in their variety. A breeze raised a noise like a distant calling of geese caused by the halyards hitting the metal masts. The noises died down, only to be raised again by another breath of wind wafting through the harbour. Somewhere in the distance, a rusty squeak of gangplank wheels could be heard rubbing against the pontoons. Joanna slowed down, trying to take it all in and nearly lost David in the darkness which, in this part of the world, came on suddenly. At last, he stopped in front of a white, fibreglass ketch.

'That's her,' he said, mopping his brow.

Joanna looked up and saw the name *Zainda* registered in Greece painted on the stern. This was going to be her holiday home for the next six weeks. Two metal masts swayed gently against the sky. The main mast was covered with blue cotton tarpaulin, laced securely round the boom. The aft deck was slightly raised to accommodate the aft cabin and there was a deep, centre cockpit from which two doors opened, one forward to the companion way and the main cabin, the other to the aft one.

As they stepped on board, a man in his forties appeared from the main cabin. He was tall, his sandy-coloured hair parted to one side, a long, sallow face, and an air of a carefully maintained languid detachment. When he spoke, to introduce himself as Simon, his accent confirmed a public school background. Only the earlier mention of a girlfriend by David betrayed that he must be capable of an emotional involvement.

'Ah, yes, Joanna, is it? Had a good flight?' he asked, not waiting for an answer. He behaved as if her appearance allowed him to cross out an item on his to-do list.

'Hello,' she said, stretching out her hand. 'Yes, I am Joanna.' It wasn't taken.

'Sorry, I have oil on my hands, been trying to fix the engine.' He turned to David. 'Had a mechanic here all day and it's still not fixed. A bit of a bore, that,' then checked himself, remembering her presence. 'I don't need to tell you to remove your shoes before coming on board. David will show you to your cabin. Now, if you'll excuse me …' With that, he disappeared into the darkness, carrying a piece of metal in his hand.

Joanna followed David in silence, stepping carefully as they made their way to the main cabin. The whole place was in an incredible mess. The cockpit floor was open, revealing the engine, an oil drum, and all sorts of containers and coiled lines. The cabin inside was stuffy and dark. Smouldering in a corner was a small paraffin lamp, a replica of an old ship lamp, casting a feeble light. The walls were inlaid with wooden panelling as if to make up for the lack of wood outside. To one side was a galley with a gimballed stove, a small sink and a fridge below. Opposite the galley was the captain's table, covered with charts and sheets of paper. All kinds of electronic gadgets and controls were fixed above it. Joanna was able to recognise a radio, but it was too dark to figure out the rest. On a small shelf lay various rolled-up flags, ensigns and books, amongst which Joanna recognised the Reed's Almanac and the Mediterranean Pilot.

In the middle of the cabin was a table and a surrounding seating arrangement. It was cluttered with tools, scattered among the remains of a meal which had clearly been eaten some time ago. There was also a quarter berth behind the chart table. A door at the far end led to the fo'csle with the so-called heads – the toilet and shower – and two berths on either side partitioned by a thin wall. David threw her kitbag on the bunk in one of them. 'I sleep opposite,' he pointed to the dividing wall. 'Try and find your way around, if you can. Must go and help Simon. I think he's in a bit of a state.'

Joanna thought that on the contrary Simon sounded very relaxed, but perhaps there were some understated signs of inward turmoil, obvious only to David. She peered around in the semi-darkness and decided to investigate the bathroom facilities, but got up too quickly, bumping her head on the ceiling. 'Damn!' she swore, feeling for a bump through her hair, at the same time accepting it as a kind of christening, a sort of "Welcome to life on board". The tiny toilet contained a complicated set of pumps for flushing the loo, a washbasin and a shower. Another door opened to a cupboard completely filled with oilskins and life jackets.

Nobody came to the boat that evening. When Simon and David returned, the three of them had a rather silent meal in the local taverna before retiring for the night.

Chapter 2

Joanna was woken up by the sun making playful patterns on her face. It passed through the hatch, making the little cabin even hotter. Her mouth felt parched, her throat swollen, her memories of last night in the taverna wrapped in a haze. Simon had kept the conversation confined to the technical details of engine failure, all. directed at David. Obviously, he had not been too impressed by her, thought Joanna, and only maintained the minimum of politeness required to convey good manners. She winced at the prospect of having to spend six weeks in his company. However, she was too tired to brood over it that evening as his languid voice droned above her head like the sea washing over a stone on a beach.

Now she was splashing cold water on her face and hands in the tiny toilet, trying to work out the intricacies of the loo pump. Emerging into the cockpit, the heat and the sunlight almost stunned her. She forgot it could be this hot. Simon was already working, rubbing engine parts with a dirty rag. A man of dark complexion, in blue overalls, the mechanic on whom the hopes and frustrations of the *Zainda* crew centred, was bending over the engine. His English was obviously not very good because Simon kept repeating his sentences in increasingly louder tones, as if talking to a deaf man, punctuating them with any language he could think of.

'She cuts out, no go, kaput, water doesn't come out, no water, *ohi nero*,' he kept repeating in exasperation.

The man, still bending over the engine, wiped his hands on the dirty overalls and mumbled, 'You got spanner, big spanner, like so?' gesturing with his hands the colour of slate.

'Ah, here you are,' Simon said and looked up, just noticing Joanna and obviously wanting her out of the way. 'We normally have breakfast in the café where we had our meal last night. When you come back you might like to tidy the place up a bit. We should be leaving this afternoon, if everything goes well, that is,' he said, pointing at the engine.

Leaving in the afternoon meant night sailing. For the first day of the cruise, it might not be a good idea, she decided, munching a roll speckled with sesame seeds and drinking cold coffee from a cardboard container. Her gaze fell on the harbour in the daylight with renewed curiosity. Gone was the mellow atmosphere of the night before. Now, everything was sharp and shiny in the glare of the sun, even the dust seemed to glitter in the harsh light. Already the heat made her sticky and dirty. She went back to the boat. David was nowhere to be seen.

'I forgot to ask you if you wanted anything, so I brought you this,' she said to Simon, handing him a cartoon of coffee. His face stretched into a sort of acknowledgement as he mumbled, 'Thanks.'

I think he's made of rubber; I don't think he's human at all, reflected Joanna. They were joined by David who looked Joanna up and down with an appreciative glance. Joanna became conscious of her lack of tan – her long, pale legs stood no comparison with some of the girls she saw lounging on the yachts on the way to the café. Still, it felt better to be with David than having to put up with Simon's rubbery indifference.

She began by tidying the cabins, sorting out the mess the two men had ignored. Having swept, washed and put things away with a feeling of smug superiority (women could never make a mess like this), it made her wonder if the satisfaction derived from this thought was an adequate compensation for the sheer hard work it required. She was wet with perspiration, dirty and thirsty. There was only lukewarm mineral water to drink, and it tasted vile. The fridge wasn't working. It could only be switched on when the battery was charged, but as the engine wasn't working, it wasn't charging. All this was explained by David; they didn't expect it to function as a fridge any time soon. Just then, it was used as an extra cupboard full of cardboard boxes which, on closer inspection, turned out to be dehydrated food packets. The suspiciously colourful pictures of mouth-watering dishes on the wrappers were bound to hide their tastelessness which no amount of cooking could change into a decent meal. Was she supposed to eat as well as cook them? The cupboard next to the fridge contained an assortment of glossy packets of powdered soups. A greenish powder oozed from one of them, leaving a trickle of sticky stuff on the shelves. She threw the offending packet into the dustbin. *There goes the asparagus soup, and there go I. I'd rather starve.*

In the afternoon, even more sweaty and dirty than ever, shoulders and skin sore from too much sun, she went down to the cabin to put on a soothing lotion. There was a sound of footsteps on the gangplank. A man was already on the aft deck, bending down to remove his shoes before throwing his kitbag into the cockpit as if it had no weight at all. That must be the other crew member they were waiting for. As Joanna watched him through the hatch in the cabin, her conscious mind slowly registered that she was looking at a very good-looking man. Tall, thick hair, stubble, deep-set eyes the colour of bleached blue, age about thirty-two, maybe thirty-five. At the same time, she became conscious of her dismally dishevelled dirty appearance. That's how Cinderella must have felt when the prince found her in the kitchen. First impressions are most important. Trust my luck. Oh well, there was nothing for it but to come out.

'Hello, I'm afraid the skipper's not here. I'm Joanna.'

'Colin. One of the party.' His voice was low and rather pleasant, the smile making him even more handsome.

'Please make yourself at home. Simon and David shouldn't be

long; they went with the mechanic to repair the engine.'

'I'll leave my things and come back later.' He gave her a perfunctory glance, put his shoes on again and disappeared.

I am not surprised – I probably stink as well. She grabbed a towel and went under the shower.

In the evening, the whole party assembled in the cockpit. Simon took a taxi to the airport and came back with Brenda, a thin blonde in her early twenties, heavy eye make-up, curly blonde hair, buck teeth making her mouth permanently open. She said little throughout the evening, but laughed a lot showing those teeth and a pink gum. Joanna was surprised. She had tried to imagine what kind of a woman Simon would be associated with, expecting someone incredibly good-looking, sophisticated, mature, a model, perhaps. Instead, here was this conventionally pretty girl with prominent teeth, almost half his age.

David, sitting in the cockpit, legs stretched across the seats opposite, cradling a can of beer, greeted Brenda with cold familiarity.

'Hi, Brenda, had a good journey?' Without waiting for an answer, he stood up to get himself another beer.

Colin arrived moments later. He was already tanned, she noticed, so perhaps hadn't come straight from England. His movements, compact and athletic, reminded her of the springiness of a large cat. She found herself increasingly conscious of his smile which lent warmth to the otherwise rather severe features. However, that evening she was firmly monopolised by David who stayed close all the time and sat between her and Colin at the restaurant.

The engine had not been repaired in time for the afternoon sail. Thus, the departure was postponed till the following morning. Meanwhile, they dined *souvlaki* the Greek skewered meat, salad with plenty of olives and crumbled cheese, and they drank a lot of wine. In the course of conversation, she managed to find out that David had just graduated with a not very good degree in a subject chosen by his father. Colin admitted to a spell in the armed forces, but did not elaborate further. The moon shone high in the sky as they walked back to the boat, making silvery patterns on the water, glistening between the anchored yachts. She looked around and swore she could see several rats scuttling near the litter bins. Or were they cats? She was too drowsy to care. Brenda and Simon eventually disappeared in the aft cabin after a ritual which involved a lot of giggling and bottom pinching that others pretended to ignore. Joanna reached the bunk in a dream-like state and fell asleep even before her head touched the pillow.

Chapter 3

It had been a hectic morning. Joanna was struggling with a hangover, at the same time as trying to figure out how much fresh food to buy for the journey. She caught up with Simon and Colin on the way to the mechanic's workshop.

'How far are we going, Simon? Where would be the next place to buy fresh provisions?'

Simon hesitated, then turned to Colin. 'We're going to Kea, isn't that right, Colin?'

Colin nodded. Joanna was surprised. How come Simon was consulting him about where to go? The hesitancy in his manner made her wonder who was the *real* skipper, but then it was none of her business. She soon forgot about it on the way to the shops and the market. The sun was high and it was already very hot.

The long, crusty loaves of freshly baked bread made her wonder if there was anything in the world that could smell more delicious. Laden with lemonade bottles, fruit and bread, she made her way slowly back to the harbour. David disappeared on last minute errands after gulping a mug of instant coffee. There was nobody to help carry the shopping across the gangplank. She wobbled half-way, terrified of dropping the bags into the water, and only just made it to the aft deck. While struggling with the bags, the door of the aft cabin opened and Brenda came out. Tussled and without her makeup, she looked pale, yellow and blotchy in the sunlight. Joanna wondered again how she had managed to attract Simon, or anybody else for that matter. Still, she was far from sorry for Simon. If that's how he likes his women, good luck to him, none of her business. Her irritation grew as Brenda did not offer to help; instead, she watched calmly as one of the bags split, scattering the contents on the deck, and a rolling bottle of lemonade crashed into the cockpit. On the contrary, Brenda seemed to take Joanna's duties as cook and Girl Friday quite literally.

'You couldn't fix me a drink, could you, Joanna?' she asked, watching Joanna carefully stack the food away so that nothing would roll out during the passage on a heeling boat. Joanna was torn between settling this matter once and for all by telling her she could get it herself, but there was some uncertainty about where her duties lay. She let it pass this once.

'What would you like? There's orange juice and there's lemonade.'

'Orange juice would be fine,' sighed Brenda, revealing a significant cleavage (*a boob job?*) through a loosely tied kimono-style jacket that she wore as a dressing gown. It was white satin and had an embroidered black tiger biting its tail on the back.

'Ugh, it's warm,' she shuddered.

'The fridge isn't working. We have to charge the batteries first, and we can't do that without the engine working.'

'Oh God, how dreadful.' Brenda gave a visible shiver of disgust as she put the plastic cup down on the table and lit a cigarette. She gave the cabin another look, then, picking her way delicately past the shopping bags as a cat might round puddles of water, went back to the aft cabin.

The rest of the party re-assembled around noon. The engine had been put back together and at last it was working.

'We'll have lunch on the way,' said Simon with firmness in his voice. 'We're late as it is. Everything ready, Joanna?'

She nodded. A trial run would reveal all the things she had no doubt forgotten, though she couldn't think of anything she had missed. Brenda was sunbathing on the aft deck in a scanty, yellow bikini which blended with the colour of her skin, making her look naked. She stretched her skinny legs and waved 'Hello there!', the tone of welcome reserved only for Simon. Simon grunted, tightening something on the engine. Colin and David busied themselves with the mooring lines tied to the pontoons. They jumped on board as soon as the engine showed signs of life. A looker-on threw in the remaining line tied to a bollard. They fended off the yacht next to them and slowly putt-putted their way out of the harbour.

As they wove their way between the moored yachts, the sea changed colour from molten lead to bluish-green. Once beyond the outer walls of the harbour, it stretched out, covered in small wavelets glittering in the sunshine. Simon was at the helm, David on the fore deck coiling the mooring lines as *Zainda* met her first wave and dipped in a curtsey on meeting the sea. At last, thought Joanna, the open sea.

The breeze soon picked up enough for Simon to suggest they might put up the sails. David and Colin sprang into action, while Joanna kept looking at the sea, the fenders she was meant to stow still in her hand, fascinated by those depths so full of colour, at once green then blue then pewter grey. She could never have enough of the sea – applying for this job had been the right thing. The waves heaved up from the depths, ran towards the hull licking its sides, only to disappear underneath and out on the other side. The boat heeled over as soon as the sails caught the wind. With the engine silent at last, they moved, propelled by the force of the wind on the sails, in supreme harmony with the elements.

Her moment of rapture was shattered by a shower of sail ties David dropped into the cockpit. She caught them, stowed them and put away the fenders. As the boat heeled even more, she saw Brenda slide to one side as she tried to catch hold of something to stop her. She gave a squeal, one arm flung out getting hold of the sealed square box which contained the life raft while the other let go of a towel. It flew away, but luckily caught on the life lines. Rule number one: always make everything fast while sailing! Joanna hoped Simon would say so, but he only stretched out his hand to help Brenda into the cockpit and said nothing, looking as if he had expected something like this to happen. Colin and David took no notice. They were talking in low voices on the fore deck, tidying up, oiling hunks on the jib, coiling various lines, and doing all those little jobs that on a boat never seem to end.

Joanna watched Colin standing on the bows as they sliced through the foam and spray, silhouetted against the sun, spanner in hand. He could have been a god, an ancient Greek god, riding the waves as he moved with the rising and dipping bow. His teeth gleamed as he smiled, perhaps, like her, acknowledging the magic of the sea. Watching him, she could feel a sensation rising within her, but wasn't sure whether it was exhilaration or an ache. *Oh Alex, where did we go so wrong? And now you are an expectant father, and here's me, eyeing handsome men!*

That moment should have lasted for ever, but life, unlike fiction, does not provide fade-outs or breaks, and instead continues uninterrupted in its own whimsical way. After a time, somebody decided it was time to eat; there was bread to be cut for sandwiches, salad to be prepared, drinks to be passed round and then everything to be cleared away.

The sun was already setting when they were able to pick out the columns of Poseidon's temple at Cap Sounion. This temple, remembered Joanna, was the ancient sailors' last landmark before they pointed their "well found" ships into the unknown sea, and also the first to be seen after a long voyage to tell them they were nearly home.

The wind blew stronger down the Macronisi channel and they had to tack. Again, it was David and Colin who did all the work. Joanna sat watching them idly from the cockpit. While those two seemed to revel in the physical exercise, she dreamt of Greek gods with golden hair and magnificent bodies. She stole a glance at Colin then firmly made herself look at something else. Her eyes rested on Brenda. On her, all that magic was wasted. She was pasty-coloured and moaned, holding her head with both hands. Simon was propelling her gently to the leeward side of the boat, where she hung limply over the lifelines and was sick.

It was dark when they approached the island of Kea. The wind dropped to almost nothing after sunset. Somewhere in the distance the lights of the Kea beacon winked, patting the dark sea with cat's paws of light. In the deepening darkness which felt almost like velvet, nobody stirred to switch on the engine as *Zainda* came almost to a halt in the dying wind. Even Simon looked pensive in the glow of his pipe. The peace was shattered by a moan from Brenda:

'My God, how far is it to the harbour?'

Chapter 4

Kea. It had not changed much since the last time she saw it, in that other closed chapter of her life. The sweet smell of rosemary and other aromatic plants wafted in through an open hatch into her cabin. Joanna looked out, taking in the scene before her eyes. Everything was still as she remembered it – the excavated grounds of the newly discovered ancient site, the beach and, further out the quay and the houses lining the shore. *Zainda* was under anchor in the bay, swinging gently. The sound made by the wavelets rippling against the hull and the creaking of lines was all that could be heard. Outside, in the morning sunshine, silence was perfect.

She went into the main cabin and found nobody there. Up in the cockpit David mending something. On seeing her, his face lit up.

'Slept well?'

'Mmmmm, marvellously. Where is everybody?'

'Colin took the dinghy out somewhere,' he waved his hand vaguely in the air. 'Simon and Brenda are still asleep.'

'Well,' she said, feeling the warmth of the sun on her face, 'how about a swim before breakfast?'

'Good idea,' he rose with alacrity.

She changed quickly into a bikini and went on the foredeck. David's eyes lit up. He followed closely, almost rubbing himself against her. Joanna became conscious of his body and the few hairs on the chest.

'Race you,' she said, feeling hemmed in by his presence; he made her feel conscious of having very little on.

'All right,' he stopped and smiled. 'You go first.'

'OK. To the opposite side, there …' She stepped over the life lines. 'Ready?' Her body made a graceful arc as it hit the water. Its coolness gave her a delicious shock. After surfacing, she began to swim with long, measured strokes. David followed, puffing and splashing. She was seized with a desire to be left alone, of not having to share this exquisite moment with a stranger, and began to swim quickly away from him. But it only had an opposite effect as he puffed and spluttered, trying to keep up. She was beginning to be embarrassed by this, what she was beginning to recognise as juvenile infatuation. What sort of forces operated between men and women, causing an attraction to one without the slightest effort on the part of the other, she wondered. There was nothing she could do about David apart from not give him the slightest encouragement. *He's bound to snap out of it.* In the meantime, for the sake of a peaceful and frictionless holiday, it was better to ignore the whole thing the best she could.

When they swam back to the boat, Simon and Colin were already there, bending over the chart table. Simon was measuring distances along the chart with callipers, while Colin was fiddling with a ship-to-shore radio. It emitted loud groans and whistles to the accompaniment of background crackling sounds. She went past them, dripping wet, cheerfully calling out, 'Breakfast will soon be ready.'

Colin turned round, his casual glance changing to a more attentive one as his eyes moved over her figure, but when she looked back, his attention was focused on the radio. Oh well, at least he was not immune to feminine charms.

'We're going to Skiros,' announced Simon at breakfast. 'Better put your skates on, we want to leave as soon as possible.'

David nodded thoughtfully, biting on his fourth piece of bread and jam. Brenda opened her sleepy eyes wide. She had had to be woken up for breakfast, and was wearing her usual kimono with the black tiger, while the others were in shorts and T-shirts.

'Better take a sea-sickness pill,' suggested Simon.

Brenda sighed and lit a cigarette.

As they motored to the entrance of the bay, the line of the horizon where the sea met the sky was waving and moving. The sea was breaking round the cliffs and plumes of spray reeled back on contact with them. David went forward to check the sails which began to flap as soon as he removed the ties, which he tucked into the waistband of his shorts.

'Good force five to six on Beaufort scale I shouldn't be surprised,' commented Simon, adding more revs to the engine. The bow swung up high on meeting the open sea only to plunge down with a thud, sending plumes of spray on either side of the hull. It was accompanied by a metallic clang of crockery and saucepans as *Zainda* slammed into the waves.

'We'll set the sail as soon as we get out of the bay and get on course,' said Simon to David. Colin was still in the cabin, busy with the radio, not once glancing at Joanna who was trying not to lose her balance as she put away everything that moved in the cabin. Meanwhile, Brenda disappeared into the aft cabin.

After a long time, or so it seemed to Joanna, Simon decided to put up the sails and switch off the engine. *Zainda*'s movement became less violent.

'We'll have her on jib and mizzen only,' Simon was saying. 'Here, Joanna, give us a hand with the mizzen. I'm afraid the wind's head on. We'll have to tack once we get round the headland. Bang on north-westerly, I'd say. Bit of a bore that if we're to make it in good time.'

After a time, they rounded the tip of Kea and took the course for Euboea. The wind was on the beam now, and the movement became more comfortable. It was a beautiful, sunny, cloudless day. Joanna lay sunbathing, head resting on the rubber dinghy. Time was of no interest at moments like this; it didn't matter if minutes passed or hours. The only important thing was the sun, the sails shaking slightly, making a pattern of white against the blue sky, and the swish of water as the hull sliced through the sea. Occasionally, she would get droplets of spray on her face, leaving a smudge of powdery salt as they dried.

Once round the tip of Euboea, the bliss was shattered. The wind turned head on, and the movement became more violent. They sailed close to the wind, tacking every so often. It meant sailing in the direction of the coast, then having to tack and face the open sea while the land receded from view and, after a time, head back again. In this zigzag fashion they plodded, for every twenty miles sailed making five miles forward. The wind did not let up and even increased to the top of force six as measured by Simon's little hand-held anemometer.

Joanna decided to cook soup on the wildly swinging stove. She soon forgot to ignore those glossy packets that offended her ideas of decent cooking, and instead, in a quick mental turn, blessed them for their convenience. The stove, though gimballed, moved a lot. There was no belt to strap oneself to the galley to prevent slipping. Instead, she had to wedge one foot firmly against a cupboard, hold tight to the edge of the sink with one hand and try to mix the soup powder with the other. The saucepan was at eye level one moment, only to move precariously downwards the next. Cutting bread was also a dodgy business. It kept sliding on the board which resulted in her stabbing the empty air one moment, the board with the bread the next, while the knife met with the bread at infrequent intervals. By the time she managed to serve the meal, she was quite exhausted, but the looks of the three men rewarded her efforts. They were all ravenously hungry and everything handed up to the cockpit where they had assembled disappeared in no time. David's appetite was double that of the rest of the party, though he showed it least.

Looking at his lean, almost thin, body Joanna wondered where he put it. Brenda, on the other hand, refused to eat. She held tightly to the seat in the cockpit, wet and bedraggled, staring miserably into space, shaking her head in dumb refusal every time food was passed round.

So, they went on, sailing for hours in the 'wrong' direction in order to tack back again. Simon and Colin were involved in endless discussions as to which sail to put up every time there was a drop in the force of the wind. Once they even managed to put up the big genoa, but it had to come down quickly as the wind picked up and *Zainda* heeled so precariously that her gunwale touched the water.

It was dark when they found themselves outside Kimi on the mainland. Simon and Colin had a long discussion in the cabin, the upshot of which was to put into Kimi for the night and sail to Skiros the following morning. The harbour wall stretched in front of them like a wispy straight line smudged between the darkening sky and the grey sea. It wasn't something one could see – it drew attention to itself by being straight and therefore man-made. Natural things were never straight, they tended to curve, flow, envelop. Joanna's guess that it might be a harbour were confirmed when lights began to appear on land – in clusters on mountain slopes, indicating they might indicate villages, and separately along the coast where there were scattered houses, moving cars and neon signs. The air became increasingly balmy as the wind dropped. Everyone on board was tired, battered by the wind and stinging from the salty spray which had caked round their faces, making their hands and hair sticky and forming white lesions on Joanna's blue waterproof jacket. She vaguely wondered whether it was expected of her to cook a meal in the evening and whether there were any shops to buy fresh provisions; she didn't really fancy tinned food.

Meanwhile, Simon manoeuvred the yacht pointing into the last of the fast-dying wind and the sails began to flap. Colin and David went up on the deck to fold and tie them with the sail ties. The engine spluttered, whined and barked into motion. *Zainda's* bow swung round and pointed to the winking red and green lights marking the entrance to the harbour. *Ah, yes, red for port meaning left, green for starboard meaning right.* Joanna remembered that. Everyone was on the move now, getting fenders and mooring lines ready. The galley was a mess of unwashed plastic bowls rimmed with grease and remains of the soup. Empty corned beef tins and onion peel were everywhere. Joanna retrieved half a packet of margarine which had jammed in the gimbals of the cooker. So, that's why it hadn't been swinging properly! In addition, it was dripping with soup which had spilled over. Now that the boat was on an even keel, she tried to clear up while the others were busy, ready for anchoring. The sea water pump jammed, and she tied a piece of line round the handle of a bucket, trying without success to fill it from overboard but the boat was moving too fast and she was afraid of losing it. Colin noticed her dilemma.

'Here, give it to me, let me do it. I say, Simon, slow down a bit, will you?'

Simon bit his lip with impatience. He looked like a man late for an appointment. 'Surely it can wait till we anchor ...'

'The water in the harbour might not be very clean and I'd like to clear up the mess,' said Joanna. 'Are we eating on board this evening?'

'Don't know, we left it rather late. What do you think, Colin?'

'No point in staying on board. We might as well go out and eat,' said Colin.

Goodness, thought Joanna. They sound as if they were meeting someone, though nobody mentioned it to her. She took off her jacket and busied herself in the galley. David's head appeared in the companionway.

'Any chance of some bread and jam?' he asked wistfully like a man who hadn't eaten for days. Joanna remembered he had had a whole tin of corned beef only a couple of hours ago and innumerable slices of bread.

'We're going out for a meal as soon as we anchor. Can't you wait till then?'

'That'll be ages.' David looked like a disappointed child about to wail.

'Oh, all right then, just let me clear some of this mess.'

She sliced the bread which, now in calm waters, presented no problem, and spread it thickly with margarine and Greek apricot jam. David gave her a thankful look from behind his dark-rimmed glasses as his teeth sunk into it. He managed to swallow enough to splutter: 'I say, before you put it away, could I have another slice?'

Brenda came into the cabin and lit a cigarette. She wandered aimlessly along the length of the cabin and started rummaging around in the cocktail cabinet where she found a bottle of red wine. She opened it and pushed the cork back in.

'Pass me a glass, will you?'

Joanna peeled off a transparent plastic cup from a tube of cups coiled round the saucepans and handed her one, without bothering to wipe off the greasy marks her fingers made on it. *That's for not saying "please".*

Brenda moved up the steps towards the cockpit, holding the bottle in one hand and a cigarette in the other. At that point, *Zainda* lurched as a bigger yacht passed by, making waves throughout the harbour. Brenda lost her balance, dropped the bottle and fell into a bucket of slops. The bottle hit the chart table and the cork popped out, spilling wine over the chart which lay on top.

'Oh, watch it!' exclaimed Joanna, trying to help Brenda and catch the bottle at the same time. She slipped and lost her balance. In the meantime, the bottle gurgled joyfully, spilling its contents on the floor. If anything, it had a paralysing effect on Brenda. With an intake of breath, and an *Oh, oh, oh!* she half lay in Joanna's arms and allowed herself to be supported without making any effort to pull herself upright. Joanna went down under her weight and grabbed the nearest support which happened to be the gimballed stove. It swung, sending down a dirty saucepan with a crash.

'Help!' shouted Joanna.

Curiously, no one above noticed what was going in the galley: all were too busy looking for a suitable place where to drop the anchor. Colin's calm voice could be heard above the others. 'Bit more to the starboard, Simon. What's the depth now…' followed by the clang of the anchor chain as it uncoiled itself from the chain locker. Joanna made a tremendous effort to disentangle herself from Brenda's grip and get up. She was furious.

'Stupid bitch!' she said to herself. However, it would not do to show her anger. Instead, she said:

'Are you all right, Brenda? Funny how nobody noticed anything, we must have made enough noise to wake up the dead. Oh, just look at this mess!' she exclaimed with genuine horror.

Brenda was trying to scramble to an upright position. Her face wore a miserable look and her voice had a sort of unnatural brightness when she answered. 'I'm all right, I think. Thank you.' Absentmindedly, she picked up the by now empty bottle and handed it to Joanna to throw away. Round her feet swirled a revolting mixture of slops and wine. Joanna suppressed a giggle – it was such a disastrous mess it began to seem funny. Simon's head appeared through the porthole.

'What the hell …' he began in his slow, languid voice as he took in the scene. 'Having a spot of trouble, you two? What's that?' he asked, pointing to the red stain on the chart.

'Wine,' said Joanna.

'It stinks in here,' said Brenda, her voice fully recovered. As she straightened up, her eyes rested on her wine-splattered legs. 'I'll be sick any minute if I don't get out.' With that, she disappeared into the cockpit.

Clearly Joanna was expected to clear up. Well, she *was* the cook and, it seemed, Brenda's dogsbody, too. She seethed as she mopped up the slops from the floor. *Bitch, bitch, bitch!* She worked furiously, head down, only going up to the cockpit to throw the contents of the bucket overboard. Out of the corner of her eye she noticed that a big white motor cruiser had entered the harbour. It was one of those luxury cruisers with a bridge above the cockpit for deep-sea fishing. The crew were all in white and the man at the steering wheel was talking to a couple at the anchor winch through a walkie-talkie. The cruiser glided smoothly, like a huge swan, and came to rest in the middle of the harbour with a barely audible grating of the anchor chain.

Joanna looked at it again with more attention. A man in white shorts was standing in the cockpit while another followed, carrying a tray with drinks; she swore she could hear ice cubes clinking in the glasses. The cruiser swung round, revealing the stern: *Jemima II* she read, then looked down at her wine-splashed shorts and canvas shoes and went back to the reeking cabin with a last look at the cruiser. *Bloody gin palace.*

'Leave it now, Joanna,' Colin's voice interrupted her reverie. 'Just open the portholes and hatches to air the place. Let's go out.' He watched as she continued to mop the floor. 'There, that's enough now. Go and change, I'll wait for you.'

Joanna went into the tiny toilet and looked at her face in the mirror. *Does he feel sorry for me? Oh well, at least he noticed me.*

Jemima II, Jemima II,' crackled the radio. As she came out of the cabin, having changed into clean clothes, she saw Colin playing with the knobs. He moved the chart with the big, mauve stain off the chart table. 'Wait for me on the quay; I shan't be a moment,' he said without looking up. Joanna did not dare look at his face. *I bet he's furious about the chart; just the one we need for this part of the world, too.*

David was already outside, checking the mooring lines tying *Zainda* to the quay. 'Ah, there you are, pass me a fender, will you, Joanna. Mind passing me another line? We'd better take the strain off of that stern warp. What d'you think, Simon?'

Simon grunted in assent and handed him a coiled line. 'Here you are,' he said then waved towards Brenda and Joanna who were already on the quay. 'Why don't you girls go ahead, get yourselves a drink? We shan't be long.'

The radio burst into crackling sounds from which only "roger" and "over and out" became distinct as Joanna and Brenda made their way towards a neon sign, the word *Taverna* flickering between the trees. Brenda was walking ahead, smoking a cigarette, her tight, white trousers cutting through the darkness like scissors. David caught up with Joanna (who was still inwardly seething about Brenda's earlier antics) and tapped her lightly on the shoulder. As she turned round to face him, he caught her arm and looked down. For a moment she thought he was going to kiss her, but his usually smiling mouth was set in a firm line. She took a step backwards, in case he changed his mind, but he only gripped her arm and propelled her forward, striding purposefully towards the Taverna. 'Come, let's go and eat. I'm famished.'

They sat under a leafy tree decorated with multi-coloured bulbs on those hard-backed, reed-plaited chairs so typical of Greece. The wobbly table was covered with a plastic tablecloth. A boy of about twelve placed glasses of cold water in front of them and continued to stand waiting for the order.

'Salad and *souvlaki*,' said David, looking intensely at Joanna and seemingly ignoring Brenda. 'Is that all right with you?'

'That's fine.' Joanna, unable to cope with his gaze, shifted her eyes towards Brenda, who was smoking in silence. She was afraid to see something in his eyes that she did not want or could not reciprocate. But he only looked puzzled, as if trying to figure something out.

Chapter 5

The following day, the passage was uneventful. The wind came from the north-west in fits and starts. Inexplicably, Skiros was no longer their destination. At some stage they had changed their minds and decided to sail to Limnos. So, there was Skiros, a few miles away, a blurred outline in the poor visibility and haze. The heat was oppressive. There was no conversation, everybody sitting in silence and looking into space, until such time as one or other of them would stir to go down to the galley to fetch a drink. In no time at all, the cold drinks were gone. The heat and the sun stunned and stupefied them while they waited for the cool of the evening to rouse them. The breeze which gave some respite from the heat stopped completely. David started the engine. Colin, who was steering, wound a scarf round his head, giving him an air of an oriental pirate. Brenda and Simon were stretched on the aft deck sunbathing. Simon would jerk up from time to time to place a playful slap on her bottom. Brenda in her scanty bikini was turning a dangerous lobster pink. Joanna, in a sensible, long-sleeved, thin Indian cotton dress to protect her from the sun, felt she ought to warn Brenda, but her attitude had hardened after the wine fiasco. Then, deciding that was mean of her, she was about to speak up just as Simon leaned over Brenda and began tickling her chin. It felt like an intrusion to notice them, so she said nothing.

They motored into the Limnos harbour in late afternoon and made fast along the quay. Nobody felt energetic enough to moor stern-to as *Zainda* was notoriously fickle in reverse.

Actually, Limnos had appeared on the horizon hours before they reached it. David saw it first through the binoculars, causing a stir of interest, and they were passed round, everyone able to see the town's faint outline above the sea. The movement stirred Joanna enough to make spam sandwiches and pass round tomatoes and salt. She squeezed lemon juice into the drinking water to quench their thirst, but it was horribly lukewarm. Their appetites, however, especially David's, were unaltered by the heat.

The moment they tied up to the quay, officials spilled out from the customs house nearby. There was a visible ripple of disappointment on learning they did not come from Turkey but were going there. Interest flagged, and only one official remained to take the crew list and passports which he told Simon to collect from the office the following morning. Joanna was sent out to do the shopping for the evening meal after Simon had implied they were eating too many meals out and it was now time for a few economies. However, that was not to be as all shops were closed except one advertising "Greek Art", displaying a rail of cheese-cloth shirts and tube-like dresses with small holes for head and arms. In the shop window was a display of silver jewellery draped on a piece of cardboard, coarse woollen jumpers impossible to contemplate in the heat, horribly shiny lobsters encrusted with thick layers of lacquer, and stuffed baby lambs with ribbons round their necks.

Joanna walked down the deserted streets. The town bore signs of Turkish influence in the appearance of the houses with their wooden slatted balconies, the disused fountains, the tiny shops like those found in Turkish bazaars. There was one other shop open where she saw a man through a small window outlined against the light of a paraffin lamp selling honey from a large vat which he ladled into jars brought by the buyers.

On the way back to the boat, empty-handed, the lights were already winking from the direction of the hill where a castle stood. Colin and Simon were in the cabin doing something with the radio. They looked preoccupied, and it was clear they were trying to contact someone but without success. People are funny, she thought. First, they go sailing to get away from it all, next they're playing with gadgets to get back in touch again. Why not stay in a hotel with access to a telephone? Such thoughts she kept to herself. She joined in to have a good time, and so far, it was all quite enjoyable. In the meantime, the crackling noise cleared and a voice was spelling something out. Another whirr and a crackle and Colin spoke: '*Zainda* calling *Jemima*. Are you receiving me?'

Jemima? Wasn't that the gin palace anchored in Kimi? Why would Simon and Colin try to contact her? Surely they didn't need to ask the crew on *Jemima* about the weather or the state of the sea? At that moment, David's head appeared in the hatch.

'Hello. Back from town early? How is the food situation?'

Joanna told him all the food shops were closed.

'In that case, let me take you out.'

'OK. I'll get ready,' she said, sensing he was anxious to get her out of earshot of whatever was going on with Colin and Simon.

'We're going out,' he shouted to them. 'The shops are closed so no food. You might want to join us later if you like.'

To Joanna it sounded more like: 'Let me take her out of your way before you proceed.' Then she scolded herself for her vivid imagination; the conversation sounded harmless enough.

'Where's Brenda?' asked Simon.

'Asleep,' said David. 'If you ask me, she's had too much sun.'

'Tell her to put some calamine lotion on.'

'Shall I do it, or will you?' asked David mischievously.

Simon's answer was inaudible. Joanna appeared from her cabin, having changed into a white dress and sandals. Her suntan and thick blonde hair contrasted well with the dress. She saw an appreciative flicker in Colin's eyes and felt attractive. But his interest, if it was that, was quickly extinguished as he turned to fiddle with the radio again.

Nothing, however, was extinguished in David's eyes. They lit up as he bounded out of the boat like a young dog and stretched his hand to help her step onto the quay.

'You're looking great!' he beamed, his glasses glistening in the light of the street lamp. 'Did you know you have lovely blue eyes?' he added whimsically, putting his hand round her waist, almost lifting her and bounding forward. 'Let's go and find somewhere to eat. I'm famished.' Joanna couldn't help laughing out aloud.

They went to the nearest restaurant overlooking the harbour where they were served a good meal accompanied by *retsina* wine. Joanna wondered, not for the first time, how many different tastes could be obtained from crushed grapes.

Conversation, however, was halting and uneasy. David was staring at her with admiration which only confused her and needed to be ignored. At some stage, in the future, she knew she would have to disappoint him if he persisted. At the same time, she didn't want to hurt or upset him. He was so young, almost vulnerable and frankly rather absurd. She felt guilty because if it was Colin sitting in his place, looking at her as David did, she'd have melted with pleasure and excitement. This realisation spoilt her appetite. There she was, getting emotionally involved again, as if that ruined marriage had taught her nothing.

She felt David's leg rubbing against hers under the table and blushed furiously.

'I'm sure the others will be joining us any moment.'

'Let them,' said David, still gazing at her with admiration. But he moved his leg and continued to inspect the dishes arriving steadily at the table. Fortunately for him, Simon and Brenda passed by, apparently not having seen them. Joanna saw Colin walking on his own. She made an involuntary wave towards him, but he was looking the other way with the intention of catching up with Simon and Brenda. Her movement and subsequent disappointment did not escape David's attention as he watched her over the rim of his glasses. To cover up her confusion she said, 'I am curious how you decide where to sail next. I mean, you say Skiros one day, then you change your mind and go somewhere else. It just seems so spur of the moment, here, there, without any plans.'

A wary look appeared on David's face. She could see he didn't want to talk about it, but he answered casually enough.

'Why, isn't that the idea just to drift? Rather nice, don't you think?'

'Don't misunderstand me. I'm happy doing what we're doing. I don't wish to pry or anything like that, it's just that people usually make a plan when they're going on holiday, but here nobody knows anything until Simon or Colin think of something in the evening.'

'There's nothing wrong with that,' David's voice grew noticeably colder. 'Some people like their holidays unstructured. Still, if you like, I'll tell them you'd like to be presented with an itinerary.'

'Oh, don't take it like that.' Joanna was quite vexed for having brought up the subject. 'All I said it was a bit odd, that's all.'

As to *Jemima,* better say nothing she thought to herself; don't ask why they were so anxious to maintain contact. To cover up her annoyance, she drank too much wine and became quite light-headed. They finished eating and went outside. The balmy air only made her head worse. There was a clear feeling of duality inside her. One of her two selves was walking along the cobbled quay, the other remained suspended between the earth and the universe. Ah, *Zainda* at last. Joanna had enough sense not to attempt to walk the gangplank. Seeing her hesitate, David, who was behind her, swung her round to face him. *He must be some six inches taller than me,* she thought irrelevantly. *Now, if I am five foot seven ... that should make him*

... *six foot and* ... Then his lips were on hers but it wasn't her he was kissing – it was that other self. She gave an unsteady, 'Oh please,' then added in a slow, carefully articulated voice: 'I'm going to bed. Thank you for a lovely evening.'

Not daring to look back, she made straight for her cabin, undressed and flopped on the bed while her head did battle with the alcohol, David's kiss and an overpowering drowsiness. *To hell with cleaning my teeth*, she thought as she wrapped the sheet closely round her naked body.

Chapter 6

They were on their way to Turkey. The food shopping had been done, with Brenda's help this time. The cabin smelled of freshly baked bread, still warm from the local bakery. The desolate air which had hung over the town the previous evening had disappeared completely with the morning sunshine. There were cars and errand boys on the roads, shops were being opened and huge baskets of fruit and vegetables were brought out from the dark recesses of corridors and courtyards.

Their shopping completed, breakfast things put away, they motored out of the harbour. Simon and Colin decided to investigate the bays to the south of Limnos town. They entered one but found it too shallow, moved on further south where they found another called Koudia, according to Simon. The surrounding countryside was bare and treeless and a number of small, open fishing boats snuggled close to the narrow strip of the beach. Other boats moved to and fro in the bay, one man rowing and the other working a kind of a rake in the water. Joanna was curious. What could they be looking for? Octopus, crabs or simply sea weed for fertilisers? But as they rounded the headland, her attention was drawn to a big yacht in the middle of the bay. The white bow, the high bridge – the unmistakeable *Jemima*! It gave her a start but she tried to hide her surprise as she looked at her companions. They all said nothing, no comment on the coincidence, nothing. She could swear that indifference on David's face was brought out through conscious effort. Simon's face never betrayed anything anyway, except perhaps an air of languid haughtiness to which she tried to get accustomed.

'How about some coffee?' Colin's voice cut through the air of studied indifference. 'Would you mind, Joanna?'

'No, of course not. Anyone else for coffee?'

'Wouldn't mind one,' drawled Simon.

'I'd love a cup, too,' chipped in Brenda. 'I'll come down in a minute to help you.'

'Like hell you will,' muttered Joanna under her breath, going down into the galley. In all fairness, Brenda's face was the only one to register total innocence at the sight of *Jemima*. Joanna looked through the porthole as she waited for the kettle to boil. Next to *Jemima* was a dinghy with Colin in it, talking to one of the crew. *So, what about that coffee?* Obviously they wanted her out of the way; her conversation with David must have alerted them. Her curiosity was now aroused. She resolved to be on the look-out for further clues but she'd say nothing to anyone. Perhaps it was silly to have mentioned her suspicions to David because now they were on their guard, keeping her out of the way. But what was it all about? She'd have to be cleverer in the future.

They entered the Dardanelles in daylight. The wind was head on and the *Zainda* was making slow progress. Once past the Gallipoli peninsula, they had to start the engine. Joanna looked at the peninsula with mounting interest: it was the site of the famous war campaign she had read about. The books she had read on the subject left her with the impression of fluctuating front lines amidst senseless slaughter which historians had tried to cover up as being not in vain. Those who died here were now commemorated by little grey plaques stuck into the ground, some by name, some by the words "Known only to God". From where she stood, they looked like scattered pebbles. Since then, countless wars had been waged as if no lessons had been learnt. Perhaps that was the biggest insult to their memory. Of course, the Gallipoli campaign threw up two giants at the front line of politics – Churchill and Ataturk – but this stony earth holding those little grey plaques was not concerned with the big events of history. Rather, it emanated futility, the fragility of human life and, above all, the pity of it all. 'Oh, the human body,' wrote a poet whose name escaped her, 'the most noble of dusts!'. What a fool he must have been: this dust was far from noble. On looking up, her eyes filled with tears, she noticed a monument shaped like a huge table on elongated legs with a flat dome on top.

'What are you thinking about?' Colin's voice broke through her reverie. His eyes registered an attentive surprise. 'You are crying.' It was something between a statement and a question. Quickly, she wiped her face and blew her nose. 'It's the Gallipoli campaign, the futility, and ... stuff,' she added, lamely.

'Yes, I feel like that about it, too. Poor show on our side. Unnecessary loss of lives.'

His face showed a momentary softness followed, as if on reflection, by putting on an expression of indifference like slamming down the visor of a medieval knight's helmet. He went down to the cabin and started looking intently at the chart.

They entered Canakkale, their port of entry, towards the evening. Their attempts at mooring were marred by a cross current pushing the boat towards the shallow end of the harbour. When they circled for the third time round the harbour, the wind pushed them sideways while they tried to reverse and tie the stern to the quay. Their activities were watched by a crowd gathered on the quay, everybody gesticulating and shouting well-intended advice. Joanna, standing on the deck, fender in hand ready to push it against a neighbouring boat so as not to scratch the hull, felt they were providing the spectators with a rare performance.

There were about sixty men lining the quay. From time to time, a small boy with a closely shaved head would wriggle his way through the solid wall of adults and shout something in a shrill voice. Others waved their hands like windmills. The wall parted to reveal a policeman in uniform, holding a bicycle in one hand and gesticulating with another, at the same time blowing a whistle held in his mouth. Joanna looked for women in the crowd but there were none. Simon and Colin continued their attempts at mooring as if nothing whatsoever was happening on land. To add to their difficulties, a lopsided local ferry, festooned with old car tyres, appeared at the entrance to the harbour. It carried a crowd of people (*more people*, sighed Joanna), two dirty lorries, a thin cow and a flock of sheep. In one swift manoeuvre, it described an arc on the muddy water of the harbour and docilely made contact with the quay. It didn't take more than a couple of minutes.

At long last *Zainda* followed suit. Simon, in a subdued mood, received the policeman who failed to take off his shoes before coming on board although Joanna pointedly threw down a mat as he stepped on. Street shoes tended to scratch the fibreglass decks, it was expected to take them off before coming on board. Three uniformed officials followed, each carrying a briefcase. The crowd, with the little boys at the front, watched the proceedings silently from the quay. One of the braver men approached, knocked on the hull to see what it was made of, the fibreglass so unlike the wood they were used to, and one of the boys touched the life lines. Joanna and Brenda were posted on the aft deck to keep the unwanted guests from entering and to rescue the gangplank in case it fell into the water. They could feel their curious eyes, Brenda getting more eyefuls whenever she bent down, revealing a lot of cleavage in her low neckline.

Simon emerged from the main cabin, shaking the uniformed men's hands, smiling genially, and saying: 'Naturally, of course, by all means, my dear fellow, yes, of course.' There was another smile, a handshake and a pat on the arm as he led them towards the gangplank. Having waved them goodbye, still smiling, he turned back towards the cabin and said through clenched teeth: 'I need a drink.'

They went to the restaurant on the quay, leaving the hatches open so as to make the cabin less stuffy but they sat in such a way as to watch out for possible intruders. They need not have worried. Although many people came to look at the yacht which was so different from their boats that it looked like an exotic bird among sparrows, no one made an attempt to get on board.

'You English? Where you from?' a local man said to Colin while they sat at the table.

'Yes, English,' Colin nodded.

'I have sister in England, in Bir-ming-ham. You come from Bir-ming-ham maybe? You must drink, please. Turkish hospitality!' said the man taking a chair next to him. '*Raki*!' he shouted towards the cavernous interior. A waiter appeared and almost ran towards their table. He had a thick, handlebar moustache and wore a white butcher's apron. A bottle of *raki* and glasses soon appeared, followed by another bottle, this time of water. The *raki* was deftly poured into the glasses and topped with water, turning the contents milky. To Joanna it tasted like a throat gargle except that it turned out to be quite potent. However, once begun there was no end to Turkish hospitality. Simon offered to stand the next round, but the man wouldn't hear of it. Several men carrying chairs joined them at the table, all insisting on standing a round of drinks. Everybody drank *raki*, passed cigarettes round and attempted to establish a conversation, though English was obviously not spoken widely in Canakkale. After a few rounds, Brenda became quite giggly and tried to sit on Simon's knee. The men looked at her without registering surprise even though such behaviour was unthinkable in their society. There were very few women about as far as Joanna could see, and none at all in the restaurant. She concluded that they did not think of women tourists as belonging to the human race as they knew it, rather they regarded them as some fantastic creatures who descended on them on a migratory stopover, only to disappear goodness only knows where.

During the conversation, such as it was, it had been decided that the girls would visit Troy, only a few miles away from Canakkale, the following day. The men opted out for a trip to the war cemeteries of the Gallipoli campaign. A taxi driver was produced from among the locals sitting round the table. He smiled, revealing a golden tooth, bowed, and shook hands. Joanna accepted the arrangement with misgivings, not trusting any of those men once they found themselves alone with two female tourists (fantastic creatures notwithstanding), nor the way they surreptitiously ogled Brenda in her low-cut dress. But Simon and Colin were insistent, offering to pay the taxi fare and expenses. David said nothing and looked away. *They want to get rid of us,* flashed through Joanna's mind. *And David knows that I suspect something. Perhaps I should confide in Brenda.* But she changed her mind and said nothing, still smarting from Brenda's condescending attitude to her as dogsbody and cook.

The following morning, the taxi arrived on time to pick them up. As the girls came down the gangplank, the driver rushed out and sprinkled their hands with scented water before opening the doors of the taxi. Inside, the thoroughly cleaned car was heavy with an oriental perfume. 'Turkish hospitality,' he murmured and bowed.

'Christ, what a stink,' said Brenda once they were seated she took out a paper handkerchief to wipe her hands. Joanna wanted to do likewise but felt constrained. It didn't seem very polite to thwart the gestures of friendliness or "hospitality" even though the unwanted smell made her sneeze. Instead, she smiled more broadly than usual, in an attempt to cover up Brenda's rudeness. It failed.

'Your friend, she don't like perfume, no?' said the taxi driver as he sat down in the driver's seat.

The whole of the dashboard and the steering wheel was covered with a bright green fur fabric. From the driver's mirror hung an assortment of mascots. Scattered about the car were little apes with plastic faces, a huge felt dice forming a cushion, and a cardboard hand on a spring which swung up and down as the car moved. By each side window was a small vase holding artificial flowers.

They drove at a slow pace set by the crowds making their way towards the local market. A flock of sheep had just been disgorged by a dirty ferry, and the animals dispersed in all directions. Small boys were chasing them towards the core of the flock with much shouting from everybody around. The town had a devastated appearance in the sunlight. The main streets were lined with dug-up trenches, there was no pavement, heaps of rubble were piled at irregular intervals. The houses had plaster walls at ground level and wooden balconies on the first floor. From time to time, a woman's face would appear, usually elderly, staring impassively at the street below. The houses must have been partly sunk into the ground because the doors and windows were very low, just a few feet above the street level. A number of them had a big pipe, probably a stove pipe, stuck through one of the windows or through a hole in the wall, enough to give a fire inspector a heart attack.

An attempt to redress the ramshackle appearance of the streets and houses was made in the square where stood a monument of a military figure surrounded by a few wilting flowers resigned to their fate in the full glare of the sun.

The taxi finally made it through the town, out into the open country, and stopped at the entrance to the ancient site of Troy. The driver let them out, then, finding a spot in the shade, parked the car and promptly went to sleep. At the entrance stood an enormous wooden horse, a monument to the Trojan horse of the Iliad and Odyssey fame, doing more credit to the imagination of Walt Disney than to Homer's. This naïve object Joanna regarded as an insult to ancient history, soon to be forgotten once they got through the ticket booth and entered the site.

It met them with a riot of field flowers. They walked round the walls and promptly got lost, confused by all those layers of excavated Troy – Troy II here, Troy VII there. It was better to give up trying to make sense of it and simply imbibe the atmosphere of the place. Brenda soon got tired of the whole thing and went to sit in the café by the entrance. But the spell of the place captured Joanna's imagination. She climbed to the top of the walls where the view left her almost breathless. The plain of Troy where all those battles of the Iliad took place stretched in front of her. She tried to imagine the Trojans and the long-haired Achaeans, the "swift and excellent Achilles", and Ajax, and Agamemnon king of men whose face she had seen impressed on the golden mask in the museum. She climbed further and looked directly below. The stone wall was fairly high where she stood. From here, the women of King Priam's household must have watched the battles taking place on that distant, shimmering plain. Here must have stood Priam's elderly wife, and Helen, the most beautiful woman in the world. How did it feel to be the most beautiful woman in the world? Were her loyalties divided between her husband and her lover? Who did she really want to win? Did she ever feel remorse for being the cause of all that bloodshed? Another scene from the Iliad came to her forcefully – Hector and Andromache. Somewhere on these walls, perhaps on the very spot where she now stood, Hector said goodbye to his wife and their little son Astyanax before going to battle. The baby became frightened by his glittering helmet with the horsehair plume and burst into tears. His parents began to laugh when they realised what caused them and Hector took it off before kissing the little wet face goodbye. Not long afterwards, Hector was killed and baby Astyanax hurled down the ramparts to his death.

The plain shimmered in the heat haze where now a tractor made its way slowly along the fields. In the distance was the sea. No hollow or beaked ships were beached there, or any other for that matter. Joanna walked right round the ruins and was surprised by the size of the immortal city – it was so small.

Slowly, she made her way back to Brenda who was sitting on the café terrace where sun and shade patches filtering through the leaves of a nearby tree did a slow-motion dance. Scattered around the terrace were bits and pieces of ancient masonry, grinding stones and pestles, bits of columns and flat stones with funeral engravings. Brenda was playing with a ginger cat. Joanna ordered a Coke, brought to her by a wistful-looking man with a long moustache. Brenda prattled on, glad of the company as if no animosity or short duration of their acquaintance existed between them. It was all about clothes and flat-sharing with a girlfriend, an unhappy affair with a boyfriend who drove her mad, the time when she met Simon at a party somewhere in St. John's Wood, and when he took her back to his flat.

'He was terribly supportive after all I'd been through with Kevin,' she was saying. She had moved in with Simon for now, but kept her flat on, just in case things didn't work out between them. Both she and Simon were now into self-analysis. 'Once a week, there's a group therapy we go to. You see, we're working towards a committed relationship,' she explained seriously, eyes round with introspection.

Joanna was fascinated in spite of herself. 'What do you do there?'

'Oh, well, we've only just started. You just lie there, relax, and touch each other without speaking. You see,' she said in the tone of a lecturer addressing a particularly unintelligent group of students, 'touch is terribly important, especially if you're striving for fulfilment.'

Joanna nodded, none the wiser.

'I should be in a more advanced group; I've been to classes before,' continued Brenda. 'Simon needs more time, you know, to function fully, if you see what I mean. And there's the food question. I mean, what you eat is what you are. I can't stop Simon from eating meat, though he said he'll give it a try.'

Joanna's head was spinning. Meat, fulfilment – how did it all fit in? Meanwhile, Brenda continued, her protruding teeth smudged with the lipstick she managed to apply while talking. 'I said to him, I said, darling, you are not giving yourself a chance, are you? Mind you, he had a dreadful time with his last girlfriend, and there was a wife too, now his ex, but he doesn't want to talk about that.' She lowered her voice. 'I have a feeling he's still not quite liberated, he's suppressed, if you see what I mean. He needs an emotional workout. I used to be like that, you know, I mean, I know what he's going through. I can be supportive, I know I can,' she sighed, sipping her Coke.

They were interrupted by the appearance of the taxi driver making his way towards them. 'I suppose we should be going,' said Joanna getting up. 'Our time's up.'

'No hurry, please,' said the man and sat between them. 'Cigarette?' he asked in his heavily accented English as he drew a packet from the breast pocket of his shirt and made a sweeping movement with it. Joanna shook her head, but Brenda took one. He lit it for her, then his own, inhaling deeply, then eyed both girls speculatively from under his bushy eyebrows as if sizing them up. Joanna felt uncomfortable under the scrutiny, like a lamb being inspected by a possible buyer. She didn't like the man at all.

'Would you like a drink, a Coke perhaps?' she asked for the sake of politeness.

'Yes,' he nodded, shifting his heavy, speculative gaze towards Brenda. He must have found something more to his liking in her face because he moved his chair nearer to hers. The wistful waiter with the long moustache appeared. The driver growled something in Turkish. The waiter nodded and came back with three bottles on a tray, the straws bobbing on the foam at the top.

'Fruit juice,' said the driver laconically, his acceptance of Coke ignored, and pulled at the straw.

'What, no beer?' laughed Brenda.

'No.'

Joanna blushed furiously, ashamed by her gaffe. Surely she ought to know Muslims didn't drink alcohol. But then last night's round of *raki* could have confused anyone. Obviously, some people here were more orthodox than others.

Meanwhile, the taxi driver was concentrating his attention more and more on Brenda who, to Joanna's amazement, did not repel his advances. On the contrary, she seemed rather to enjoy them. Joanna felt in the way and caught herself feeling sorry for the pink and freckled Simon, who, it would seem, would have to compete for Brenda's favours with men like this thick-set, heavy-featured and admittedly testosterone-oozing Turk. Brenda seemed to have momentarily forgotten her supportive role in Simon's life, and the presence of Joanna, giving the driver her undivided attention. She bit the drinking straw in a suggestive manner while looking at him; by now he had his arm round her chair. Joanna looked at Brenda with wonder. Anyone who could bite a straw like that, prominent teeth notwithstanding, suggesting a sex play, must have hidden talents. The driver leaned forward and whispered something in Brenda's ear. She responded with a loud, deep-throated laugh. Joanna couldn't take it any more and stood up abruptly. They both looked at her.

'Don't you think we should be going back?' she said, hoping to bring Brenda to her senses.

'Why, what's the hurry?' she drawled. 'I haven't finished my drink.'

Joanna felt the urge to put a stop to this scene which was beginning to disgust and at the same time slightly alarm her. These Turks probably considered any blonde tourist girl their prey, an easy lay. Being older and most likely more travelled, she felt it her duty to warn Brenda not to lead the man on. Just now, Brenda's behaviour only justified any ideas about women tourists being easy.

'I'm going to wash my hands. You coming Brenda?' she hinted heavily.

'I'll stay where I am.' Brenda gave Joanna a brazen smile and laughed again, showing the fullness of her throat and the pink roof of her mouth.

Coming out of the washroom, Joanna came to the conclusion that it wasn't the Turks who had the "wrong ideas", but she herself. By this time, the driver had his arm round Brenda and his bullet-shaped, close-cropped head was tilted towards her neckline. The top buttons of Brenda's blouse were already undone.

'Are we going then?' she asked sharply. 'I've got masses to do on the boat.'

'You not like here?' asked the driver. His face in the dappled sunshine gave him a mottled, sinister look. Suddenly he laughed. 'Ah, perhaps you not like Turkish men?' He addressed himself to Joanna while pressing Brenda closer to him. Brenda emitted a sort of neigh, and did not move. Joanna turned abruptly. 'I'll wait for you outside,' she said and walked indignantly past the ridiculous statue of the horse into the car park. She could have kicked herself for allowing her disapproval to show; Brenda was old enough to know what she was doing. Slightly mortified, she waited by the taxi for them to catch up.

Her mood on the drive back was subdued. Brenda sat in front next to the driver and attempted to put her head on his shoulder. The numerous bumps on the road soon put a stop to that, but she continued to laugh a lot. Joanna, sitting in the back, presumed they were trying to pet but by now was past caring. All she could think of was how to get out of the stifling taxi quickly. The opportunity did not take long to present itself as they drove past the entrance to the bazaar.

'Would you please let me out here? I need to do some shopping.'

The driver, however, was busy changing gears, at the same time massaging Brenda's leg, and not listening. His other hand, hairy at the knuckles, gripped the steering wheel trimmed with green fur. A big signet ring with a flashy artificial ruby adorned one of the fingers. He managed to stop eventually, well past the entrance.

'Let me pay you now,' she said, then with a side glance, 'You coming, Brenda?'

But Brenda sat there without moving, not even looking at her, rather at something in the distance and pretended not to hear.

The driver waved her money away. 'No worry, I come to boat later.' He leaned through the window and winked conspiratorially. 'I come with friend for you. So, we will be four, yes?' and laughed.

Joanna turned away, furious. She could have slapped that stupid, leering face and only an inbred horror of creating a scene in public stopped her. So, he thought she was cross because he did not pay attention to her, just Brenda. Well! The taxi melted into the busy street before she could trust herself to walk calmly through the gate into the market. Once there, she walked disconsolately for a while before going back to the boat.

As expected, there was no one on board; they were supposed to be at the Gallipoli all day. She was struck by the mess in the main cabin and the smell of stale cigarette smoke, unusual as none of the men smoked, and certainly not in the cabin. All boat owners have an intrinsic horror of starting a fire and Simon was no exception, only just being able to tolerate Brenda's smoking and that with ill-concealed grace. In the galley, Joanna noticed with surprise that the cupboards were open, crockery and saucepans strewn around. The chart table was also a mess, with cigarette ash all over the charts. The top chart was heavily smudged, as if someone had been pointing at something with a dirty finger. It was all rather odd, especially as the men were fastidious about stowing everything away neatly.

I bet some officials came back this morning, and then they must have been in a hurry to leave for the tour of the cemeteries. She set herself to task, working out her bad mood caused by the taxi driver's remarks and Brenda's behaviour, emerging from the cabin a couple of hours later when everything was cleared up and put away. The sun was still up. She settled herself with a book, sunbathing on the fore deck, and was soon immersed in the trials and tribulations of sea battles between England and France in the eighteenth century. There was nothing like a good sea story on a sailing holiday. The hours flew by and the shock of Brenda's behaviour was beginning to wear off.

There was no sign of Brenda returning, however. After a time, Joanna's good mood gave way to a nagging worry, changing into a feeling of guilt. How could she have left that silly goose alone with that man? Anything might happen in a strange country. By now, she could almost see Brenda stabbed, lying somewhere in a pool of blood, victim to the taxi driver's criminal inclination. Rising abruptly from her sunbathing spot, she scanned the quay with anxious eyes. It was bathed in the sharp afternoon sunlight, the air shimmering with heat and dust. There was nobody about. The only movement came from a rustling newspaper held by a man sitting in the shade of an umbrella outside the restaurant where they had had their drinks the previous night. Joanna caught a momentary glimpse of his face as he turned the pages. It was a rather handsome face, that of a middle-aged gentleman, too fair to be Turkish. A tourist – most likely English. Only an Englishman would sit in this hot sun on an empty quay while everybody else was having a siesta. The phrase *mad dogs and Englishmen* came to mind and she smiled involuntarily in spite of her anxiety. Now, what would be the best course of action? Stay and wait or go and look? Simon must never be told about this little episode if it could be helped. Anyway, it would be like telling the teacher on your school friends – just not done. To grass on Brenda was unthinkable.

She looked at the quay again, but there was no change; the streets were deserted as before. The sun was by now fairly low, and its reflection on the water made the cabin very hot. She noticed the doors of the aft cabin were not locked. That was rather careless. She opened the door gingerly and looked in. It was in an even worse state than the main cabin. Brenda's clothes were strewn all over the double bunk bed, and a stale, stuffy, unwashed kind of smell hung in the air. 'What a slut,' said Joanna to herself, closing the door. It would be better to go to a café, get a nice cold drink and wait for Brenda under a sun umbrella. The man, the tourist had gone, for which Joanna was grateful. She disliked those forced conversations with people in foreign countries when the only thing in common was language. On such occasions, she wished to turn into a dog so that she could wag a tail. It would spare all those meaningless platitudes and the racking of her brain for something to say. She'd have wagged her tail instead to show friendly intentions without having to say a word. Spared the tail-wagging conversation, she sipped her deliciously cool lemonade and went back to her book. Then, the sound of a car horn made her start. Brenda jumped out of a car, safe and sound by the look of her, followed by the taxi driver and another man she recognised as the wistful waiter in the café who was holding a camera.

'Hello,' waved Brenda, 'come and have your picture taken.'

'No thanks,' shouted Joanna, relieved to see her. The moment she knew Brenda was safe, her anger returned. 'Where have you been all this time? I've been worried about you.'

At that moment, she saw Simon, Colin and David in the distance. Brenda saw them at the same time and said something to the taxi driver who was leaning against *Zainda*'s hull, being photographed from different angles. Without another word, the two men walked quickly away, jumped into the taxi, and drove off without saying goodbye. 'I never paid him,' flashed through Joanna's mind while Brenda was making desperate signals with her eyes. 'Pretend nothing's happened,' she managed to whisper. 'Tell you all later.' Her lips stretched into a wide smile as soon as Simon came within hailing distance.

'Simon, darling, how was your day? Joanna and I had a marvellous time, didn't we, Joanna? So interesting,' she drawled.

Joanna nodded thinking hard of something non-committal to say, but nothing presented itself quickly to her mind.

'Enjoyed yourselves?' asked Simon.

'Yes, good, thank you, and you?' asked Joanna. They all made appropriate noises without elaborating on the day's events except for David who came close to Joanna and whispered 'Missed you!'.

'My goodness,' said Joanna brightly as the conversation was flagging, 'you must have been in a hurry to leave the boat this morning. It took me over an hour to clear up all that mess.'

The remark, meant as a gentle reproof, caused more consternation than intended. The three of them looked at her with unconcealed surprise. Colin was first to speak.

'A mess? What sort of a mess?'

'Oh, please don't think I'm complaining,' said Joanna. taking a step back. 'It's just when I, I mean, when we came back, there was quite a bit of ... you know, things spilled out and stuff. Not to mention the cigarette smoke! Was it something you were looking for? Anyway, I put it all back. It doesn't really matter, I didn't mind doing it,' she finished lamely, feeling wretched. Colin looked very serious, as if it was her fault. Oh, why had she opened her big mouth! Actually, they all looked puzzled, with Colin the first to recover.

'Well, I'm sorry to have put you to all this trouble. If you have any more shopping to do, perhaps Brenda or David could help you.' He made it sound like a command, in a *get out of the way* tone.

As it happened, both David and Brenda were glad to join her. David in his usual way bounded rather than walked towards the bazaar, so that the girls had trouble keeping up with him. He bought himself a ring-shaped bun from a boy who was carrying stacks of them on a tray held by a strap round his shoulders, and was munching steadily.

'I'm sorry, David,' panted Joanna trying to keep up. 'About mentioning the mess in the cabin. I know I'm supposed to do those girl Friday jobs, so I don't want to appear like I'm complaining. What I mean is, I'm enjoying this trip, and I don't mind doing it, really.'

'Forget it. I'm sure Simon didn't take it that way,' he said, then added quietly, 'and you know I think you're wonderful.' He looked at her lowered head and sighed. 'I mean, I think you're doing a wonderful job.' Then in a changed voice he turned to Brenda. 'Your dress is quite dirty at the back. What have you been doing?'

'Nothing,' muttered Brenda, shrugging her shoulders. Joanna nearly laughed aloud, but tried to keep a straight face.

Chapter 7

The following morning, they left for Istanbul. No more was said about the mess, and if Joanna sensed a kind of suppressed feeling among the men, she put it down to the general excitement generated by the next leg of their journey. Not a breath of wind stirred as they left Canakkale, so, unable to sail, they had to motor. From time to time, big ships passed them by – huge naval vessels, tankers, cargo boats, fishing boats, the usual traffic going to and from the Black Sea. All produced big wakes which made their yacht roll enough to raise a clatter from the cutlery and the saucepans like a cackle of frightened hens.

Brenda was obviously avoiding Joanna while lavishing her attentions on Simon. Sitting in their usual place on the aft deck, Brenda began putting segments of an orange into his mouth, saying 'Mmmm' every time he opened his mouth for more. Joanna, dozing in the sunshine, looked away disgusted and caught Colin's speculative glance. He seemed to be paying her more attention lately before slamming down that proverbial visor.

Her attitude to Colin was beginning to be a source of vexation: it annoyed her to discover she was becoming more and more aware of him. It would have been better not to feel attracted to men, at least not so soon after the fiasco of her marriage. The flattery of David's attention was more than counterbalanced by its lack in Colin. She had the impression Colin was deliberately shutting her away from his mind, much as she was trying to keep him away from hers. Only, it seemed he was succeeding admirably while she was failing. Maybe he too had been hurt in the past and didn't want to get involved again, but it wasn't flattering. A woman liked to know she was attractive, but if Colin thought that she was, he was extremely good at covering it up. She did catch an appreciative look once or twice when diving off the deck, as if he couldn't help himself, but it disappeared quickly, leaving her wondering whether it was her imagination playing tricks, or, as was most likely, wishful thinking.

It was unfortunate that Colin was handsome in that rugged, outdoor way which appealed to her. She liked the way he moved, slow and calculated, the kind of deliberate slowness like a jungle cat that she had watched in nature films. His tanned face with its golden stubble, his athletic body, the broad shoulders, his close proximity, all confronted her daily in the confined space of the boat where everybody was in physical contact with each other whether they wanted it or not. Often, the boat would lurch so that they bumped into each other, or had to squeeze past in the narrow passage. They all wore next to nothing in the heat, spending most of the day in bikinis and swimming trunks, only putting on shorts and a T-shirt in the evening when going out to eat. *Trust my rotten luck*, she swore, recognising the unwanted sensation of an electric discharge whenever her body touched Colin's, while he didn't seem to have *any*. Only David's attentions restored some of her confidence, while at the same time keeping the sensuality within her awake. It was a vicious circle.

This time, Colin's gaze was steady as he moved towards her. Joanna brightened up considerably in spite of her resolution to keep a grip on herself.

'How did you spend the day yesterday? Was everything all right?'

'Oh, very nicely, thank you. That trip to Troy was most interesting.'

'The taxi driver didn't make a pass at you?' he made it sound like a joke, but his eyes were not smiling. The question made Joanna jump. Had he found out about Brenda? But that was impossible, he couldn't have, they had been too far away to see Brenda alone in the taxi. Also, even if they *did* see the men take photos of each other by the boat, he couldn't possibly know she wasn't with Brenda all the time. She still had the money Simon gave her for the taxi. Better spend it on food so that no one would notice; no good giving the money back and risking awkward explanations. No, it must have been one of those polite questions, though it did unsettle her a bit.

'No, no, how can you even suggest it? Dreadful man!' she shivered at the recollection, hoping Brenda wasn't listening.

'Well, I don't know, an attractive woman like you.' *Attractive, he thinks I'm attractive!* Could he be thawing out at last?

'Somehow, he managed to resist me. Though I don't know how,' she added with a twinkle. 'And you, did you enjoy your trip to the cemeteries?'

'Yes, we did. Look ...' he said seriously, putting his hand on her arm as if about to confide in her, but at that moment they crossed a wake of a cargo ship and *Zainda* rolled madly. Both lost their balance in the unexpected motion and had to cling to whatever was at hand. There was a loud clatter in the galley, a basket of fruit and vegetables rolled on the floor, spilling the contents. Joanna jumped to the rescue. When everything was returned to normal, the moment of intimacy, such as it was, was gone. Colin seemingly forgot what he wanted to say and was bending over some piece of machinery he was oiling.

It was Joanna's turn to steer. She took over from David, who was whistling a tuneless song, and only a slight paleness under his tan betrayed that he had been watching Joanna talking to Colin. Joanna saw the grim look he gave Colin and was confused. The boy couldn't be that serious about her, surely? To give her something to do to relieve the monotony of steering she picked up the binoculars and scanned the shore. They were passing the town of Gelibolu. She focused on the minarets, then on the rest of the town, the houses, people, cars, and finally the entrance to the harbour and the jetty. She started. There, tied to the jetty, was *Jemima*! It could not be any other cruiser, though it was still too far to read the name. The same hull with that characteristic white bow, the high bridge. Two crew in white were walking on the decks, one standing by the anchor winch. The radar on the mast was making slow circular motions. *Some people need their heads examined*, she thought contemptuously. *What do they need that for, what do they expect here – fog?* Then she reflected. It could be to do with radio communications; sailing is now full of high tech, my girl, none of that sextant and a wet finger pointing to the wind stuff anymore. She put the binoculars away and concentrated on steering, saying nothing about *Jemima* to anyone. A crackling noise came from the radio in the cabin. Colin was trying to establish contact, but his voice was muffled and no words that made any sense reached her ears. However, his activity was not lost on Simon.

'Any luck?' he shouted from the aft deck, trying to extricate himself from Brenda's arms. One of her hands fell on the deck with a thud. 'Sorry, darling, never mind, there, there,' he rubbed her affectionately like a bruised child. Brenda pretended to whimper.

'Not really, Simon,' said Colin. But Joanna heard him transmit something and knew it was a lie. Simon muttered, 'Too bad, carry on,' and, spreading himself on a towel, resumed sunbathing.

Towards the evening, they arrived at the island of Marmara. *Zainda* entered the little port on the north side of the island where the breakwaters were made of pure marble blocks, glistening white where they were cut, dull yellow where they were in contact with the ground. As they cleared the entrance, they saw what must have been the whole population of the island standing shoulder to shoulder, watching them in silence. Simon took over the steering and went twice round the harbour to find a suitable place for mooring. There wasn't one, at least not near the village, if that was not too grand a description for the few houses scattered round the water's edge. A number of small, open fishing boats were tied loosely to the quay.

'If they would move some of these boats, we could squeeze in here,' Simon pointed to a couple of bollards on the quay. David threw the dinghy in the water and rowed furiously towards the shore. Somehow, he made himself understood, for very soon a number of figures detached themselves from the living wall, jumped into a couple of boats, nudged them along the quay and started re-tying them. Soon, the gap between them widened which Simon judged sufficient for *Zainda* to squeeze in.

While the girls were tying fenders to the life lines, Simon reversed the boat, this time successfully. Colin was now on the stern, from where he jumped off onto land to fend off if necessary, before making fast to the bollards on the quay. Joanna gave a sigh of relief. She did not cherish the repeat of the spectacle at Canakkale, not in front of all these people lining the quay. If there were fewer of them than in Canakkale, they made it up with curiosity, those standing in the second row craning their necks to see better. The silence was complete. One or two boys climbed the tree by the local café which was festooned with string shopping bags filled with bread, lettuces and long green tails of spring onions. Under the tree, stood a rickety table with a television set on it. It was switched off. Joanna wondered about the cause and effect: had they switched it off to watch them moor, or were they watching them because the programme had finished? As in Canakkale, there were no women in the crowd, just one or two little girls with tussled hair wearing baggy trousers. Joanna managed to slip down to the cabin and put on her cheesecloth dress over her bikini. It helped to overcome the shyness she felt when so many people stared at her. She was beginning to understand the short temper of celebrities beseeched by staring crowds and clicking cameras. Brenda, however, had no such scruples and walked up and down in her scanty bikini, drawing all eyes from the shore to herself before bending down to shorten the length of the finder, revealing a lot of her ample breasts. Not for the first time Joanna wondered if she'd had a boob job. The human wall swayed but no sound was emitted. Or rather, it was a swish of many people moving at the same time. Joanna muttered some pretext and went down to the cabin to hide. The others pretended not to notice the crowd or simply ignored it. Simon was busy at the wheel, David stood by the anchor winch. At last, the engine was switched off and David lowered the gangplank.

'Let's see if we can get a cold drink in this place,' suggested Simon. 'There's no ice left in the fridge, is there, Joanna?'

Joanna nodded in confirmation.

'We'll try to get some here,' said Simon in a mood of unbounded optimism. 'Come on, old girl,' he said as he gave Brenda a playful slap on her bottom. 'Put something on and let's get out.' Brenda gave a squeal and disappeared in the aft cabin.

Joanna walked down the gangplank towards the café. The wall parted for her but still no sound. It unnerved her. There was one word in Turkish which came to mind – their equivalent of 'hello'. '*Merhaba,*' she said shyly. Whether it meant 'hello' or not, it proved to have magic properties for unlocking the silence. Suddenly all the faces broke into smiles. '*Merhaba, merhaba,*' they said, trying to shake her hand and saying something else she couldn't understand. Several men beckoned to her to come and sit under the shade of the tree by the café. A bottle of lemonade mysteriously appeared in front of her. She had become a focus of attention, surrounded by overwhelming friendliness and hospitality. The contrast between this and the silence only seconds before was almost too much. She was glad when the others came to join her to dilute the almost overpowering attention. However, even with the others present, it was all rather difficult as nobody had a language in common. There were nods, winks, gestures, cigarettes passed round. As it continued, it became more and more tiresome. Simon was his usual supercilious self which made Joanna's teeth grit and Brenda's behaviour was no better. Her attention was concentrated on Simon and she laughed a lot, showing those protruding teeth and pink gums. *I bet she wants to throw him off the scent after what happened with the taxi driver*, thought Joanna. *I wonder where they got it together. Was it in the taxi or did he have a cousin who found them a hotel room, nice and quiet, arranged with a knowing wink and a nod? Ugh, how could she do it with a man like that?* She shivered. Unknown to her, David's eyes were on her.

'Are you cold?'

'No, of course not.' Unable to take any more of Brenda's and Simon's company, she stood up. 'I'd like to look at the island before it gets too dark. How about a short walk, David?'

The alacrity with which he accepted the invitation made her feel almost guilty. She turned to Simon. 'Are we having supper on board tonight? I could make a curry if you like.'

'Good idea. Don't be too long.'

'Have fun,' drawled Brenda, giving Joanna a knowing wink. How she managed to make it sound like an indecent proposition was beyond her. Not for the first time on this trip, Joanna felt strangling Brenda would be a pleasure.

Colin lit a cigarette and looked away.

They walked for a while in silence. The men who lined the quay to watch them had now lost interest and sat in small groups, crouching on the ground and obviously waiting for transport. Their string bags trailing greenery like feathers lay beside them, so that the loaves of bread were covered with dust. A couple of lorries arrived from behind the hills, and the men jumped into them and disappeared. There was little sign of life in the houses now: the whole place, so full of people moments ago, was empty. They walked towards the breakwater and laughed, struck by the same thought – they were going to have a look at the sea, having spent the whole day looking at nothing else. 'But then, it looks different from land,' said Joanna.

They stepped over rubbish and sleeping dogs, then walked round the huge marble blocks on the quay waiting for shipment. The heat absorbed during the whole day of sunshine now emanated from the blocks, making them warm to the touch. A narrow footpath led from the quarries to the hills. There, the whole area was dug up revealing white, glistening marble. The whole island, it seemed, was made of marble, only thinly covered with soil and vegetation.

'Maybe the word 'marble' came from Marmara: it sounds similar,' suggested Joanna.

'Could be,' agreed David listlessly as if he didn't care much one way or the other.

Looking at him as they walked side by side, Joanna wondered how long ago he left school, then remembered he had mentioned a uni and a not very good degree. So, must be around twenty-one. She was reminded of a Great Dane dog: he was all arms and legs, loosely joined as if their movement was independent of each other and the general idea of propelling oneself forward was just one of the many options. He bounded up the path and only stopped at the top of the hill for Joanna to catch up. As she approached, he took off his glasses to wipe them. His eyes, focused on her, had an innocent, almost vulnerable look. *He's like a little boy with a crush. Why did he have to choose me?* she thought helplessly, playing down the urge to scold him, tell him not to be silly, find someone his age, but knew she couldn't. Somehow, he managed to melt her defences, or perhaps her maternal instincts. 'Oh damn!' she said aloud, without thinking and kicked a stone.

'Why, what's the matter?' he asked anxiously.

'Nothing, just nothing,' she muttered crossly. 'Oh look,' she said, pointing to the field, glad to be able to focus his attention on something other than herself. There, ahead and below, was a clearing on which lay scattered stone sarcophagi. 'How very interesting! Let's go and have a closer look.'

David bounded ahead obediently, and she followed. A steep path took them to the field on which were at least twenty sarcophagi, all open. Some were simply rectangular stone coffins, others had curious, dome-shaped lids with ear-like protrusions at each corner. Several were lying in deep trenches only partly excavated, others were scattered on the ground together with bases of columns and plinths for monuments lost long ago. There was a complete, unbroken statue standing among the stones of a two-headed man in a flowing robe, possibly a toga.

'Looks like Siamese twins,' said David, walking round it. The statue cast a long, double shadow in the setting sun.

There was a notice at one end of the field in several languages, warning visitors not to deface or damage the exhibits. In a token gesture, it had a trailing wire fence sunk into the ground half way round the field. There were no visitors here besides them, and no cow would have been deterred by that wire fence. Needless to say, there was no guard.

'Isn't it fascinating?' said Joanna, inspecting the stones. 'This must have been a cemetery, Roman or even earlier.'

'I suppose so.'

She was very excited, her interest aroused not only by the ancient historical site but the way they found it, almost discovered it, and had it all to themselves without having to share it with crowds of people. The setting was romantic, too, a lovely remote corner of the world, rich in history.

'Let's go up a bit,' said David, taking Joanna's arm. 'I'm not too keen on cemeteries lately.' He said it in such a strange, serious voice that Joanna looked at him with surprise, but he avoided her eyes.

They retraced their steps slowly up the hill. The path took them to a tiny quarry on the other side where a man was sitting under a canvas roof stretched on four poles. He was chipping a block of beautiful, pristine white marble. A small boy was sitting next to him, occasionally sweeping the chips out of the way. The man was holding what looked like a short steel comb in one hand, hammering at the block with the other. What appeared to be a finished product lay nearby. Joanna said *merhaba* again, and the man grunted in response. Any further Turkish being non-existent, she pointed to the grooved, chiselled piece of marble and asked in English: 'May I see?', reinforcing her question with gestures. Surprisingly, the man answered in English.

'Please,' he said and continued to work on his piece of marble. The object looked like a small basin with two flat flaps on either side that looked like ears. For the life of her, neither she nor David could make out to what use this object could be put.

'What is it?' she finally asked the man, turning the object this way and that.

'Wash basins for Turkish baths,' he replied.

'Oh?'

The man got up and patiently pointed at the object. 'Here for water,' then pointed to one "ear", here for soap, 'Here,' he said and pointed to the other one, 'for cup. Water into cup,' he gestured, pouring the imaginary water from an equally imaginary cup and pouring it on himself. 'Soap,' he said, making another gesture as if lathering. 'Turkish [which he pronounced *Toorkish*] bath,' he concluded, then sat down as if exhausted by this long explanation and continued to chip the marble block.

'Yes, I see,' nodded Joanna who had never had a Turkish bath. 'Thank you.'

The man didn't look up, seemingly absorbed in his work, and the boy got up to sweep the stone chips as they left.

'Rather interesting, a bit of local colour,' said David.

They walked down the hill while the sun slowly sank behind the horizon. The light from the lighthouse hidden by the hill began to pat the surface of the sea at regular intervals and the first star appeared on the darkening sky. The ground on which they were walking cascaded to the sea in a series of terraces on which grew all kinds of field flowers, exuding an overpowering smell of herbs flowering bushes and small trees. It was truly nature's own garden. The narrow footpath took them round the hill. They stopped to view the panorama spread below, standing side by side.

'Isn't it …' started Joanna and stopped. David's hands were drawing her to him. He looked at her in the falling dusk for what seemed like ages, then bent down and kissed her, burying his lips in hers. Her reaction was at first to draw away, followed by the realisation either that she couldn't or didn't want to, and didn't care which. Whether it was the atmosphere of the place, or whether he struck a chord in her subconscious no longer mattered. She could have melted in his arms as long as the evening lasted. The smell of flowers wafted around them, the stars twinkled, the sea shimmered like nowhere else in the world. Finally, the need for breath drew them apart. They stood somewhat stunned, facing each other in the deepening dusk, not saying a word. David looked as if he wanted to etch her image in his mind for ever, taking in every detail of her face and hair.

'You are beautiful,' he murmured at last. Dazed by his kiss, she stood still. Suddenly, her eyes grew wide. 'Oh my God, David,' she exclaimed grabbing his arm. 'I promised to cook a meal before it gets dark. Come on, let's run.'

David laughed. The mood and the tension gone, he ran after her swiftly disappearing figure.

'We must hurry, whatever will Simon think? He'll give me the sack on the spot, he's bound to,' she panted, running down the hill, glad not to think what that kiss had done to her. Just now she couldn't cope with her emotions, wanted them to vanish. There was too much in that kiss, augmented by the smell of flowers, the sunset, the readiness of her response. It must have lurked in the depths of her innermost being, unknown and therefore frightening because she had not been aware of its existence. She was reminded of seeing a dog once as it watched an open fire, its eyes fascinated, mesmerised by the flickering flames. Something primitive, ancestral lurked there. A similar thing had happened to her just then when David kissed her, a flashback into the interior of her very core. Or perhaps somewhere nearer, the split from Alex, the betrayal, the emptiness left in its wake. Whatever it was, it would not do to disturb it, in spite of having read somewhere that the only adventure left to man (and woman) was the discovery of oneself. It was too disquieting, and she ran down the hill, prompted not so much by her duty as cook on *Zainda* as to put distance between herself and the place where it happened. She wished her life to be filled with ordinary, mundane things, not to be disturbed by sentimental youngsters who bounded like dogs on Turkish hills.

A rattling noise greeted them as they approached the quay – the local generator came to life, its noise dispelling any romantic notions nature had provided. She ran into the cockpit, trying to catch her breath. Colin and Simon were having a beer in the cockpit, the light in the aft cabin betraying Brenda's presence nearby.

'Oh, there you are,' said Simon, barely inclining his head in her direction.

'Sorry I'm late,' panted Joanna. 'We've seen a Roman cemetery, ever so interesting. Tell you about it later. Supper won't be long.'

Colin said nothing, only looked at her flushed face and then at David's who was grinning to himself. If a fleeting grim look crossed Colin's face, it must have been due to a trick of the light thrown by the cabin lamp …

'I'll get myself a beer,' said David, rubbing his arm against her before joining the others in the cockpit.

'Are we staying here tomorrow?' Joanna turned to Simon as she stirred the curry paste into the tinned meat.

'I don't think so. Might as well sail to Istanbul. Ought to leave reasonably early, say, five? That should give us plenty of time to get there, see the sights. What d'you say, Colin?'

Colin, whose face was in the shadows and only intermittently relieved by the glow of the cigarette he was smoking, nodded in agreement. So did David, by this time holding a can of beer, his long legs stretched out so that they touched the opposite seat of the cockpit. They all went to bed soon after the meal was finished, having washed down the curry with quantities of surprisingly good Turkish wine. Joanna slept soundly and dreamt of David kissing her. His face vanished slowly, replaced by Colin's. It was then that a warm glow flowed through her body.

She woke up feeling guilty, uncomfortable and thirsty. There was a movement of the boat which somehow didn't seem right. She looked through the hatch. In the bright moonlight she noticed they were not facing the same way as the evening before. *Funny, I didn't hear them re-moor. I must have slept like a log after all that wine.* She slipped on a T-shirt and shorts and tiptoed past the sleeping figure of Colin towards the galley to get herself a drink. Having poured herself some water from a bottle kept in the fridge, she went up to the cockpit to enjoy the fresh air and gasped with horror at the sight that greeted her. They were adrift in the middle of the harbour, the wind, or perhaps the current, pushing *Zainda* towards the outside harbour wall. Already they were very near those jagged marble blocks. She jumped down to the cabin and shook Colin by the arm.

'Colin, wake up! Quickly!' In that moment, there was a scraping sound as *Zainda* made contact with the harbour wall.

'Why, what's going on?' he answered sleepily. In that moment, the boat gave a lurch followed by a thud, as though her hull was being knocked out. He jumped. 'Christ, what was that! David! Need your help!' he shook him, putting on his shorts at the same time. Both were out in the cockpit in a flash, grimly surveying the scene.

Joanna was lowering the fenders to take the brunt off the edge of the marble rocks.

'Quick! Joanna, get Simon!' She knocked on the door of the aft cabin. Simon's tussled head appeared after a seemingly indeterminable time. He looked like an old turtle in a wig. 'What's going on, Colin? Don't take her out now, it's much too early.'

'Come up!' said Colin. 'We're adrift. Give us a hand with the engine, we're too near the wall. David, get down to the dinghy, get the kedge out. Pass the boathook to Brenda and tell her to fend off the best she can.'

'I say,' David's voice sounded worried. 'The dinghy's not here,' he said, pointing to the painter which dangled loosely by the side of the boat. If adrift, it was nowhere to be seen. With grim fascination, Joanna watched the hull repeatedly raised by the waves and dropped, rubbing against the rocks with an ominous scratching sound. Her efforts of cushioning the contact with fenders met with little success, a mere plaything in the hands of the elements.

Her thoughts raced. Who could have done it? It was obviously a premeditated act. Somebody must have silently and efficiently untied them, and set them adrift while all were asleep. Now why should anyone do such a monstrously hostile thing? What have they done? Her thoughts became more and more confused. She jumped on the wall, pushed the hull away, while it swayed, bobbing on the waves, up and thump, up and thump.

David jumped into the water to help push the boat off the wall, while Simon tried to start the engine. Colin, tight-lipped, was at the anchor chain, the idea being to drop the anchor and pull away. It came to nothing. Joanna wondered how long a fibreglass hull could take this kind of punishment before it finally gave way and tore a hole. Colin was now standing over Simon as he gallantly fought with the engine starter. It sounded as if had been flooded, giving a loud whine like a nervous dog, only to peter out into silence. Brenda stood shivering in a see-through pink nylon nightdress, holding a torch.

'How is it going, Simon?'

A hiss through Simon's teeth rose above the whine of the starter. 'She won't start, there must be something missing, a pin, I think. Brenda, kindly move to the left, that's better, hand me that spanner, more to the left, thank you, darling, now go and get dressed,' his voice, always so languid, had a sharp edge to it. Brenda obediently went back to the cabin, teeth chattering. A wave bigger than the previous ones lifted the hull and dropped it on the rocks with a sickening crunch. There was a sound of the tearing of fibreglass and wood. Colin appeared by Joanna's side. 'Anchor's not holding. Go and see if there's a hole right through. Stuff some rags into it if necessary.' His voice was drowned by the burst of engine noise as it suddenly came to life. There was a dark cloud of smoke, the boat moved forward, but then the engine cut out.

'What happened?' There was no mistaking the tenseness in Colin's voice.

'Don't know,' Simon said, sounding weary. He brushed his long hair away from his face. 'Bit of a bore, that,' he said, then buried his head again in the engine compartment.'

'Can you see anything, David?' came Colin's voice again.

David, who had been left behind on the rocks as the boat moved forward, was now swimming towards them, and circled round the boat.

'Can't. Try and shine the torch here. Ah, yes, I can see now, we've got the dinghy painter wound round the propeller. Pass me a knife, I'll see if I can free it.'

Joanna dropped him a knife on a piece of string which she tied to the lifeline and watched him in the feeble circle of light made by the torch as he kept spluttering, diving and coming up for air.

'I'm afraid I've got to get out, I've got a cramp!' he called out. 'It's wound very tightly round the prop shaft, so it won't come off easily.' He stood dripping and shivering in the cockpit.

'Would you put the kettle on, Brenda?' called Joanna. 'Make David a hot drink.'

'Brandy would be better. And put some dry clothes on,' said Simon.

David disappeared into the darkness of the cabin, leaving pools of water behind him.

The nightmare continued. Colin took over hacking away at the rope, as long as he could hold his breath under water before coming up to the surface with a splutter. Strangely, nobody could find a snorkel. A cool wind blew over. Then Simon decided to take over from Colin, but he didn't stay down long. As the men took turns, the boat kept rubbing against the harbour walls. Miraculously, there were no holes right through and the bilges were dry, only deep scratches on the outside of the hull. While the men were resting from diving, Joanna stood on the rocks, pushing it off with a boathook while Brenda moved the fenders from the deck to cushion the jugged, protruding edges. After an interminably long time, Colin's voice was heard.

'Try and start the engine now.'

It worked the first time; the gear engaged and the boat moved forward and away from the rocks. Joanna's arms felt like lead with all the pushing. The relief of seeing *Zainda* move away from the harbour wall made her legs tremble so much she had to sit down. Simon circled the boat round the harbour and steered towards their mooring place. Colin swam towards the quay and came out where Joanna was standing.

'Are we going to stay here for the rest of the night?' she asked.

'Might as well. I think that whatever's left of the night we all need a bit of a rest, don't you'? he pointed to the sky. In the darkness, the edge of the horizon was becoming visibly lighter, a paler blue tinged with a narrow golden band.

'Who could have done this? And whatever for? They all seemed so friendly, those men on the shore. And yet, someone deliberately meant us harm! Why? What do you think?' blurted Joanna, gingerly picking her way along the quay in her bare feet as they walked to meet the others back on the boat in the harbour. The huge blocks of marble awaiting shipment threw long, sinister shadows in the fading moonlight. Not a soul was about, but, in Joanna's distraught state, vicious men were watching them from behind every stone. Colin, though still shivering in the cool night air, walked easily, rather like a proverbial jungle cat. Although Joanna walked behind him so that his face was hidden and she could only see his back, she sensed a grim determination emanating from his every movement. He walked quickly, in silence, and didn't bother to answer her.

'Colin, wait!'

'What is it?' he replied impatiently, not slowing down.

'I can see our dinghy – I think.'

He stopped. The dinghy, the grey, slightly battered Avon was snuggled in the nook of the harbour, bobbing among the rubbish accumulated there. They got in and pushed away with a boathook. There was no one about, nothing stirred, the open fishing boats swaying gently in the gathering breeze, the water with all its floating debris lapping the breakwater walls. They helped to tie *Zainda* to the quay then Simon got into the dinghy to examine the damaged hull.

'I don't think there are any holes right through. A bit of luck, that. We'll patch the dents up in the morning.'

'Might as well catch up on your sleep, Joanna. Not much we can do right now,' he said, then turned to Simon. 'I just have to go and see about something.' Having changed into dry clothes, he stepped out, quickly swallowed by the darkness.

Joanna struggled with the stove and the kettle to make tea. When at last she reached her bunk, the sky was already pale yellow. A widening band of pink and orange was spreading from the east, adding to the colours of the coming day. Ah, the rosy fingers of dawn! Before falling asleep, she heard a noise – it was Colin coming back. Where had he been? Had he been up watching all night? She went to sleep again, determined to keep those worrying thoughts at bay till daytime.

Chapter 8

They were now sailing towards Istanbul. Who could have done it and why? That question went round Joanna's mind round and round till she thought she'd go mad. It was no accident, that much was sure, it had definitely been deliberate. A slight breeze accompanied them, and soon they came across a school of dolphins – or were they porpoises? She could never tell the difference between them. Everybody grabbed their cameras, trying to photograph them as they leapt out of the water. Their playfulness was fascinating. They approached the hull at great speed, then dived under just as it seemed the bow would slice them in half, zigzagging in front, leaping in an effortless, beautiful arc to submerge gracefully into the blue-green depths. She was sure they squeaked as they sped along the water. No matter how often it was repeated, Joanna could not have enough of it.

Another puzzle which preoccupied her as she stood poised with the camera pressed against the pulpit was that nobody had referred to the incident again. Somehow, she expected endless comments, discussions, possible reasons for it happening, attempts to contact the police, enquires from the fishermen, anything in fact except their silence. When she tried to raise the subject over breakfast, Simon dismissed it out of hand. Somebody must have played a prank: 'Y'know, a joke, a sick joke admittedly, probably kids, lots of them about. Ignorant natives, they don't know any better, y'know, best to forget it and press on. No need to make a fuss.' And that was that.

What he said made some sense, and yet the puzzle continued to niggle. Who could it have been? Kids? A dispossessed fisherman who came back in the middle of the night to find his mooring space occupied? No fisherman would set them adrift, it just wasn't possible, there was such a thing as camaraderie at sea. People understood the precarious nature of the sea, whether they went out on it for a living or for play, and stuck together irrespective of divergence of interests or language. The sea united them all in a common bond, even if it were the *only* bond. Simon was right, it must have been the work of mischievous children. But to get up in the middle of the night, tow them out quietly – could that possibly be the work of *children*? It made no sense. Her head was reeling. She had to admit the incident had scared her. She tried to calm herself by applying doses of common sense, but her fears kept returning. She even tried to corner Brenda to see if she shared any of her misgivings, but ever since their eventful trip to Troy Brenda had been avoiding her. Once she had come to the galley as Joanna was busy cutting sandwiches for lunch.

'If you mention anything about me to Simon ...' she hissed. 'I'll – '

Joanna stood up abruptly, white with anger, so that Brenda did not finish whatever threat she had in mind.

'If you're not here to help, Brenda,' she managed to say, 'I'd be glad if you'd move out of the way.'

Brenda shrugged her shoulders and climbed back to her usual place on the aft deck, by now monopolised by her and Simon. Moving next to him, she managed to rub herself kittenishly against his body. Ever since the incident at Troy, she had become extremely demonstrative in her affections, in an almost continuous celebration of their liaison. 'What a bitch!' muttered Joanna to herself. She jabbed a serrated knife into a tomato until the juice squirted all over the table. 'Bitch.'

They were entering Istanbul. The sea was very choppy and there was a lot of traffic: ships, boats and ferries, crossing to and fro. Joanna looked with curiosity at the houses and buildings lining the water front. Beyond them, slender minarets of numerous mosques pointed towards the sky like long fingers above the general outline of the city. A lot of noise was coming from the land now, the steady buzz of traffic, honking of cars, mixed with the hooters and sirens from the boats and ferries crossing the Bosphorus Strait. Where the waters were most turbulent, a number of little anchored open boats swung precariously back and forwards, each with one or two fishermen fishing with grim intensity in their bobbing crafts. Just looking at their boats in that constant, bobbing motion made Joanna feel seasick. From time to time, big cargo ships passed through, adding their wake to the general turbulence.

The current must have been pretty strong because *Zainda* made slow progress on their way up. Eventually, they found the bay Colin was looking for, a kink in the smooth line of the built-up sea front, a haven full of buoys, one of which they selected and made fast.

'What's this place called? We seem to be miles from the city centre,' asked Joanna.

'If you can trust my navigation, it should be Tarabya,' said Colin.

Colin had changed considerably since that eventful night. Maybe that was one reason her instincts were aroused enough to tell her it had not been an innocent prank carried out by spiteful children as Simon had suggested. If, before the incident, he was, if not communicative at least relaxed, now his face was set in grim concentration with an occasional tick in his tightly clenched jaws. He had withdrawn into himself as if trying to work something out, and was impatient if anyone was in his way. Whatever he was trying to do, she certainly was no part of it. As soon as they moored, he said to her:

'Look, I'm sure you'll be glad to be off, see the sights. Why don't you and Brenda go in to town, come back for supper later? We'll be here, doing the repairs.'

With that, he dismissed her and started working the knobs of the radio set. *He's behaving as if he he's in command and wants me out of the way*, realised Joanna, bridling inwardly at the thought of having to spend a whole day with Brenda.

'I wonder why they want to get rid of us?' she blurted to Brenda on their way to the bus stop.

'They don't,' said Brenda placidly. 'Simon wants me to have a good time and knows I'm not mad keen on sailing. Not like you,' she added. 'Here,' she said, brightening up considerably. 'Let's go and have a drink in that hotel over there. I don't feel like going to town right now, I'm much too tired.'

The hotel to which she pointed was a new, multi-storey building not far from where they moored. It looked like one seen anywhere in the world, exuding an international, soulless, 'airport' kind of atmosphere. For Joanna it had nothing special to recommend it, no local interest. She considered this international type of architecture a waste of time. They could be visiting something more characteristic of the country instead. But Brenda was not easily dissuaded and Joanna was too tired to argue. Anyway, the city centre was far, and she was experiencing 'sea legs' walking on the firm ground. They always came after spending a long time on a moving boat. Although she felt alright and perfectly balanced on the boat, as soon as she stepped ashore there was this swaying sensation as if the ground was about to give way, making her stumble because, of course, it didn't. She reached the hotel on unsteady feet and gratefully sunk into a chair, holding tight to what seemed like a tilting table on which the waiter had placed a glass of iced water, followed by a Coke. The rest of the day was spent, as expected, in utter boredom, watching people pass by, to the accompaniment of Brenda's not very profound comments.

The following day, the men continued to address the damaged hull, as well as dealing with the formalities their stop at Istanbul entailed. The girls were told again to take time off, enjoy themselves and not bother to come back until the evening. Joanna groaned at the prospect of another day with Brenda for company, reflecting that it was perhaps better than none in this unknown city. Often a sightseeing tour in a foreign city ended in having to fend off unwanted attentions of men who simply could not understand why women tourists on their own would not consider them a gift from the gods sent to relieve them of the boredom of their own company. Or perhaps they were simply looking for a fleeting adventure. Whatever the reasons, it seemed particularly true right now of Turkish men, where a young woman who was blonde, attractive and foreign seemed to combine the qualities irresistible to them, hence rarely left alone.

As they dressed to go out, Simon stopped them. 'I say, you might like to stop for the night in Istanbul, y'know. Saves you all that journey back. Expenses paid. We could do the repairs properly, spread ourselves out a bit, couldn't we, Colin?' he said, turning to Colin for support.

'Good idea,' shouted Colin from the cabin, too heartily for Joanna. She was more than startled. Simon was prepared to pay to keep them away? Brenda however almost jumped for joy. 'Oh, splendid! We could have a long bath and sleep in a proper bed.' She went up to kiss Simon who pressed money into her purse.

'Come on, Joanna, don't just stand there, get your things and let's get going.'

Joanna hadn't seen Brenda so enthusiastic about anything so far, apart from that taxi driver. Obviously sailing didn't suit her. She packed her bag and joined Brenda on the quay, shoes on, waiting impatiently.

It didn't take long to get a bus to take them to the city centre. They decided to find a hotel first, leave their bags, and set off sightseeing. The day was sultry, overcast and even drizzled intermittently, unusual for the time of the year. The bus made its way slowly through heavy traffic. If Istanbul was in Joanna's imagination a shining city of oriental charm filled with wonderful, historical relics, she was disappointed. All those historical buildings, together with the rest of the city, were almost wrapped in smoke and drizzle. Her first impression was of a pervading greyness. The overcrowded bus crawled through the narrow streets and most of the pavements were dug up as if whoever started the construction works had changed their mind half way through.

They judged to be in the centre of the city once the mosque of Suleiman the Magnificent with the slim minarets appeared through the misted windows. They alighted, not sure which way to go. The Hilton and Sheraton hotels were out of the question – Simon's generosity did not stretch to that. As far as Joanna was concerned, any reasonable, clean hotel with a bath would suit. They walked along the grey streets disconsolately, pushing their way past the milling crowds, when at last they came to the part of the city where several houses had "Hotel" signs above the entrances. They chose the nearest, eager to leave their bags and begin sightseeing, especially as the sun had now managed to part the heavy clouds so that the city lost its grey look and became very hot.

A pale-faced man with a moustache and a protruding belly sat behind the reception desk at the end of a big entrance hall with tiled floors and a tall ceiling. Their footsteps made a hollow, echoing sound on the tiles as they walked towards him. He nodded and said, 'Yes,' several times to their enquiry about a double room with a bath, indicating he understood English, then picked up a key from an array on the back wall and beckoned to follow him.

The room he opened was on the first floor. It was sumptuously furnished with large, heavy pieces of furniture of which by far the largest, taking up most of the space, was a four-poster bed. The predominant colour of the room was pink – a pink satin bed cover, bedside lamps with pink lampshades, pink curtains framing the window, pink cushions scattered on the chairs. Joanna fingered the satin bed cover.

'What would you call this shade of pink, Brenda? Brothel pink?' she asked with a straight face.

The man opened a small door leading from the room. It revealed a bathroom with a big bath, a shower and a toilet just few inches from the ground. He opened one of the taps over the washbasin and water cascaded from it. If the pink colour of the bedroom had nearly put Joanna off, the sight of so much water obtained without having to laboriously pump the toilet on board *Zainda* sent her into rapture. 'We'll take it, shall we, Brenda?

Brenda nodded in agreement. The man looked as if it didn't matter which way the transaction went and kept looking into the space above their heads. He bowed slightly on hearing Joanna's decision. 'Please, your passports. Key downstairs when you go,' he said and waddled out of the room. His feet, clad in cheap sandals which were simply rubber soles held up by two straps fixed between the toes, made a soft, shuffling noise along the corridor.

'Right,' said Joanna as soon as he disappeared. 'Who's first to the bathroom?' Without waiting for an answer, she peeled off her clothes, grabbed a bottle of shampoo and dived under the shower.

They emerged from the hotel an hour later, washed, shampooed, feeling wonderfully clean and ready to "conquer" the town. The key, however, would not fit the lock in the door and they had to leave it unlocked.

'Must see him about this,' said Joanna. 'It should be all right; we can leave our things here; I'm sure nobody steals in Turkey.'

They went downstairs to find him but the hotel was empty, lifeless. Somewhere, far away, they could hear women's voices and a child crying. Then, all went quiet. The man was not at the reception desk. Brenda rang the bell and they stood waiting. Nothing happened.

'Did he say he wanted our passports?' whispered Brenda. The hall had this effect on them, as if their voices were unnaturally loud.

'I'm not leaving mine here,' said Joanna. 'We can hand them in when we come back and tell him about the key at the same time.'

Once out on the street, the sky had resumed its overcast appearance. They walked along the streets slowly, noticing that the men who passed them were weighed down by objects they carried on their back which made them look hump-backed. On closer inspection, these objects turned out to be saddles, to which all kinds of things were strapped as the men moved to and from the bazaar. It was the only sensible means of transport in these narrow, partly dug-up passages, but Joanna found them degrading, as if they were pack animals.

The bazaar – the covered Turkish market – was a world of its own. Lining the labyrinths of narrow, vaulted passages were tiny, lit cubicles displaying all kinds of goods. From each a man, or sometimes two, gazed, ready to pounce on the passerby. There was not a language they couldn't speak. To be a shop keeper in the bazaar required more than mere selling. It was not so much an art but an elevated calling, with no room for amateurs.

'Come, where you from? English, Deutsch, Français, Polski, Ruski? You want bag, carpet, jewellery? Come, my friend, I give you good price, tell me what you want, come look, please not have to buy, just look, sit down, sit down,' and a place would be made on a tiny chair or a chest. 'You want tea, coffee, juice? Please, Turkish hospitality, sit down, what price will you give me, eh, just tell me!' It would go on and on. In that little world, each man produced his own climate, sucking into his cubicle both the unsuspecting tourist and the seasoned veteran who had already tasted, to his own considerable cost, the force of these micro-elements. There was no way to extricate oneself easily without losing money or giving offence. An utterance of 'Come, you are my friend, how much will you give me, just tell me the price', and one had to stop and ponder even if there was not the slightest intention of ever wishing to possess the offered object. During one of these encounters to appease and shake off the man, Joanna mumbled a figure. 'You think I am thief, eh?' the man screamed back. 'That price is for thieves. I give you good price, not thief price.' He looked thoroughly offended. It was quite a show.

They made their way through the maze of passages progressively wearily, and finally managed to get lost. Soon they were besieged by a crowd of little boys, street urchins who, for some reason known only to them, shouted, 'Alemaine!' in shrill voices as they trailed behind them. Joanna was wearing a high-necked blouse and jeans but Brenda had taken no such precautions. It simply didn't help to wear shorts just about covering the buttocks and high heels. Men stared at her, their eyes sticky like the tentacles of a weird insect, moving up and down her figure, eventually fastening somewhere in the middle of her chest, half-bared by the low-cut blouse.

Brenda, being less disciplined than Joanna, finally emerged from the bazaar carrying a stuffed toy camel, its eyes unevenly placed on either side of its head, a brass ashtray and a jumper she didn't like once seen in the daylight. Joanna, in turn, bought a turquoise ring she didn't want and blamed Brenda, who kept stopping at the jewellery shops and agreeing to have tea with them. After taking up the owner's undivided attention for the best part of an hour and being shown literally hundreds of pieces of jewellery, she was about to leave without buying anything but Joanna felt the man's efforts had to be rewarded. The man continued to show them more goods, reluctant to let them go. Finally, Joanna was prepared to pay almost anything to be able to get out of that stuffy, overheated cubicle where the hot, sweet tea made her perspire uncomfortably. Brenda had no such compunctions: she drank tea, followed by a Coke, laughed a lot and tried numerous rings, twisting her hand this way and that, then the bracelets, before rejecting the lot and dismissing the fawning proprietor. Joanna looked at the modest turquoise ring on her finger which secured their release, mixed with pity for the man who had tried so hard, wondering who of the two was the weaker.

Having left the bazaar behind them, they trailed round the city. Joanna wanted to see the mosque of the great Suleiman with its slender minarets that she had admired from the distance, but it was not to be. At the entrance sat several men, making sure the tourists took their shoes off. One pointed to Brenda's shorts and shook his head from side to side in disapproval. 'Proper dress, proper dress,' he screeched, pushing Brenda back with his arm. The man next to him took a mop out to wipe the steps. Apparently, she had moved too near the entrance while still wearing the shoes that everybody was supposed to take off at the bottom of the stairs. She shook herself free from the man's grip and walked away. Joanna followed.

'Too bad,' she said to Joanna. 'Those places bore me anyway.'

It was getting late and they were tired so they collapsed at the nearest restaurant, somewhat restored by a delicious steak and a salad with crumbled cheese on top. The thought of that huge, soft bed drew them back to the hotel. They found it as they left it – empty. Even the key was lying in the same place on the reception desk. Brenda rang the bell. It echoed strangely in the reception hall. After several attempts, a small door opened from behind the desk and a woman appeared in the doorway, holding a white scarf to cover half her face. Brenda went up to her.

'We'd like to register now, and could you see about the key, please? This one doesn't fit the lock.'

The woman looked at Brenda, her eyes mystified as if she had never seen a woman in shorts before. It was obvious she understood not a word, but stood there without making a movement or a sound. Eventually she nodded and disappeared.

'I'm not going to stand here for ages,' said Brenda. 'Let's go upstairs. If they're not interested in our passports, it's their look-out.'

They went up to their room. Although tired, Joanna couldn't sit still and kept pacing up and down. The stillness of the hotel was getting on her nerves. It did not seem to affect Brenda who had already undressed and was wiping off her make-up.

'Tell you what we could do,' said Joanna, stopping in the middle of the room. 'We could fix a chair under the door handle, then nobody can open the door from the outside. I'll feel safer that way.'

Her feeling of uneasiness had not communicated itself to Brenda who was sitting in front of the dressing table, putting dollops of cream on her face and working them into the skin with circular movements. Her face registered placid repose. Joanna, on the other hand, had her ears cocked for any sound or movement outside. Nothing, however, disturbed the eerie, empty silence. They seemed to be the only guests. Business couldn't be very good, she reflected, although this was the peak of the summer season. She looked out onto the small, narrow alley below, forgotten by the main traffic. The darkness was relieved by a feeble light from a single lamp further down the road and a neon sign blinking intermittently from the building on the opposite side which was also a hotel. It was new, squeezed into a row of older ones, gleaming with fresh whiteness like a false tooth. If there was any life in that street it was concentrated in that new hotel. It was obvious they took all the business from the one she and Brenda had chosen, which they now realised was practically empty, deprived of its lifeline of tourists.

The bathroom was hot and stuffy. The window looked out to the back of a row of houses. Joanna had to struggle to open it to let in fresh air; clearly, it had not have been opened for some time. After further attempts, it flew open, hitting an obstruction, but miraculously did not break. An iron staircase serving as a fire escape was fixed there, extending half way in front of the window.

She went back to the bedroom, suddenly no longer tired. Her pulse and heart were pounding while she tried to sort out her irrational anxiety. Obviously that night on the island of Marmara had unsettled her more than she knew. Now this gloomy hotel was getting on her nerves as she listened, trying to detect sounds in its cavernous silence.

'Oh, come on, Joanna,' drawled Brenda. 'Don't just sit there, come to bed. It's bliss here! It's ever such a soft mattress,' she said as she patted it lovingly.

Joanna's uneasiness continued to rise. How to explain it to Brenda? Anything, any excuse would do, if only she could think of something quickly. A sound of a car pulling in front of the hotel made her start. After a while, she could swear there were soft footsteps on the corridor, drowned by the whine of the car engine moving in the reverse gear. Then the footsteps became audible again.

'I believe I can hear our man coming to give us the key,' said Brenda. 'Too bad, I'm not getting up to get it. My, you are on edge, aren't you?' she said, looking at Joanna who jumped towards the window. 'You should relax more.'

'It's not that,' said Joanna, turning away from the window as she watched the car. There seemed to be something familiar about it. Quick, think of something. 'I'm just particular about hotels generally,' she lied. 'I'm scared of bed bugs. Do you mind if we have a look at that mattress?'

'Bugs,' exclaimed Brenda, jumping out of the bed in a flash. 'You don't think we've got bugs here, do you? I'd hate that, I really would.'

'Let's have a look then,' said Joanna, pulling off the sheet, bending her head, ears cocked as she listened to the sounds outside while examining the mattress.

The footsteps hesitated, came nearer, were joined by more. Joanna's face was wet with perspiration. She dug her nails into the wet palm of one hand as her finger drew slowly along the seam. Fate, it seemed, decided to be on her side. The finger encountered a soft lump. A bug! She drew back in disgust mixed with relief.

'I've got one,' she hissed triumphantly, picking up the half-squashed bug and throwing it on the floor. 'I'm not staying here another minute,' she exclaimed. Was it her imagination or did the door handle slowly move? 'Not another second. Brenda, we're leaving.'

'What, leave?' Brenda protested feebly. 'Now?'

'Yes, now, I don't care. Hurry!' This time she swore the door handle moved.

'But how? What do we say to the man? He'd make us pay anyway,' she almost wailed.

'Not if we get out so he doesn't see us. Hurry up and get dressed,' she said, nearly pushing Brenda into her shorts. There was an audible rattle at the door, even Brenda noticed it. 'What was that?'

'I don't know!' Joanna's voice was urgent and at the same time very calm. This time it was obvious that out there, in the corridor was a man, maybe more than one, who was trying to enter their bedroom without knocking. Someone who meant them harm. Her head was clear now that those vague suspicions that had so tormented her emerged from the shadows and crystallised into a concrete threat. All the inexplicable questions as to why anybody should be after them could be sorted later. Now was time for action.

'Maybe ...' started Brenda, but Joanna pushed her firmly into the bathroom. 'Don't put the light on. Got all your things?'

'I suppose so,' Brenda's voice sounded doubtful. 'I can't see here in the dark, can I? What are you doing?' Her voice rose into a pitch.

'Shhh, be quiet.' The rattle of the door handle became louder. There was no doubt this time – someone had dropped all pretences and was trying to break in. Joanna wondered how long the chair would stand up to it.

'Was there a knock at the door?' asked Brenda and stopped to listen. 'Look, Joanna, it's probably the man with the key. Shouldn't we go back, talk to him? I think all this is rather stupid if you want to know.'

Joanna sighed. This was no time for explanations, like pointing out the man hadn't knocked or called out, and by the sound of things there was more than one outside in the corridor. Also, she couldn't put into words her anxiety, the feeling that something was just not right. In response, she swung her legs through the open window and stepped on the iron staircase. It wobbled under her weight.

'Here, give me your bag and pass me mine. Now, give me your hand.'

Brenda squealed as the staircase swung with a loud creak about a foot from the wall, like a swing in a park.

'Shhh, don't make such a noise.'

They tiptoed down the iron stairs with what, to Joanna's ears, sounded like a loud clatter. There was a drop of about five feet from the last step to the ground which fortunately turned out to be quite soft. They found themselves in a dark, dank garden surrounding the hotel on three sides, overgrown with shrubs and full of rubbish. They tiptoed alongside the tall, iron fence separating the garden from the street and almost trod on a cat. It sped in front of them, tail erect, making loud, angry noises, Joanna ready to forgive it for not being a rat. They found one railing that was bent enough for them to be able to squeeze through. They must have been no more than fifty yards from the hotel entrance, where a car was parked, mounted half-way on the pavement. There was no one in it. Again, it looked familiar. In the dim light of the street lamp, Joanna could make out a dice and a hand on a spring in the rear window. The dashboard and the steering wheel were covered in a fur fabric. It was too dark to detect the colour. Was it possible this was the taxi which took them to Troy? Would Brenda have planned a rendezvous with the taxi driver? Surely she couldn't have, they hadn't known in which hotel they were going to stay. Her thoughts raced faster than her legs. She had to stop herself from running and appear to be walking normally. Brenda followed her closely and seemed to notice nothing. Joanna looked at her with suspicion. If she didn't plan it, how did the taxi driver, if it was even his taxi, know where to look for her? Had he been following them? Her fears welled up again as she looked over her shoulder.

'Where shall we go now?' panted Brenda. Her voice implied she had humoured Joanna so far but was finding the present situation beyond a joke.

'Why, the hotel opposite,' said Joanna with a lightness she didn't feel.

As luck would have it, they managed to mix with an English party who had just arrived and were crowding round the reception desk. Brenda's nightie tucked into her shorts raised no eyebrows: it could have been a frilly blouse.

As soon as they were alone, locked in their room, Brenda took the sheet off and examined the mattress carefully. 'I'm not going through that rigmarole again. It's not my idea of fun to prowl round stinking gardens in the dark.'

Joanna, too, gave the mattress more than a perfunctory look, carried on only a minute longer than Brenda for the sake of appearances. Were they being followed? Would the taxi driver have gone to such lengths to see Brenda again? Was he after the money they owed him for the fare? But was she sure it was even his taxi? There were plenty of cars like that in Turkey, decorated with fur and mascots. All those questions kept revolving in her head. She looked through the window onto the street and the hotel they had left in such a hurry. There was a light in the window on the first floor, the room they had vacated. Shadows were moving against the light, flitting quickly, gesticulating. Somebody leaned out of the window, scrutinised the street, then shut it. The light was switched off. After a while, two figures emerged from the entrance, walked quickly to the car and drove away.

'None here, I can swear.' Brenda's triumphant voice cut through her whirling thoughts. 'We'll be all right, Joanna. What are you staring at now? You are funny. Fancy not liking hotels. I love them. Give me a holiday in a hotel every time.' She stretched luxuriously on the bed and closed her eyes. Joanna moved away from the window and switched off the main light. Had one of those figures been Brenda's taxi driver? She looked at her with renewed suspicion, lying on the bed, breathing evenly, eyes closed as if already asleep. Suddenly she gave a giggle without opening them.

'I'd love to see the look on that man's face when he finds we've gone. And we had a bath for nothing.'

Chapter 9

It was late the following day when they eventually sat down to rest their weary legs in a café overlooking the Golden Horn. Joanna looked at it with tired eyes after a night of intermittent sleep and a morning of sightseeing. The Horn wasn't golden at all, in fact it belched black smoke from the sawmills below. She stood up wearily in order to find the ladies' room. Weaving her way past the tables and chairs, she saw an elderly man reading a paper not far from theirs. There was something familiar about him; she was certain she'd seen him somewhere before. It bothered her because she prided herself on remembering faces. Where might she have seen him? It was most annoying not to be able to place the man. So far, they had had no visitors on *Zainda* apart from port officials. Wherever they anchored, always in close proximity to other yachts, Joanna could not remember being visited by any of the owners or their guests making friendly calls. Could he have come from that gin palace? Even though they had sailed along a similar route, their crew and owners had kept themselves aloof. No one had ever been invited on board by either party. It must be her overwrought imagination. God, what a night!

'David seems quite fond of you.' Brenda's voice cut through her thoughts as she sat down by the table again. 'He keeps looking at you all the time.'

Joanna was annoyed, not prepared to discuss David, least of all with Brenda. 'Oh, when did you notice that?' she asked acidly, at the same time wondering how she could have witnessed anything. Brenda avoided the galley whenever she could, rarely helped if at all, spending most of the time in the aft cabin or sitting on the aft deck, sunbathing, or reading what Joanna considered trashy novels.

'Well, I have,' pouted Brenda, lighting a cigarette. 'I notice all sorts of things.'

Joanna brightened up considerably. She must have noticed that something was wrong last night, that it wasn't just her overwrought imagination. They were being followed, or watched, and it wasn't all in the mind. Somebody did try to break into their room last night, but who and why? Perhaps if they talked about it, they might sort something out. Two heads were better than one.

'What sort of things?' she asked, managing to keep the excitement out of her voice.

'Puppy love, that's what.'

'Oh,' came a sigh from a deflated Joanna. If that was all Brenda noticed about last night, then she was as thick as she had always suspected. But then the incident with the taxi driver stabbed her memory like a thorn. Was she trying to deflect her attention from it? Had it had any significance, or was it merely a holiday interlude, perhaps a sort of compensation for Simon? Brenda had sort of implied Simon was not satisfying her. Or could she be part of a sinister plot?

Meanwhile, Brenda discarded her shoes and was wriggling her scarlet-painted toes. 'And don't tell me you don't enjoy it. His attention I mean. I know you do, but then,' she nodded with mock seriousness, 'you've got your sights on someone else, haven't you?'

Joanna felt the colour rise to her cheeks. So, her feelings for Colin were so obvious that even a goose like Brenda had noticed them. Brenda was watching her with half-closed eyed, gauging the effect of her words. Joanna tried to pull herself together. 'I don't know what you are driving at, Brenda,' she managed to shrug.

Suddenly, she started, as it hit her. The man – of course! The man in Canakkale. The same man! She rose as panic gripped her. Why was he here? *Why not?* said the calm voice of reason. The sightseeing circuit was the same for all tourists – Troy, Istanbul, etc. Of course. She sat down again. That stupid Brenda set her nerves on edge, and she looked at her with renewed dislike.

Brenda, blissfully unaware, sat looking vacantly into space. Her legs were crossed, stretching the material of her shorts, exposing the bulging flesh of her thighs to the elements and to the lingering looks of delight of the male passers-by. 'I'm not driving at anything, but don't think I don't notice things.'

Joanna turned round to look at the man again, but the seat was empty – he was gone. She felt panic again, like a fist in the throat, and dug her nails into the palms of her hand. She simply must pull herself together.

They arrived at the harbour of Tarabya after a tiring journey by bus lasting more than an hour. The bus stopped at frequent intervals, held up by the crawling traffic. The traffic lights, of which there were only a few, did not seem to mean anything to the drivers. Either they were not used to them in Istanbul or they broke down too often for anyone to take notice, so that the drivers just ignored them. The lights flashed red and green intermittently, the traffic stopped and moved, propelled by its own law, which stated that if you saw a space ahead you moved into it irrespective of the changing colour of the lights.

The sun was casting long rays over the hills on the opposite side of the Bosphorus Strait and the harbour was already in the shade when the girls, hot, sticky and aching, arrived back at *Zainda*. The gangplank was tied up which meant there was no one on board. Lights were just beginning to appear in the cafés and restaurants on land, illuminating also the little kiosks of the street vendors selling ice cream and fruit juices. There was the sound of the theme music from the film *Zorba the Greek* loud enough to reach them in the harbour. Suddenly, the lights of the modern hotel were switched on, flooding one end of the quay with bright luminescence. They watched this gradual night-life take over from the receding day, sitting in the cockpit, sipping not very cold lemonades and stretching their aching legs. Brenda's eyes were trained on the hotel, yearning, no doubt, for the lights of the big city, thought Joanna. She, on the other hand, looked towards the distant hills where the setting sun was making a last effort to tint them with its golden hue. She noticed a new arrival in the harbour – a big, gleaming white cruiser bearing a Panamanian flag flapping in slow motion from the aft deck. It was similar to *Jemima*, but clearly built for deep-sea fishing, with a bridge above the cabin where all the controls were arranged, almost like a cockpit of an aeroplane. The bridge was festooned with rods and harpoons which swayed in the breeze. In the centre of the bridge was the steering wheel and a chair intended for the big fish hunter, enabling him to swivel round as he surveyed the watery jungle without having to get up, then take over the steering wheel from the paid underling sweating in the control cabin below and having spotted his quarry strike with those gleaming harpoons. While she was pondering all this, the cruiser came to life with a loud roar of the engines. Billows of smoke came out of the exhaust, wafted across the waters of the harbour and reached their cockpit. The hull shuddered and swayed on the moorings while the noise continued unabated.

Joanna gasped for breath. 'They're charging their batteries. It'll go on for ages. We might as well head off and have something to eat or we'll suffocate here.'

They put on their shoes and walked along the quay, Brenda gravitating towards the modern hotel.

'Come on, Brenda. It's much too expensive there. Let's go find another place. I'd like some local food anyway.'

But Brenda kept walking ahead. 'We don't have to eat there. Or …' she added with a glance at Joanna, '… sleep there. Let's just have a drink, that's all. Oh, come on, this is more fun than sitting on that boring old yacht.

Joanna had no energy to disagree and didn't feel like going to a restaurant on her own. As they passed the tables of the various eating places set out in the open air, men's eyes followed them with the inevitable chorus of 'Where you from? English, German, French?' trailing behind them. They entered the hotel bar where Brenda ordered a tequila, Joanna contenting herself with a Coke, thankfully cold this time.

'Oh look!' exclaimed Brenda conspiratorially. She was playing with her drink, scanning the place with the precision of a radar scanner. 'My God,' she drew in her breath and exhaled with a loud: '*Wow*! Just look behind you but don't make it too obvious.'

'Where?' asked Joanna, looking absentmindedly at the people near her, wondering which man took Brenda's fancy this time. Obediently, she followed Brenda's gaze and froze. A man and a woman had just entered the bar at the far end, opposite to where they were sitting. She recognised Colin instantly. He was dressed as she'd never seen him on board: he was wearing an immaculate shirt, which set off his tan handsomely, and beautifully pressed trousers. His head was bent down towards a woman on his arm as he steered her through the crowd. The woman was stunning, there was no other word for it. 'She must be a model,' thought Joanna miserably. 'Women don't look like that naturally.'

The woman was dressed in a light, close-fitting dress which accentuated her magnificent figure. Shoulder-length hair framed her exquisite features with a dark, almost liquid cloud, kept back by a pair of sunglasses. Her enormous dark eyes, fringed with long thick eyelashes, were focused on Colin. He must have said something which amused her because suddenly she smiled, revealing a row of dazzling, white teeth. She left no eyes unturned.

'She is beautiful, professionally beautiful,' whispered Joanna. There was constriction in her throat and chest. So, this is what "defeated, not the slightest chance" feels like. Sort of weighed down and crushed. Just as the feeling of pain is delayed after the cause of it has struck so Joanna sat there, feeling not so much hurt as numb. This, so soon after she had allowed herself to think Colin was beginning to show some interest which had made her feel elated in spite of herself. Now, that feeling of hope lay smashed like a Christmas bubble. Mesmerised, she watched Colin and his companion make their way between the tables. The last thing she wanted at that moment was to be seen by them. With an effort she stood up. 'I'm going outside. It's too stuffy in here.'

Hey eyes hot and stinging, she stumbled past the people sitting at the low tables in a hurry to leave before being seen by Colin. She bumped her toes against someone's feet and nearly fell on top of a man sitting in an armchair. 'I'm sorry,' she mumbled and straightened herself up, recovering her balance and rushing towards the door. Agitated as she was, a shock of recognition pierced through the inner turmoil. The man in the armchair – it was the same man who was in the café where they spent the afternoon, the same man from Canakkale. Her feelings were too disturbed by the image of Colin bending solicitously towards the woman to be able to reflect over the coincidence. 'Joanna, take a grip on yourself,' she told herself firmly. 'No way can you compare yourself to that stunner.'

What a fool she'd been, what a bloody fool. How had she ever allowed her emotions to sink that deep in the first place? She should know better by now. Hadn't her broken marriage taught her anything? And what had happened? She'd allowed herself to be hurt yet again. Served her jolly well right. Had Colin ever encouraged, promised, made advances? No, those occasional glances she'd interpreted as appreciative were simply her wishful thinking. Oh, how did this beastly, idiotic feeling for him ever come about? And all against her will, in spite of all the good resolutions? What was the cause of the sudden, lucid awareness whispering in the innermost depths of her soul: *this is it; this is love.* The ancients were right to depict love as a mischievous little boy shooting love darts at all and sundry. But if the ancients were right about Eros, they were also right in treating love as a random thing, and therefore something that couldn't be helped. Heaven knows I didn't want it to happen again. Maybe I'm sex-starved, maybe it's not love but something more basic. Maybe I have built my fantasies round a person to fit my subconscious yearnings, but what I basically want is a man. She tried to think when she had sex last time, and had to admit it was a considerable time ago. The image of Colin and the beautiful woman floated again in her mind's eye. Joanna gave another sob as she hurried along the water front towards *Zainda*. If sex or the lack of it was the underlying cause, then there was David. He was willing enough, that much was becoming more and more obvious.

On board, she found a box of matches in the cabin and lit a cigarette from a packet Brenda had left on the table. She sat smoking in darkness and was only jerked from her misery by Branda's cutting voice: 'Oh, help yourself.' Her face appeared through the door leading to the cockpit. Joanna wasn't sure if she meant it or not, and didn't care.

'Aren't we going to eat?' continued Brenda. 'You shot out so quickly I could barely keep up with you.'

'I'm not hungry,' said Joanna, puffing at the cigarette. She inhaled deeply and felt dizzy. 'I ... felt sick. It was so stuffy inside.' Unused to cigarettes, her head was swimming.

'Poor Joanna,' said Brenda vaguely. 'Perhaps I can get us a hot dog or something.' With that, she clambered out of Joanna's field of vision.

Joanna sat in the darkness, relieved only by the flicker of the street lights. She puffed at the cigarette for a while and felt very sick indeed. In the nick of time, she made her way to the cockpit and was leaning over the side just as Simon and David were about to step on the gangplank.

'Are you alright? Is anything the matter?' asked David anxiously,

'It's nothing. I must have eaten something that didn't agree with me. I'll go and lie down. I'll be alright in a minute. Perhaps you could make your own supper? I can't look at food right now,' she mumbled on the way to her cabin.

'Poor Joanna,' said David. It was the second time in the last half hour and it set her teeth on edge. 'Are you sure you'll be alright? Want to take something for it?'

'Quite sure, thank you.' She closed the door of the cabin and lay on the bunk bed. 'What a fool I've been! Of course it's not Colin, it's plain and simple sex I want,' she mumbled into the pillow. But that didn't stop her from crying until she fell asleep.

Chapter 10

The next day, the sun shone and there was a magnificent freshness in the air. Joanna rose with a throbbing headache and only hoped the experience of the previous evening did not show on her face. Happily, the others noticed nothing. As far as they were concerned, she'd eaten something that didn't agree with her, not an uncommon complaint in a hot climate. There was nothing more to be said.

Colin was conspicuously absent. She didn't want to ask about him, afraid that her feelings which she was determined to keep to herself might show. Anyway, Simon didn't keep her in suspense for long.

'We're leaving today. Colin will be joining us in Kusadasi in a couple of days. Let's provision and be off. No time like the present. Chop, chop! How are we for fuel, David?'

David got up and said he'd see. To check the fuel level in the tank was not as simple as might have seemed. He had to roll up his bedding, take the mattress off his bunk bed, then find an opening to the tank in the dark recesses of the bilges. It was stoppered with a tight-fitting screw which could only be undone by a mole wrench. This part of the procedure had so far not run smoothly. There was always a bruised hand or finger when the wrench or the screw gave way suddenly. This time was no exception. There was a muffled cry of "Ouch!", a hiss of breath drawn in, followed by a string of swear words of which "bloody" was the most acceptable.

'You couldn't get me a plaster or a bandage, Joanna? I'm bleeding in this wretched hole,' came a more distinct request.

Joanna obliged. She kept cotton wool and plasters in the galley for just such occasions. The men were forever bruising themselves against something or other, usually involving metal bits and pieces such as anchor chains, winches and parts of the engine. It was no good unpacking the first-aid kit which formed part of the survival kit stored in several layers of waterproof material that came together with the life raft to be used in an emergency. Emergency was a euphemism for total sinking, and it was better not to think about that.

Once David's hand was patched up, the rest was relatively simple. A dry measuring stick had to be found in the bilges but, inevitably, it had been lost. Joanna had to move various tins of food and paint stored there to find it, tucked away in a damp corner together with all the accumulated crumbs and rubbish. Then it had to be wiped dry, inserted into the tank, taken out and the wet mark examined to see the amount of fuel in the tank.

'Quarter tank full,' announced David triumphantly half an hour later, brushing the hair off his face and wiping his steamed glasses with a piece of rag. Without them, he looked defenceless, like a little boy. The impression was compounded by a dirty smudge across his face as he brushed his curly hair back. 'What are you smiling at?' he asked Joanna. 'If it's about my crushed thumb, it's not funny,' he said and pointed to his hand where a few drops of blood coagulated on the now dirty piece of cotton wool. Joanna looked at him full in the face. 'You got yourself quite dirty,' she said in a low voice, holding his hand a touch too long, and smiled again.

'I'd better go and wash after I put my bedding back,' he grinned back at her, rising to the bait.

'If it's sex I want,' she thought to herself, 'it won't be too difficult. Love? Forget it. I'll never make a fool of myself by falling in love again, never.'

The sail to Kusadasi was uneventful. They sailed close to the Turkish coast, not wishing to stray too far over to the Greek side in case they were seen by a patrol boat and made to re-register in Greece, which would have involved a lot of bureaucratic hustle. So, the island of Lesbos remained in the distance as a solid outline etched against the sky while Joanna let her thoughts dwell on it as she lay sunbathing in the warm sunshine.

Lesbos, or Lesvos, had been the home of the poetess Sappho who was allegedly attracted to women, and gave women with "those tendencies" her name. Was Sappho really a lesbian? Some fragments of her poetry were interpreted as implying it, but they were not convincing. Joanna was much more interested in the story of her unrequited love for a shepherd, the cause of her suicide – a dramatic leap from the white cliffs off the island of Levkas. What was this woman of intellect doing there, anyway, chasing young shepherds far from her home island? What could she have had in common with this young, doubtless virile young man? It must have all boiled down to sex. There, my girl, is an example for you. It's what you too should be after, not hankering for love. He must have been a great catch if Sappho had loved him so much as to commit suicide. Was he in any way to blame for her death? An aging poetess, most likely quoting poetry at him – what could she offer a virile shepherd? Would *he* have harboured secret longings to turn a summer flirtation into an intellectual passion as he tended his sheep on lonely vigils? Well, she, Joanna, had not gone so far as to contemplate suicide, and thankfully David was not a shepherd. She sighed and turned over to get a deeper tan on her face. The suntan suited her. It made an attractive contrast with her blue eyes and blonde hair. In fact, with her hair worn loose and in the scanty two-piece swim suit which showed her trim figure to an advantage, she was a much-changed woman from the prim one who'd boarded *Zainda* on the first day in Athens. She put more cream on her nose which was beginning to go red. If she let her skin burn, it would peel and then flake. She slapped more cream on the neck and shoulders and continued to sun bathe in the pleasantly warm sun. The wind had blown fitfully since the morning but was now fizzling out. The sails occasionally flapped heavily, only to fill out with a loud clang under the influence of the remnant of a breeze, only to flap again. The main boom swayed dangerously across the cockpit and clanged as the sails alternatively swelled and collapsed. She opened one eye and saw Simon and David take them down.

'Here, give us a hand with the sail ties, Joanna. We'd better motor,' said Simon.

The engine spluttered and coughed before finding its own regular rhythm. Vibrations shook the hull, and the saucepans and the cutlery began their usual rattle. The surface of the sea was almost flat and although never completely motionless, this time reminded Joanna of a huge, smooth, pewter-blue animal heaving gently in its sleep. The air was so still that a passing boat in the distance emitting smoke left a trail above the water long after it was gone. There was no distinct line between the sea and the sky, and the few open fishing boats in the distance seemed suspended in the air.

'A bit of a bore, that,' drawled Simon, surveying the becalmed scene, his long hair lying limply across his face. 'We're low on fuel. Hope we can make it to Kusadasi.' He went down to the main cabin to look at the chart.

Joanna closed her eyes and faced the sun again. It was nice to be on a working holiday, lie in the sun and not worry where she was going or when she'd arrive. In the sunshine nothing seemed to matter, only the warmth and a pervading sense of well-being. Who cared if they arrive early or late at Kusadasi? Oh yes, Colin was going to meet them there, like a sleek cat brimming with contentment, after making love to a beautiful woman. Joanna was not looking forward to seeing him. She could practically see the expression on his face, the cat who got the cream, a small satisfied smile playing round the corners of his mouth. He was probably one of those men who had to have some stunner around them; stunners were, after all, a social asset. Millionaires and celebrities were always photographed in the company of beautiful women, never with the plain ones, however successful *they* might be. It was so unfair. A woman with good looks had everything going for her, everything handed to her on the plate as it were, thanks to the gift of nature. Her plain sisters, in which category Joanna – always self-deprecating – included herself as it simply did not occur to her that she could be attractive, had to try harder, sparkle in a conversation, develop a sense humour, learn to listen, and try to be generally useful. And the beautiful ones? They were the centre of attention everywhere they went; men helped them, sought their company, excused their silly remarks and interpreted their silences as depths of intellect rather than admit that in fact they had nothing to say. After trying hard, she thought bitterly, what do the plain ones like me end up with? Marriage down the drain, a fiasco with a man I fancy. She sighed again and concentrated on the events in Istanbul. Admittedly she was considerably rattled by them. Did the men who were trying to get into their bedroom have sinister intentions, or was that the product of her overworked imagination? Perhaps the man on the desk *had* wanted to give them the right key and had brought a locksmith with him? He could have done. She was not one hundred percent sure the car she saw was the same as their taxi to Troy; it was too dark to see properly. Brenda had nothing to do with any of it – by now she was certain of that. But there was something else ... a discordant note thrummed in her brain. Her mind searched through the images deposited there, lying in a heap like a shaken-up jigsaw puzzle. *The man*, the middle-aged man! Of course! Was he following them? Surely three times in a short period of time was no mere coincidence? Could he have something to do with Brenda? If Brenda had allowed herself to be ... Joanna searched for the right word ... *seduced* by that awful taxi driver, who else might she have picked up in the past? Granted, the man did not look the type who was after young women; in fact, he looked very respectable, but appearances were deceptive. Joanna remembered once looking at a man reading a pornographic magazine in a sleazy Soho bookshop. She was interested to see what type of man would read such filthy trash and had to admit to being greatly surprised: he looked like a distinguished city broker, or a lawyer, perhaps. He certainly was not a dirty old man with sex-hungry eyes as she had imagined. *This* man, who might be following them, had a precise, military air about him, certainly not lecherous, but that didn't mean a thing. All those men one reads about in the papers who committed heinous crimes were often model husbands, loving fathers and respectable neighbours. But could Brenda be involved somehow? Although there was no love lost between them, Joanna could not credit Brenda with being so devious or, for that matter, so clever as to be part of some mysterious plot.

A warm haze pervaded the air. The sea continued to heave slowly like a huge sleeping animal. Everything seemed to contribute to make it a time of happy contemplation and pause her worries about lecherous men chasing an amorous Brenda around Istanbul. All fears and worries could wait for later; right now, nothing mattered in this golden warmth. All that did matter was to enjoy the peace and harmony of the sea and the sky. Even David, whose eyes kept straying towards her from time to time, lay slumped in the cockpit, exposing to the sun his bare chest on which a few hairs sprouted. His eyes were closed, yet Joanna sensed imperceptible vibrations emanating towards her, as if his thoughts were caressing her body like tiny wafts of air. Speech, after all, was not the only means of communicating with another human being. But she was too bruised by recent events to respond, switching her attention to Brenda who lay flat as a pancake on the aft deck, hipbones protruding from above the bikini line, showing a lot of red skin. Joanna concentrated hard, but there was no response, no vibrations from Brenda. A complete blank. 'Come on, Brenda,' Joanna was coaxing her inwardly while suitably composing her outward appearance into relaxed indifference. 'What sort of men did you have in your life who'd be chasing you all over Istanbul? Are you part of a sinister plot?' It really did seem unlikely; no, she was sure it had nothing to do with her. Joanna tried to calm herself, the rising fear turning into anger. Why should she be involved in something of which she had no part and knew nothing about?

The wind picked up slightly and Simon and David stirred to put up the sails and conserve the remaining fuel which was getting dangerously low. Joanna woke up from her day-dreaming and went down to prepare lunch. Simon looked preoccupied, or worried, it was difficult to tell which. Why should *he* be worried anyway? It wasn't *he* who had been followed in Istanbul! So far, they weren't late for this appointment in Kusadasi, either. In an unlikely case of a delay, Colin might have to spend the night in a hotel. So what, life under sail was like that, it had its own existence in which the concept of time had no part. Being on time for appointments never fitted in with sailing. Sailing was about nature and harmony, but time, divided superficially by the pedantic humans into hours and minutes, was not of its world. Simon obviously didn't see it that way – he looked worried as he drank his lukewarm beer.

Eventually, the harbour of Kusadasi began to etch itself on the hazy horizon. Joanna was surprised to see it was a few miles away from the town. It was quite new and looked very much like the one of the new marinas which had recently sprung up all over the Mediterranean coast. There were only a few yachts and boats inside tied to the new moorings, and a lot of earth-digging equipment, used in the building of the harbour, was still dotted around. David spotted a fuel sign above the pump station and they motored towards it, using the last drop of diesel in the tank. There was nobody at the pumps so David went ashore and managed to collar a man with whom, as Joanna was able to figure out even from a distance, he had difficulties in being understood. Eventually he came back and said the man had said the fuel pumps were not working, so it would be better to moor next to a crane from where they would arrange to bring fuel in tins. They moved away and made fast to the crane, which was working, moving blocks of stone from a wooden caique and depositing them on the quay.

The caique was a lovely wooden boat with a wide stern that looked like a big, comfortable rump. She had a high aft deck surrounded by balustrades, a short mast and a primitive rigging of hemp ropes. It was obvious she was rarely sailed, propelled most of the time by a big diesel engine controlled from the dog house in the middle of the deck. However, there was a smell of wood and tar about her in spite of the diesel. Altogether it was a much more romantic boat than her white, shiny fibreglass counterparts littering the marina, in which tourists came to play in the warm waters. How insignificant must these smooth, shiny toys appear to the crew of this working boat!

The crane on the quay creaked and groaned while the diesel motor which operated it made loud, barking noises and emitted clouds of dark smoke. The man with whom David had spoken helped them to tie the mooring lines, then shouted something and another man sprang from the holds of the caique and approached Simon. He might be able to help Simon negotiate the transaction of purchasing fuel not far from the harbour, explained the first man, and bring it back in tins in a taxi. Brenda offered to go with Simon, saying she had been cooped up on the boat for far too long.

Joanna sat on the aft deck, watching the scene around her. The crane continued to creak, belching black fumes. A few children in ragged clothes were watching her from a distance. Suddenly she saw movement in the direction of the fuel pumps and sat up.

'I say, David,' she shouted. 'Look, there is a man at the pumps after all.'

'So there is!' he agreed, coming up from the cabin.

'Don't you think it might be an idea to fill the tank from here?'

'Oh, I don't know. But what would we do with the tins Simon will be bringing?'

'But then again, he might not. You can never be sure, but if he does, we can keep them as spare. We're bound to use it sooner or later; we're always having trouble getting fuel: either we're too late and everything's closed, or we are in some remote place and there isn't any.'

'You might be right,' conceded David. 'Let's do it now before that pump attendant goes away again.'

Joanna deftly jumped onto the pontoon and untied the lines. David started the engine. A puff of wind carried the bow instantly away. from the pontoon and *Zainda* swung away towards the fuel pumps.

'That was a neat little manoeuvre,' congratulated Joanna, but her hand poised to pat him on the back was suspended in the air, interrupted by a tremendous crash. They both jumped and looked back. A huge block of stone had slipped from the hook of the crane and dropped into the water where they had been just seconds before. As it dropped, it produced a huge spume of water. One of the rough corners caught on *Zainda*'s stern, splitting part of the rubbing strip and sending a shudder through the hull. Joanna and David looked at each other in horror. The consequences of. what might have happened to the boat – and themselves – if they hadn't moved the boat flashed through their minds simultaneously. Colour drained from Joanna's face as she stood immobilised, one hand on her mouth. David expelled air with a loud 'Phew!' and wiped his forehead with the back of his hand. Beads of perspiration ran down his face.

'That was a narrow escape,' he finally managed to say.

They became conscious of the silence around them. Curiously, there were no shouts from the men on land, no spectators of the scene that an accident usually attracts. Everyone was behaving as if nothing at all had happened. The driver turned the crane around, lowered the huge hook so that another man standing on the quay could attach the dangling rope from which the stone block had slipped, nearly killing them. Joanna watched the calm scene with wide eyes, while the implications of the tranquillity began to register in her brain. She started to shiver uncontrollably. David put his arm round her, his face tense and white with shock. 'It's all right, we're alright,' he said in an unsteady voice. 'We're alright,' he repeated, steering the boat towards the fuel station.

'David,' whispered Joanna. 'They … they don't seem to care.' She shivered again.

'It's all right,' he repeated, his free arm tightening. He pressed her close so that she could feel the sticky warmth of his body.

'I'm scared,' she said quietly, fighting the tears that were welling up.

'There's no need,' his voice was unsteady. 'It was just an accident. The hull's not damaged, just a scratch really,' he shrugged. But he didn't look as imperturbable as he sounded; in fact, he looked almost as shaken as she was.

'An accident! Do you honestly believe that! Look around you! Can't you see, they're all behaving as if …' she searched for the right word that would sum up this extraordinary indifference which struck her more than the block of stone had done. '… as if they were in some kind of conspiracy!'

Once the word came out, the whole incident made sense; it gave the situation a label that fitted. She repeated the word "conspiracy" to herself, with a kind of relief. But David wasn't listening. He had manoeuvred the boat along the quay opposite the pumps and was tying the mooring lines, helped by an attendant. His face was drawn, his movements clumsy. *He is as frightened as I am, but he is doing his best to cover it up,* she realised. But the strain of covering up what he actually felt showed on his young face. But why cover it up in front of her? What was going on?

Conspiracy. The word reverberated in her head. As far as she could make out there was not one but two conspiracies. One was out there, outside, obscure, sinister, stalking her, the other was right here, on this boat and David was part of it. Conspiracy not to acknowledge that something was not right. Or perhaps there was nothing wrong, it was all her imagination, imputing sinister implications where none existed. After all, it was perfectly feasible that it was an accident – they did happen with cranes. But why didn't anyone make a fuss? Maybe they were afraid they'd be sued for negligence. No, it was possible it was simply an accident. The soothing flow of reasoning was interrupted by David who was sitting by the chart table, entering the amount of fuel pumped into the tank in the log book.

'Joanna, do you know today's date?'

Joanna looked at her watch. 'Friday the eleventh,' she said and froze.

Friday, she repeated to herself. Friday was the Moslem equivalent to Sunday: they didn't work on Fridays! She looked wildly around her. The crane had been silent for a while now, which she had failed to notice before in her agitated state. There was nobody around but for the figure of the pump attendant disappearing into the distance. He had already locked up his office and was making his way towards the town. *Friday*. She leaned her forehead on the cabin door and sobbed.

'I say, steady on,' David said, sounding bewildered, flushed with embarrassment at not knowing how to deal with female tears. 'Here,' he fumbled in the galley as if a thought suddenly struck him. 'Here, drink this,' he said, pouring half a glass of warm whisky into a plastic cup. Joanna looked at the liquid and shook her head.

'Your nerves. Delayed shock and all that. You ought to drink it.'

'Okay.' It burnt her throat and tasted foul. She let her head rest on the side of the cockpit, holding the plastic cup in a clammy hand. A sort of numbness enveloped her body. She heard Simon and Brenda arrive in a taxi. They came empty handed – the petrol station in the town was closed as it was a holiday. Simon congratulated David at having spotted the petrol attendant. David mumbled something about the damage to the rubbing strip made by a stone slipping off the crane. Joanna wasn't really listening, and spent the evening in a merciful haze thanks to the whisky.

The following morning the sun shone brightly as it always did in that part of the world at that time of the year. Its mellow warmth and colours only deepened the sense of despondency in Joanna. She felt as if she were recovering from a long illness and walked around in a daze, absolutely determined not to share her suspicions with anyone. So far, whatever she said or implied had been met with a complete lack of understanding. Was she right though? Was there some kind of conspiracy? She couldn't imagine David, for instance, being part of some sinister plot, nor for that matter Simon. Admittedly she didn't particularly like him, but there was an aura of integrity about him; he just didn't behave like a crook might. Brenda? She was a bit of a goose and an easy lay. Alright, suppose there *was* a conspiracy – for what purpose? There was nothing in any way suspicious or out of the ordinary occurring on the boat, they all carried on in a normal way. So, whatever it was, it was obviously in her mind. She could be going mentally deranged, her mind disintegrating under the shock of her broken marriage, the emotional, if silent, infatuation with Colin. Yes, her mind was falling to pieces. Please God, don't let me go mad. Outwardly, she behaved calmly, only her eyes, bruised with heavy shadows, betrayed her inner anxiety.

There was no sign of Colin. Although Joanna knew she had to give up thinking about him, the situation was too fresh to be forgotten that quickly. She caught herself thinking about him in spite of all her resolutions, especially knowing that he might be back at any time. Her interest continued to flicker, every passing taxi giving her a mild stab of expectation, at the same time knowing that when once he came and was around her again, her emotions would be difficult to keep under control. The whole situation was making her despondent and miserable. It occurred to her to cut the holiday short. She pondered over it, but there were practical difficulties: they were in Turkey, her return ticket to London was from Athens. Kusadasi was far from an international airport, to get there would involve costly transport, and then she'd be obliged to pay the full fare back, something she could ill-afford. There was also bound to be a scene, the whole rigmarole of false excuses and explanations. The very thought made her cringe. She was no good at lying. At the bottom of it all there was also something else. Her curiosity had now been aroused. What was it all about? Deep down in her heart of hearts, there lay a conviction that it was not all just in her mind. There was something afoot, vague and sinister, but what?

Joined now by Brenda, she headed in to Kusadasi town on a shopping expedition. Simon had suggested they should provision for a couple of days, while he and David patched up the rubbing strip damaged by the falling block. The damage was superficial. One corner of the block had caught the rubbing strip, ripping off part of the wood and making a deep scratch alongside the stern. It required patching up with a piece of wood and filling the scratch with a fibre glass filler. As the girls set out with their shopping bags for the town, David was already mixing some foul-smelling paste in an old tin.

They were no further than a few paces from the boat when Joanna heard the wireless crackle and Simon's nasal drawl articulating: '*Jemima II, Jemima II*, this is *Zainda* calling.'

'I am surprised,' said Joanna in spite of her resolution to say nothing. 'They are forever calling *Jemima* on the radio, and yet we never meet them.'

Brenda said nothing and seemed preoccupied. Joanna noticed her silence and didn't press the matter further. She was sorry to have mentioned the subject. However, she underestimated Brenda's capacity to exhaust her favourite and, as far as she could see, the only topic which occupied her mind.

'How are you and David getting on? We left you on your own last night,' she added in a meaningful tone.

'Frankly, I was in no state to notice,' said Joanna taken aback. 'That accident shook me up a bit.'

'Poor David,' she said in a slightly mocking voice. 'What have you got against him?'

'Why, nothing,' stuttered Joanna, quite out of her depth. What was Brenda driving at? 'Nothing at all. On the contrary, I like him very much.'

'He's very keen on you — it stands out a mile. What I don't understand is what's holding you back. You really ought to come to my classes once we get back, you know. They will help you shed those inhibitions, they're tremendously supportive. I mean, look at you,' she continued walking slightly ahead of Joanna and not looking at her, which was just as well. 'You've already had one crisis in your life, you obviously need guidance. We all do, there's nothing to be ashamed of, might just as well admit it. You simply have to clear your system of inhibitions. David, for instance. I mean, we're not talking about a committed relationship, just …'

'I can't hop into the sack just like that!' Joanna interrupted her with mounting irritation. She was getting very cross with Brenda. 'Anyway, he's much too young for me.' With that, she hoped to close the subject without actually letting her temper explode, feeling that for the sake of harmony in the confined space of the boat she had to keep her anger in check. But Brenda continued, undeterred in her missionary zeal.

'Don't be ridiculous. At his age they're very good at … like that, you know what I mean,' sounding as if she spoke from experience. 'Right now, he's getting pretty morose. I can't see why you can't do something about it. Even Simon has noticed. He said he wished you two would hit it off. Anyway, what's holding you back? You're on holiday, aren't you?' she tossed her head defiantly as if the rules and restraints of normal, everyday life did not apply to holidays.

Joanna gritted her teeth while slowly counting to ten and said nothing. Again, her silence was misunderstood.

'Come on,' Brenda said as she slowed down for Joanna to catch up with her. There was a note of understanding in her voice; she spoke like an analyst to a patient lying on a psychiatrist's couch. 'You'll be saying you're frigid next. Of course, you don't want to do it with David – you've got your sights on someone else, haven't you?' Her eyes crinkled in a knowing wink. 'Well, let me tell you, nothing doing on that front, so why don't you enjoy what's available. That's what I always say.'

Joanna entered the town of Kusadasi, face white, lips pressed into a thin line betraying seething anger. It was the second time Brenda had mentioned Colin. She stopped by the nearest shop window to calm herself, not daring to speak. The window had onyx ashtrays and carved animals on display. Joanna counted twenty of them before she could trust herself to face Brenda again. That wasn't enough as there simply weren't enough ashtrays or toy animals in the whole world for that matter. She could happily hit Brenda with something hard or, better still, strangle her slowly.

Brenda, however, was quite unaware of the reaction she had provoked. Unconcernedly, she turned to look at the display in the jeweller's shop next door. Unable to tolerate Brenda's company any longer, Joanna walked away. Her feet took her along the main street, past the shops displaying copperware and other useless ornamental objects made for tourists. Outside hung colourful carpets on the walls, but she was too cross to notice or admire them. On the streets was the usual bustle of honking cars and beautifully painted small carts drawn by mules and donkeys. There was a caravanserai in the middle of the road converted into a hotel which looked mysterious and romantic. The streets were full of men and boys. Occasionally a woman, dressed in baggy trousers, shuffled past her, wrapped in a white shawl, holding a shopping bag with one hand and the corner of a shawl to her face with the other. If both hands were occupied, the shawl was held by the teeth. *So much for women's lib*, thought Joanna.

She walked on quickly to where the street gave way to the waterfront. Ahead was the sea, and boats on anchor. Looking up, she saw bobbing in the gentle swell the unmistakable lines of the *Jemima*. The big cruiser was lying on anchor, her bow making graceful little curtsies in the slight swell. Joanna could detect two of the crew on the fore deck bending over the anchor winch. There was movement by the door of the side deck. It opened, revealing a woman in a scanty bikini. Joanna's eyes narrowed. The woman had a beautiful figure, the colour of her tanned body enhanced by the pale green bikini, tailored to a hair's breadth to cover the essential parts of the body. She moved with the grace of a dancer towards the aft deck, holding her dark, luxurious hair with one hand, away from her face. Joanna realised with a shock that this was the same woman she had seen with Colin in the hotel in Tarabya. She continued to watch her, fascinated.

Behind her, a man appeared in the doorway, not very tall and considerably fat. Most of his face was hidden by large dark glasses. He was dressed in white shorts and a loose shirt revealing a protruding stomach covered in matted hair. There was not much hair on his head; it was as if it was all concentrated on his body. As he moved away from the door, another figure came out following close behind him. Colin! He appeared to be listening attentively while the man was talking, looking ahead, not bothering to see if Colin was there or not. Colin was trying to catch his words and looked like a fawning dog, all the more so as, judging by the frequent nods of his head, he seemed to be rapturously agreeing with the man. A sense of disgust rose in Joanna's throat.

The woman walked on, visibly ignored by the two men, yet at the same time, perhaps in Joanna's mind who was getting hyper sensitive by now, conscious they were fully aware of her presence. There was something about the behaviour of the fat man which proclaimed ownership of her, as if he had her on a leash. That was a comfort: at least Colin didn't have her all to himself. Joanna thought there was something rather unpleasant about the fat man. However, looking at the two of them in deep conversation, they didn't seem to be adversaries at all, quite the opposite, in fact. The man kept talking as they stepped out on the deck, gesticulating with his fat hands, in which Joanna thought she could detect a fat butt of a cigar. Colin kept nodding his head vigorously in agreement, then stretched out his hand in a gesture of goodbye. The fat man took some time to notice the outstretched hand, leaving Colin in that fawning position a little longer. Eventually his hand descended into Colin's. Colin seemed to notice nothing, smiling broadly; in fact, he looked positively happy at the contact, as if a great favour had been bestowed on him. Still smiling, he gave a small, perfunctory bow in the direction of the woman and descended the steps where a small dinghy was waiting for him, with one of the crew revving up the outboard motor. The dinghy made its way slowly towards the shore while Colin waved again towards the couple he had left on the deck. They hardly noticed him. The fat man caught up with the woman and, prodding her in the back, made his way slowly up the steps to the upper bridge.

Having witnessed the scene, Joanna was too disgusted to be able to face Colin. Colin of all people, sucking up to the rich. Well! She almost ran back to the place where she had left Brenda and caught her in the doorway to the onyx shop. Brenda was holding a carved animal mounted on a little pedestal, vaguely resembling a horse's head.

'Do you like it? I bargained with that woman in the shop till I was blue in the face. Got it for less than half the asking price. She took ever such a long time over it, though. I had a coffee and a Coke, and still she said ....'

'Let's go, Brenda,' interrupted Joanna, still panting from her run, afraid they might be seen by Colin any minute as she was loathe to face him. 'We've wasted enough time already. We must do the shopping now and get back to the boat.'

'Why, what's the hurry?' Brenda asked, refusing to be pulled along.

'We said we'd be away for an hour and an hour's almost gone. We haven't done any of our shopping yet and we're supposed to leave this morning.'

Joanna kept walking fast in spite of the heat building up. Any activity would do to erase that dreadful, fawning image of Colin. It was positively degrading the way he'd behaved; she had never imagined he could be like that. Fawning upon a man whose mistress (she couldn't imagine that woman to be his wife) he coveted. Her cheeks were burning.

'Let's get a taxi on our way back,' said Brenda. 'I'm not going to carry the shopping in this heat. I don't care what Simon says about extravagance.' She tossed her head and swung her shopping bag defiantly, clutching the carved onyx animal. The bag was of shiny plastic with a picture of a white dog with a long black nose wearing a coronet. At the bottom of the bag in big black letters were the words: "There'll always be an England".

Chapter 11

By the time they got all their things together and were ready to sail, it was late afternoon. Colin joined them after lunch with a casual "Hello". His eyes rested briefly on Joanna and he asked her in a light tone what she had been doing with herself while he'd been away, in a way that didn't require an answer. Joanna answered briefly, steadily refusing to meet his eye. He slid away quickly to the main cabin, as if glad of an excuse not to be with her, and buried himself in the charts and controls at the chart table. She could hear Simon telling him about the accident.

The scratch on the hull had been patched up, showing up in pale green against the white paint, and a piece of new wood had been inserted into the rubbing strip. Otherwise, there was nothing to show the accident had ever taken place. It was not discussed any more, at least not in Joanna's presence.

Brenda reappeared, having changed into her yellow bikini, and stood in the doorway. 'Hello, stranger,' she said to Colin. 'How was it? You must be exhausted,' she giggled, the first to see the funny side of her impertinent remark. Colin looked up from the chart table, raising an eyebrow.

'Not as much as you, kid,' he drawled and slapped her on the bottom.

'Ouch,' laughed Brenda, moving back towards the cockpit as she rubbed her behind, pretending the slap was stronger than it was. 'Macho man now, are we?'

Joanna buried her head in the cupboard, stowing away the shopping and all the bits and pieces that had piled up on the table during their absence. Now that Colin was back, she wished he'd go away, his presence disturbed her too much. She was afraid her disgust might show sooner or later if they were alone together. It was better to concentrate her thoughts on David and the conversation she had had with Brenda.

Admittedly there was something to what Brenda said. What were her reasons for keeping David at arm's length? Well, she wasn't in love with him. Sex was something one needed to have from time to time for the sake of inner harmony and peace of mind. She would heartily agree with that. More and more during this holiday she found her harmony shattered, her nerves on edge. It was most likely attributable to lack of sex. She wasn't going mad, her mind wasn't falling to pieces, the only thing that was wrong was that she was very likely sex-starved. How long ago was it when she had last made love? Ages. Things hadn't been going too well with Alex in that department lately. That one-night-stand was very likely a multiple one, come to think of it. So, what was it then that prevented her from making love to David? Everything was going for it. The stage was ideally set for a little holiday interlude – a young man ready and willing, nobody to raise an eyebrow, not that it bothered her what other people thought. Once the holiday was over, it would soon be forgotten and they would all go their separate ways, back to their normal, everyday lives. So, why was she hesitating? Mainly because what she felt for David was so different to what she felt for Colin. *Colin?* Why, she'd almost forgotten him already. An interlude with David would help to forget him totally. Anyway, she liked David, and that evening on the island of Marmaris, when he had kissed her, she had felt a surge of attraction in spite of herself. It would work out all right in the end. She should get used to the idea of having a lover from to time. Without a husband, and she wasn't going to be saddled with another in a hurry, that was certain, she should have an affair from time to time if only to remain, sort of, on the level. Otherwise, she'd go bonkers, get nervous ticks, funny obsessions, that sort of thing. Sex was fun, too, had she forgotten that? Would anyone get hurt if she had her bit of fun? Of course not. Joanna had to concede a point to Brenda. *I am just not what is called liberated. Strict upbringing, Victorian morality, that sort of thing. In light of recent research, my inhibitions should be dealt with, and the sooner I do it, the sooner I'll achieve my – what was it called? – that inner harmony. Wa? Is that what it's called? Right, I'll make love to David, restore this Wa and I won't be imagining things any more. Easy. No one will get hurt, it will be fun, everyone will be happy. Now it's simply a matter of time and place and making it all plain to David. At the next available opportunity, I'll be ready to go for it.*

She looked up into the cockpit where David, oblivious of her new resolution, was half buried under a sail, repairing the tears in the canvas. His glasses had slid down his nose, he was slippery with perspiration, and there were smudges on his face from the repair work he and Simon had done on the hull. Joanna's eyes travelled slowly down his body to the place where his swimming trunks bulged, trying to acclimatise herself to the idea. One shouldn't be shy about the whole thing, like a convent schoolgirl who'd vaguely heard about the facts of life and suspected more than was good for her. One should go for it with open eyes. David looked up as she turned away, but she managed to detect with out of the corner of her eye that he smiled at her. It was a warm, slightly wistful smile, as if seeking reassurance. *He isn't actually in love with me*, she said herself. That would be too cruel. It could only be done in fun, if both sides played the same game. She looked at him again, but his head was lowered while he laboriously stitched the sail. She might have misinterpreted his smile. *He couldn't be in love with me, he's much too young, just out of college. That makes me what – say, eight years older? I could be his aunt. Anyway, I gave him no encouragement, I'm hardly ever alone with him. Love is something that grows, is nurtured and blossoms like a flower. It's for mature people, it can't appear just like that, without a reason. Like hell! What about me and Colin? How much encouragement did he give me?* She looked at David again, who said in a normal voice, obviously unaware of her thoughts:

'You couldn't find me a new roll of twine, Joanna, could you? I've come to the end of the reel.'

She found the twine and while handing it to him rubbed herself, not quite accidentally, against his body. He looked up, surprised, but she deliberately wiped out the invitation from her eyes. It was simply accidental. He seemed to accept the message and went back to work. Joanna realised it would be very easy to get him to do what she had planned. He was too ready for her, if anything, too easy. She sat next to him and brushed his hair off his face.

'Why don't you rub that smudge off?' she murmured.

Again, a surprised look flickered in his eyes, at the same time revealing an intense emotion that made Joanna stiffen again. That boy couldn't be serious, could he? That would certainly ruin everything. At the same time, she couldn't help feeling flattered. After Colin's indifference it was rather nice to be admired.

The sun was very hot, almost unbearable as they motored out of the Kusadasi marina. Simon was steering. Colin came out of the cabin into the cockpit, his eye flickering for a moment when he saw Joanna so close to David, then went back to the chart table, fumbling with a ruler and dividers, whistling a tuneless melody through his teeth. Joanna and David stowed the fenders, while Brenda, as usual, was putting a mask of cream on her face.

'Where to, skipper?' asked Joanna in spite of herself, although she'd vowed not to ask questions.

'Bodrum,' said Simon and turned towards Brenda. 'You'll like Bodrum, Brenda, it's not a bad old place, y'know.'

Brenda got up and rubbed his shoulders and neck with sun cream. Simon pretended to purr with pleasure. 'Go on, do it again,' he laughed when she stopped and pinched her bottom.

Joanna took in his freckly face and long, sandy hair falling across his forehead and decided she had had enough. They both jarred on her nerves with their uninhibited sensuality, their showing off, not caring who saw them. Simon was so arrogant it probably never occurred to him other people had feelings. It wasn't showing off, he genuinely didn't care, almost didn't notice other people, until it suited him to do otherwise. Joanna averted her eyes and concentrated on storing away the fenders.

'Looks like a night's sailing,' she said to Colin, glad to have found a commonplace remark when they were alone in the cabin.

'Yes,' said Colin curtly, looking up from the chart table. He was reading the Mediterranean Pilot and making notes in the log book. 'Does it bother you?'

'Why, no,' she lied, though in fact didn't like night passages at all. She could never sleep properly, walked half-dazed the following day, snatching little naps whenever possible. The roll and pitch of the boat was most noticeable in her cabin, and whenever it was time to rest after her watch, she rolled so much in bed that it was hard to fall asleep. The cockpit was the best place when the boat was underway, but when she did try to sleep there, it was obvious she was in someone's way, bound to stumble over her sleeping bag and wake her up. Whichever way, there would be no sleep tonight. She sighed.

The sun was setting and clouds had gathered along the horizon. The sky glowed red, layered with gold, orange and almost translucent green on a background of deepening indigo. A few clouds made dark patterns across the bands of light.

'I say, what a lovely sunset,' she exclaimed. They all looked up.

'I don't like the look of it,' muttered David.

'Why?' Joanna was startled. 'It's beautiful! How can you say such a thing David?' She sounded almost offended.

'I think there's going to be a storm,' persisted David. 'I say, Colin,' he shouted into the darkening main cabin, 'what's the barometer doing?'

Colin came into the cockpit. 'Not very good, I'm afraid. Dropped three millibars in the last hour and seven since this morning. There's certainly quite a storm building up as you say.'

'We might be getting a bit of a blow later on, 'Simon said unconcernedly. 'On the other hand, it might miss us, you never know in the Med.' He turned to Brenda. 'I'd get a couple of sea-sickness pills in you, old girl. Go on,' he gave her a playful slap and pushed her towards the aft cabin.

'Oh no, not a storm again,' said Brenda. 'I hate taking those pills, I really do.' She looked accusingly at the offending sky.

'I know you do, old thing, but it's better than being sick. Now be a good girl. Joanna will pour you a glass of water, won't you, Joanna?'

Joanna gritted her teeth. *Here we go again.* She brought a plastic cup filled with water for Brenda, then went down to stow everything securely.

The blow, when it came, hit them several hours and a further drop of several millibars later. It was already quite dark. David and Colin went on to the deck, ready to drop the mains'l and the jib, and prepare the storm jib. There was nothing more they could do until the wind picked up sufficiently; the storm jib was too small to sail in the wind they had just then. Clouds were gathering more and more quickly, and there was by now an occasional rumble of a distant thunder. The air was warm and damp, and everything on the boat was suddenly dripping with moisture. Even the plastic seat covers and the mattresses were clammy and damp, and the wooden floors of the cabin became slippery. Joanna took out the oilskins from the locker and left them out in readiness. They had had no need for them in the last week and now they exuded a damp, musty smell.

The wind continued to be slight, easterly, and blew fitfully owing to the shelter provided by the mountains on the island of Samos. Colin was working at the chart table, trying to establish their exact position.

'We're much too near the coast,' she heard him say to Simon. Simon's expression did not change as he pointed *Zainda* more to the wind. The sails flapped and the boat came nearly to a standstill.

'Must bear away, I'm afraid. We'll have to tack later,' said Simon, chewing on his unlit pipe. 'Bit of a bore, that.' He altered course and *Zainda*'s sails filled up again. She picked up a bit of speed.

At most we might be doing six, maybe seven knots, which is what, say eight miles per hour, the pace of an old, tired pensioner out on their evening constitutional. Well, perhaps not as slow as that, thought Joanna.

All those pyrotechnics in the sky and the hushed silence preceding the storm gave her butterflies in her stomach. She wished she had a pair of wings or a powerful engine to get her quickly to a safe, snug harbour.

The frequency of lightning flashes increased. They tore across the sky, each followed by a crash of thunder. The lightning seemed not to go down in a zigzag fashion but flickered horizontally, lighting up the whole sky, bathing it momentarily in an eerie light. Brenda's face had all but disappeared into the hood of her oilskin jacket.

'Do you think our masts might attract the lightning? I mean, in the same way as the tallest tree would do on land?' she asked in a small voice.

Nobody bothered to answer her, they were all too busy preparing for the onslaught of the elements. Joanna shrugged her shoulders, feeling sorry for her as she looked visibly frightened.

'Oh, I don't know,' she said. 'I was told once something about water being a good conductor of electricity so that the lightning just hits the water, or something like that, I'm not sure. Anyway, I don't think it would do us much harm.' She made it all up, in an effort to reassure Brenda.

Standing there in the darkness, waiting for the elements to unleash their fury on them in a boat which suddenly seemed tiny and vulnerable, gave her a feeling of fatalism which made the suspense bearable. *What will be, will be, no need to worry over what might be, I'd rather concentrate on what actually happens.*

There was another lightning-thunder tandem. The storm was coming nearer.

'Can't we head somewhere for shelter, Simon?' Brenda's voice was tearful. 'We're not too far from land, are we?'

'Sorry, love,' Simon's voice lost some of its usual languid tone. There was now a firm edge to it. 'We've got to make Bodrum by tomorrow morning.'

Joanna perked up. So, they had a rendezvous, did they? But with whom and what for? Had *Jemima*, that fat man and the woman anything to do with it? Now, if this was just a pleasure trip it wouldn't matter whether they reached Bodrum one day or the next. *Why aren't they running for cover to the nearest shelter?*

'Why, we haven't a train to catch, have we?'Brenda's voice reflected her own thoughts.

Nobody answered her. They all sat in the cockpit peering at the gathering clouds and the darkness in subdued suspense. Joanna watched the moon appear from behind the clouds, illuminating the scene with its pale, rather sinister light. It was not reassuring. Black, thick clouds sped along the sky. More and more white horses appeared from nowhere, glowing with phosphorescence against the surface of the sea which, like the clouds, was inky black. They seemed to Joanna like a pack of angry dogs coming towards their small craft, smashing against the side of the hull with a thud and disappearing in a foam under the keel. More and more were coming from where the first lot came. There was also a discernible whining noise in the rigging now, as if someone was trying to tune a monotonous string instrument. *Zainda* was beginning to heel at a precarious angle until they were all slipping on the wet floor and had to stand with one leg firmly wedged against the cockpit seat opposite.

'It might be an idea to get the safety harnesses out,' said David, surveying the scene. He blinked, revealing dark, defenceless eyes as he wiped the spray off his glasses. He put them back on, then took them off again.

'My glasses are smudged with salt, I'll have to wash them with fresh water. I'll get the harnesses out when I'm down there.' He disappeared into the cabin, closing the door carefully behind him.

'Perhaps, Joanna,' drawled Simon in his measured voice, 'you could make us a hot drink, put it in the thermos flask. It might not be as comfortable later on.'

That was Simon indulging in one of his understatements again. *Comfortable!* The boat was already rolling and pitching enough to make the stove swing madly on its gimbals. Joanna had to perform miracles trying to boil water in the kettle, which kept slipping from side to side, and having boiled it, pour it down the narrow neck of the thermos flask without scalding her hands. The floor was slippery and the strap, intended to give support to the cook, had been lost. There was always so much to do on the boat, and yet there were still all those things not attended to that would uncannily crop up in times of emergency, no matter how prepared you were. They had been spoilt by the good weather which had lulled them into a false sense of security. Now, it was all beginning to show.

'Coffee or cocoa?' Joanna shouted, opening the door to the cockpit. She badly needed fresh air.

'Cocoa would be fine.'

'Okay.'

Joanna descended the slippery steps and nearly fell headlong into the cabin as the boat pitched and her feet gave way. She managed to grasp a peg on the wall, to prevent her arm from being completely torn out of its socket. She had firmly closed the cabin door in case the spray splashed inside so no one had noticed her plight. She managed to land on her feet, rubbing the painful arm. Luckily it wasn't serious. A cupboard door swung open, spilling its contents and the saucepans on the floor. They were sliding to and fro and she had to bend down in order to put them back, which made her feel queasy. Even if I *could* make a meal in gale force winds, would I be able to eat it? She gripped the edge of the table and took a deep breath, then somehow managed to make the cocoa and pour most of it into the Thermos flask by placing it in the sink and wedging a tea towel round it. The milk and cocoa powder were all over the place. By that time, she couldn't have cared less how lumpy it was, and hoped the movement of the boat would do the shaking for her. Now she had to put on proper clothes and get out into fresh air. First, she wrapped a small towel firmly round her neck to stop the water from trickling down her back, followed by the oilskin jacket and trousers. They were too big for her and she struggled with the buckles and the braces. There were no more sou'westers going spare, so she wound a scarf round her head, and no rubber boots either, only canvas shoes with special, gripping soles. Her feet were wet already, but it wasn't cold, so it didn't matter. Inside the oilskins she felt sticky and clammy. Stomach rumbling, head swimming, she wondered what in heaven's name had made her go sailing in the first place. She would have been much better off in a hotel, firmly built on solid ground. Already she had visions of a bar with a white-coated bartender serving martinis or brandy sours with plenty, *plenty* of ice, clean swimming pools and a soft bed that never moved.

No contrast could be greater between her dreams and reality as she stepped outside carrying the thermos flask. The weather had worsened considerably. The wet darkness was whining with the wind and tension of an unspent storm. There was much more movement in the sea now. Thunder, muffled in the cabin, resounded with loud crashes at frequent intervals. *Zainda* now tossed wildly in the uneven motion of the sea without the benefit of a strong, steady wind. Joanna took a couple of deep breaths and felt slightly better.

Simon was still at the steering wheel. David and Colin were on the foredeck fastening anything that could possibly become loose or even lost. David was shining a torch so that only Colin's hands were visible in the darkness. Brenda sat huddled in the corner of the cockpit, shivering. Simon, for once, was not paying attention to her.

'Where are we now, Simon?' asked Joanna.

'We just passed Samos. You can't see it, it's right behind us. We're going out a bit, so as not to be too near the coast.'

'What's that outline there?' Joanna pointed to an outline as the flickering lightning momentarily lit the scene.

'That must be Agathonissi. I'm surprised we can see it from here. We must be further out than I thought.' Simon was never so voluble as now.

'Greek or Turkish?'

'Greek, I think.'

Brenda was moaning to herself. 'Oh, why can't we go back! I can't stand this, I hate it, I hate it!' Childish tears mixed with the sea spray were running down her cheeks.

'Do you want to go down to the cabin and lie down?' asked Joanna. She felt responsible for her somehow, maybe because she wasn't feeling sick any more. 'I'll help you.'

'Leave me alone,' snarled Brenda. 'I just want to be left alone.'

'Sorry,' Joanna pulled away offended. 'I was only trying to help.'

But Brenda was immersed in her misery. She was one of those

people afraid of thunderstorms and it was no use trying to reason with her.

And then – it came. Although they were waiting for it, it took them by surprise. Through the fitful wind came a blow, laying *Zainda* on her beam. Water ran along her side deck, threatening to pour into the cockpit. They all lost their balance except for Simon who was holding onto the steering wheel. Even so, he slid across the floor of the cockpit but was able to keep himself upright. Joanna, who was on the leeward side, grabbed the first thing that came to hand which happened to be a winch, round and slippery, but better than nothing. She watched the dark figures of Colin and David holding onto the pulpit above the bow, trying to stand up. Brenda gave one big squeal as she was thrown out of her corner onto the floor of the cockpit. She managed to remain huddled there, bumped up against Joanna.

'Let's take the mains'l down now, Colin.' Simon's voice sounded reassuringly calm. 'Don't bother reefing it. Undo the sheet, Joanna, will you?' His voice was raised to a shout as the wind picked up and screamed in the rigging. The moment the sheet was loosened, the mains'l began to flap and the boom to swing wildly, adding to the general noise. *Zainda* was trying to right herself when a big wave with a phosphorescent crest, bigger than the others, hit the side of the hull with a hollow thud and a fan of spray covered the cockpit. A stream of water ran down the side of the deck and gushed over the overflowing drain.

'Drop the jib, hoist the storm jib!' Simon was yelling.

The whine of the wind reached a high note. The mains'l swung helplessly like a dying bird flapping it wings in an attempt to escape an approaching human figure. Colin was trying to pull the sail down the mast, but it was a slow job. Joanna was about to jump up and help when Simon shouted:

'Stay in the cockpit! Switch on the spreader lights!'

Even though she couldn't have been more than two feet away from him, the noise was such that he had to shout to make himself heard.

Another wave broke over the hull and a sheet of water came down, hitting them both in the face. Simon, like Joanna, wore no sou'wester. He shook the water from his face and his hair came down his egg-shaped skull like a wet mop out of a bucket. He looked ridiculous, but his voice and manner had a decisive tone. He had discarded the pose he had adopted for too long, and now commanded respect. *Maybe he's not such a useless buffoon as he pretends to be*, flashed through Joanna's mind.

David and Colin were doing heroics with the flapping, unmanageable sails which simply would not slide down the mast and be packed away easily. They worked now in pitch darkness, slightly relieved by the spreader lights fixed high up on the mast, feebly illuminating the deck. One slip and either of them could slide into the turbulent waters, seething in that hellish blackness. In a flash of lightning, Joanna saw one figure clip the safety harness to the life lines. Thank goodness someone's sensible.

'Hand me the sail ties!' David's voice sounded strained and far away.

Joanna started to look frantically for them in the locker as another wave hit her squarely between the shoulders. Water trickled down her back in spite of the towel. She wriggled her shoulder blades as the water tickled her skin. *Damn!* She handed him the sail ties and watched him tie the flapping canvas onto the swinging boom.

'Make fast the sheet!' shouted Colin. He was clutching the boom, swinging with it. Joanna did so, treading on Brenda who was lying on the cockpit floor in a foetal position. If she made any noise, it was lost in the pandemonium in which they had now found themselves.

The wind blew, screeching in the rigging, tearing at everything on the deck. Even the masts swayed horizontally, as if about to fall down. The waves continued running towards the hull, hitting it in close succession. Each hit was followed by a hissing plume of phosphorescent spray, drenching their already dripping faces and oilskins. Some waves were already crowned with spray like cockscombs, and those the wind sliced off as if with a huge, invisible machete, flinging the tops across the bow in a graceful arc to the other side. Joanna watched the bow rise, hover in the air and plunge, only to rise after what seemed an age, a spectacle repeated time and time again. The rumble of thunder added deep notes of rolling drums to the continuous noise of nature's orchestration.

In one of the frequent flashes, Joanna saw Colin on the foredeck, struggling with the jib. He dropped the canvas bag filled with the sail quickly into the cockpit. David immediately pulled the sheet which raised the storm jib. Once the sail was up, *Zainda* righted herself a little, and her movement became slightly easier. The two men made their way to the cockpit and sat panting, ignoring the splash and the spray: trying to wipe it off using their hands was a futile gesture as no sooner had they done so than a new wave drenched them. David had his glasses attached to the sou'wester with a piece of string. He gave up keeping them on his nose and just shook himself between drenches. Unlike David, Colin was not wearing a safety harness.

'What course are you steering, Simon?' he shouted.

'Two twenty,' came the answer.

'*Joanna*!' Simon roared. Though Joanna was standing next to him, she could barely hear him. 'Help Brenda to the cabin, take the sail bag with you, get it out of the way!'

Joanna beckoned to Brenda who did not move, simply clutched her knees more tightly. Joanna signalled to Colin who tried to pick her up, but she kept slipping through his hands in her oilskins. Eventually they bundled her into the doorway of the cabin, Joanna going down first. As Colin was putting Brenda on her feet, a big wave broke over the cockpit and pushed her in. She fell into the cabin, followed by a mass of water. A swear word formed on Joanna's lips as she looked at the enormous pool of water swirling at her feet, where only seconds before it had been reasonably dry.

'Get in quick!' she managed to say to Brenda.

The door slammed behind them. Brenda was moaning, clutching her stomach. The cabin was a mess: clothes, jars of cosmetics, even a blanket, just thrown on the floor which was now getting thoroughly wet.

'Good God, Brenda! Didn't Simon tell you to put everything away before a storm?' She stepped on something sharp and hairy and recoiled in horror. It was a hair curler made of spiky plastic with Brenda's hair wound round it. More hair curlers spilled out of a toilet bag, bobbing on the dirty pool of water.

'Here, let me help you take your jacket off, Brenda, please.' She struggled with her as the boat gave a sudden lurch and slammed them against the bed. Brenda lost her balance and plunged onto the bed head first.

'I'm going to die! I'm going to die!' she sobbed.

'Take your jacket off, for goodness sake!' hissed Joanna, pulling at her arm with one hand while trying to steady herself with another by holding onto the column of the mizzen mast in the centre of the cabin. She managed to take off Brenda's hat, but the ties were entangled in her hair so that she was pulling at both.

Brenda screamed. 'Leave me alone, do you hear me! Leave me alone to die! I just want to die! God, I'm going to be sick, get me a bowl, quick!'

Joanna looked desperately around her, but could see no bowl in the cabin. She scrambled to the door, but it wouldn't open. She knocked on it in a futile gesture, knowing nobody would hear her in the cockpit.

'Quick, oh quick!' heaved Brenda. Joanna gave the cabin another look with mounting panic. Her eyes caught sight of a towel. She threw it at Brenda who was doubling up and retching. Brenda managed to catch it, bury her head in it and was sick.

An awful smell pervaded the cabin. *If I don't get out of here, that will be the end of me*, realised Joanna. Frantically she fumbled with the lock, and finally succeeded in pressing something so that the door suddenly flew open. In the nick of time, she sprang into the cockpit head first, took a deep breath and closed the door behind her quickly. She wedged herself tightly into the corner of the cockpit as a solid mass of water cascaded down her face.

'Is she alright?' shouted Simon.

'Not really.'

They both shrugged their shoulders helplessly. David was already slumped over the side. At least he was sick correctly, to the leeward, without making a fuss. There was nothing anyone could do now, except hope to reach the harbour safely, and that was far away.

And so it went on. The bow rose and fell into the deep, staying there as if reluctant to rise again, only to reappear in a desultory fashion. The flashes of lightning, the crashes of thunder, an occasional glimpse of the moon with the clouds racing across its face, the howl of the wind, sometimes screaming to a pitch, sometimes dropping a notch or two on the decibel scale, went on and on. It blew unsteadily, gusting, then weakening, raising false hopes of a possible respite, only to dash them when it picked up with renewed force. Time dragged. Minutes were like hours, hours were infinity. Joanna tried counting to one thousand, then in thousands to one hundred thousand, then the number of times she got splashed on her face, then she counted the stronger waves only. Sailors say the seventh wave is bigger than the preceding six, so she counted waves bigger and smaller, glistening in the dark with their phosphorescent plumes. She found it wasn't true about the seventh wave, they came in threes and fours, so she counted every fourth wave while the elements raged and time dragged.

The three men were motionless and silent, which was just as well because every time anyone opened their mouth water poured in. Whoever said sea water was salty hadn't tasted it properly. It was horribly bitter. Colin took over the steering from Simon.

'Keep her on course and watch out for Farmakonisi!' shouted Simon. 'We want Farmakonisi on our starboard.' Colin nodded as Simon slumped on the seat, pushed down by the weight of another cascade of water. Simon was now wearing a hat pulled down tightly on his forehead. It was difficult to see what it was, but to Joanna it looked like a deerstalker. Whatever it was, it was completely unsuitable for the present circumstances.

After several eternities Joanna shouted to Simon, pointing to the Thermos flask. 'Cocoa?'

'Can't drink in this weather. Leave it till later.'

Joanna looked at David, still slumped over the side of the cockpit, looking very sick indeed. A mention of cocoa would probably send him heaving again. Her gaze shifted to Colin. His profile, illuminated by the frequent flashes of lightning, was calm and reassuring under the yellow sou'wester as if, improbably, he was enjoying himself. Looking at him, Joanna regained all the confidence the raging weather had shattered. Although she did not feel in any immediate danger, on the other hand the constant noise of the wind, the spectacular lightning and frequent drenching had unsettled her. All she wanted to do now was to sit and not have to move, while her whole being was devoted to one single, modest wish that all this, the storm, the movement of the boat, the noise, would stop immediately.

The thunderstorm was finally abating, the lightning flashes were becoming less frequent. The wind, however, so long in coming, if anything, picked up even more, and howled with greater strength than Joanna had thought was possible a few minutes ago. Simon fiddled with an object in his hand which he then lifted up as high as he could into the wind. It was a hand-held anemometer. The weather must have unsettled him, enough to speak to Joanna which he never did if he could avoid it.

'Force eight, gusting nine on the Beaufort scale!' he shouted. 'Southerly, so it's slowing us down. Will have to tack soon, I'm afraid.'

As he was speaking, there was something like an explosion above the tumult of the elements. The hull shuddered and for a split second stood still. They all jumped to their feet.

'What was that?'

Colin moved first, making gestures to Simon to take over the steering while he jumped onto the fore deck. Joanna looked at David, but he only lifted his head feebly and was sick again. She fumbled with the safety harness, took a torch from David's pocket, put it in her pouch, clipped the safety harness to the life line and, bending almost double, followed Colin. He was already on the fore deck, inspecting the storm jib. Most of the hunks of the storm jib had opened and the bottom part had torn off the sheet. There was a split at the top which spread down to an already torn half which was the length of the sail. The top part had folded over, while the bottom end with the thick metal eye and hunks was being tossed about by the wind. Joanna saw Colin try to catch it and at the same time avoid being hit by it. She went towards him and shone the torch. With one hand, she embraced the shrouds, with the other she clutched the torch and wondered how Colin managed to maintain his balance as he tried to get hold of the sail. The movement of the boat was now erratic; they were sailing under mizzen only. Simon had difficulty in keeping the boat pointing to the waves.

'Tell Simon to let the sheet out very slowly!' shouted Colin in Joanna's ear. At that moment a huge wave, bigger than the others, hit them. Joanna grabbed the shrouds with both hands, took a deep breath and crouched. The green phosphorescent mass of water engulfed her till her lungs were about to burst, and there was singing in her ears. Mercifully, it receded. She breathed deeply, freely and shook herself. But where was Colin? She couldn't see him. Only the sail flapped and tossed, and the rip lengthened so that it was folded double on its own length.

'Colin!' she screamed, frightened. 'Colin!'

She let go of the shrouds and flashed the torch around. What she saw made her gasp with horror. She could see Colin's yellow oilskin out in the water. Her voice sounded unreal to her, high-pitched and ridiculous.

'Colin's down there!' she shouted, pointing down at the sea. 'Man aboard!' she screamed.

There was no response from the cockpit; they couldn't hear her.

With her lighted torch she made a swinging arc hoping that something in her gesture would convey itself to Simon. He seemed to respond and let out the sheet so that the sail collapsed partly on the deck and partly in the water. *Zainda* came round, bobbing like a cork, swung round by the mizzen.

'Colin!' shouted Joanna hysterically, swinging her torch. In its light she could see that he had managed to grab the floating end of the sail. She dropped the torch in her pocket and pulled at the sail with all her strength. 'Please, God, don't let it tear,' she prayed. She heaved and pulled, slipping on the wet deck. Colin was nearer now, but how was he going to get back into the boat with the high, slippery bow bobbing up and down, she had no idea.

'Help!' she shouted. 'Help!'

But the two in the cockpit had not stirred; they couldn't hear her and hadn't seen what had happened. Simon's response was not the result of her shouts but ordinary commonsense seamanship.

Perspiration was pouring down her body in spite of the wetness. She tried to pull the sail in. Colin's arm was raised above the water as he tried to swim on the crest of the wave while holding to the sail with the other. It was his only hope. If he were to let go of it, he'd be lost. But he was weighed down by the oilskins and getting weaker. How could anyone swim in such high seas? It was bad enough for a boat. While her strength ebbed, her panic rose.

'Help!' she shouted again. 'Help!' She couldn't let go of the sail to run to the cockpit and tell them as she might lose sight of Colin and once he disappeared, they would never find him in the heaving sea.

'Help! Help!' Tears were flowing down her cheeks; it was hopeless.

Suddenly, without warning, another huge wave rose up, towering above the rest and flung Colin against the hull, so that his arm got entangled between the sheet of the sail and the stanchions of the pulpit. Joanna jumped and grabbed his leg and his oilskin jacket, the torch slipping from her pocket. She would never let go, no matter what, even though her hands kept slipping on the smooth surface of the oilskins. Colin, though no longer in the sea, was still on the other side of the boat, and entangled as he was in the sail, he could not lift himself up over the pulpit and onto the deck. A new gust of wind picked up the end of the sail and the metallic eye hit him on the head. Joanna could feel his body going limp and slipping away from her. That, as far as she thought, was the end. Her arms were numb, there was simply no more strength in them to hold him, weighed down as he was by the wet oilskins, let alone lift him over the pulpit. There was a burning, choking panic in her throat as she felt Colin's body slipping away from her hands. It was no good, she had no more strength. That was it. So stupid, with help no more than a few paces away. She closed her eyes sobbing. At that moment, she became aware of another pair of hands grabbing Colin: David's pale face was next to hers. He managed to get hold of Colin's arms while Joanna jumped and, with her remaining strength, grabbed Colin's leg. Together they pulled and heaved as if taking an unwieldy sail out of a bag too small for it. Eventually, his body swung over the life lines and rolled into the boat just as another wave engulfed them all. This was smaller than the others and they did not have to crouch for long before it receded. Quickly, they picked up Colin's unconscious body and stumbling, slipping, clutching to the life lines, made their way to the cockpit.

Once in the cockpit, Joanna's legs turned into jelly. She sat down gasping for breath, while David retched miserably, doubled up, over the side. Simon looked on grimly steering.

'Here!' he shouted to Joanna. 'Steer her the best you can! Point her into the wind!'

'How?' shouted Joanna, almost thrust onto the steering wheel. 'She's not responding.'

'Do your best.'

Simon lifted Colin up and struggled with him down the steps of the main cabin, leaving Joanna in the darkness. She took deep breaths, trying to control the spasms which shook her body. The effort, combined with relief at not having lost Colin, the concentration of keeping her balance on her wobbly legs while trying to steer, was all taking its toll. Peering through the darkness, she prayed for the wind to die down, for the boat to stop moving, for daylight to come, to be anywhere else but here. But the gods were deaf to her prayers. The wind continued to blow, the phosphorescent plumes continued to twist into whirlpools, their tops sliced by the wind to send spray into the helpless, wallowing *Zainda*. The mizzen gave enough steerage to point to the wind so that she could ride the waves at a reasonable angle, but Joanna doubted if they made any headway. From the corner of her eye, she could see David stumble weakly forward to fold the sail which had draped itself across the bow and bobbed up and down on the foredeck. He brought it in by clutching a handful of canvas, dragging the rest behind him.

'Have you got a spare one?' shouted Joanna.

David shook his head. 'I doubt it.'

'What are you going to do then?'

'Reef the main, I'd say.'

Simon reappeared from the main cabin and nodded in agreement.

'Just steer while we put it up!' he roared into Joanna's ear. Half of the next sentence was lost, swallowed by the sea water.

Joanna dug her heels into the floor, feeling wobbly and weak as she gripped the steering wheel. She was unable to see the compass to get a bearing because the salt water kept getting into her eyes, stinging and blinding every now and again. There was a blur in the darkness which she hoped was an outline of an island on the Greek side. It was no good focusing on the stars even when she could see them through the gaps in the clouds. She knew they changed their positions and were useless as steering points even on the calmest passages.

After another eternity, Simon and David managed to put up the reefed mains'l. Simon took over from Joanna, who collapsed on the seat. *Zainda's* movements became more purposeful now that the two sails were up, and a little more comfortable.

'Better see to Colin while I steer!' shouted Simon.

'Is he alright?'

'He'll live.'

David sat in the corner of the cockpit in an attitude indicating utter exhaustion. Joanna had to fight with herself not to withdraw into a motionless trance, oblivious to the world. With an effort, she made her way down to the cabin.

Colin was lying on the bunk in his oilskins. Simon had just dumped him there, leaving him to fend for himself. He had an enormous bruise on his forehead where the metal eye of the sail had hit him. His eyes were closed. Joanna noted with relief that he was breathing. The whole bunk was horribly wet, water dripping from his hair and the oilskin jacket. She looked at him, not knowing what to do. A long time ago, just after taking her final examinations, her school had organised a First Aid course which she had to attend with the rest of her class. But those were the giggly summer days, when the examinations were over, and the blessed release from the constraints of school rules just round the corner. Nobody paid much attention to the First Aid classes. Now she was sorry for not having listened – a futile thought. As she bent over Colin, the water accumulated on her jacket dripped down from the collar onto his face. He opened his eyes, moaned softly, and closed them again. She reflected that he looked very handsome, even like that, bruised and wet. Then the memory of the other woman who claimed him made her sigh.

A sudden, violent motion of the boat nearly threw him out of the bunk. She pushed him back roughly, not having the strength or the stability in her legs to do otherwise. He cried out in pain. Joanna took off her jacket and attempted to take off his, talking more to herself than to him to soothe her nerves.

'Now, now, take it easy. If only you had worn the safety harness,' she continued, pulling off his boots and oilskin trousers, 'you wouldn't be in this mess.'

Once the words were out of her mouth, she was sorry. It wasn't a nice or helpful remark, but it did relieve her feelings. Colin said nothing and lay still with his eyes closed. She hoped he hadn't heard what she had just said. As she pulled at his arm to take off the jacket, he gave a loud groan and something like 'Don't!' passed through his clenched teeth. He made a vague gesture as if trying to protect one arm with the other.

'Please, Colin,' she said very worried. 'I've got to take the jacket off, you can't lie like this.' She tried to pull the sleeve off very gently, stumbling with the movement of the boat, but Colin groaned louder and made more gestures with his hand to push her away. She looked at him, uncertain what to do.

'You can't lie in these wet clothes,' she protested loudly.

His eyes flickered and he blinked several times. He had regained consciousness and moved his head several times until finally his eyes focused on Joanna.

'Carry on then and don't mind me,' he said distinctly.

That was helpful; at least he wasn't concussed. Joanna took off the jacket as gently as she could but wasn't sure who suffered more in the process, her or him. His face was buried in the wet pillow while he tried to stifle the moans. After the jacket was off, she found a towel and poured fresh water into the washbasin. The boat heeled so that the spout missed the bowl, but there was enough water to soak the towel. She wiped his face. He grimaced with pain again as she touched the bruise. His arm which he kept clutching with the other hand was very red and swollen. The wave must have thrown him against the stanchions with a considerable force and she wondered if it was broken. As the boat heeled again, he rolled on it and yelled with pain.

'I could fit a canvas apron along the side so you won't roll out. Could you turn to the side and let me have a look at your arm, do you think? Just let go for a second.'

She prised his hand out of the way very gently. The bruise looked nasty and at the slightest touch of the wet towel Colin winced. Joanna remembered that vinegar was supposed to be good for sprains and bruises and started to look for some in the galley. Having poured some on the towel, the smell only succeeded in affecting her stomach in the stuffy cabin, though it did not seem to make much difference to Colin. He was obviously in great pain, gritting his teeth to stifle the moans with every roll and pitch of the boat.

'It could be broken, but I can't tell unless you let me touch it,' she said weakly.

'Don't you dare,' muttered Colin, his voice muffled by the pillow in which he buried his face again.

'If I bandage it to your side, that should immobilise it at least,' she suggested hopefully. Surely there must be something she could do for him. 'We'll get you to a doctor as soon as we reach Bodrum.'

She looked in the First Aid kit. Some of its contents had spilled out and were rolling on the floor under the table. *To hell with them*, she muttered crossly. *I can't bend down under the table or I'll be sick.* She found a large bandage and wound it tightly round Colin, so that his arm was pressed against the ribs. To do that she had to take off his shirt which took some time and he protested feebly, clutching at the soaking pillow. At last, it was done. She found a long strip of canvas that made up the "apron" which she attached to the side and round the bed to prevent him from falling out. He lay motionless, his eyes closed.

'Are you alright like that? I'm afraid there are no painkillers in the First Aid kit, only aspirins. I suppose they do work up to a point, so perhaps you should take a couple.' In a gymnastic feat, she managed to procure the pills from under the table without being sick, fill a cup with water and gave them to Colin. He swallowed them gratefully.

'Poor you.' She bent down, brushing the wet hair off his forehead. His eyes were closed as he spoke.

'You pulled me in, didn't you?'

'I tried, but I couldn't manage on my own; David helped. I'm so glad you're alive. I'd, I'd …' her chin began to wobble, and she swallowed hard to stop herself from crying. 'I'd nearly given you up.'

She blinked hard and saw him looking at her intently. His eyes were no longer hard or indifferent, but warm and soft, the colour of molten gold.

'Poor Joanna,' he whispered. 'It's all my fault. I am sorry.' His good hand sought hers and he lifted it to his lips. But Joanna's eyes were closed in an effort to keep back the tears and didn't notice.

'How is he, Joanna?' Simon's head appeared in the doorway to the cockpit.

'As well as can be expected. He must see a doctor,' she replied, getting up and going towards the door.

'It's easing a bit now, care to give us a hand?' he sounded so casual Joanna felt she'd better move double quick as he obviously needed her. She was getting used to his peculiar ways of understatement by now. Still, there was a hard core to Simon she never suspected he had in him. He wasn't made of rubber after all. Now he managed to elicit a respect she had not felt for him before.

As she came out into the cockpit, the dawn was just about breaking. There was a pale light in the east seeping through the darkness, imparting to the sea a kind of pewter colour where it had been black before. If Simon looked bedraggled and awful in that wet, ridiculous hat, he was more than matched by David whose face was ashen-green as he sat in utter misery in the corner of the cockpit, knees up to his chin, shaken by intermittent, violent spasms nearly making him fall off his seat.

'Would you mind steering for a minute while I fix the mains'l?' called out Simon. 'David's not really up to it. Better leave him where he is.'

Joanna took the steering wheel. *If they look like that, what must I look like? And another thing – I wonder how Brenda is.* She remembered the hair curlers swirling in the dirty water on the floor of the cabin aeons ago, and shuddered. It made her sick just to think about it.

The wind was making less noise, and Simon let out a few reefs. It made *Zainda* heel more but the motion was easier and more purposeful. He jumped back into the cockpit with an agility she never suspected him capable of.

'How's Colin?' he asked.

'He's got a very painful arm and a big bruise on his forehead, but he's conscious. He was trying to sleep when I left him.'

'I shouldn't be surprised if his arm is broken. One of the stanchions in the pulpit is cracked at the base. He must've been thrown right against it. Rather good of you to hang on to him like that. We wondered what was keeping you there so went to investigate. I'm afraid we lost the torch. Quite expensive it was, too,' he added as an afterthought.

Joanna realised he said it to cover up any emotion that might have crept into his voice. In fact, he seemed embarrassed by the length of his speech. She decided to rescue him from his misery.

'Cocoa?' When was it she had made it? Years ago? She felt much older now.

'Good idea,' he responded enthusiastically. 'I forgot all about it.'

She brought out the Thermos flask, poured it with difficulty, hoping it would not get diluted with sea water. She went over to David. 'Go on, David, try to drink some, even if you throw it up again.' David's teeth chattered and spasms were racking his body. He shook his head feebly. 'Can't,' he mumbled.

She didn't dare call Brenda; the smell of that cabin would have been too much. 'How much longer to Bodrum?' she asked Simon.

'Should make it by mid-day if this wind eases off. Once we're past Kos, we'll have the wind on the beam and we'll be alright.'

He was wrong. They only managed to reach Bodrum harbour late that evening.

Chapter 12

Looking back, it wasn't as awful as it had felt at the time. But that's the way with sailing – moments of adversity are quickly forgotten and all one ever remembers are the happy ones. Perhaps this explains the lure of the sea. Otherwise, why would one want to go sailing again and again?

They battled most of the day with the head winds, making slow headway towards their destination as they tacked towards the south. It was mostly Simon and Joanna who did the actual sailing, though how she managed to find the strength she couldn't say. Brenda appeared in the cockpit for a brief moment, threw the towel smelling of sick on the floor and shut herself back in the aft cabin. Her face was ashen. Asked if she wanted anything, she shook her head and said in a mournful voice, 'Only to die.' The melodramatic tone changed into a hiss when she turned to Simon.

'If I ever get out of this shit, I won't put my foot on a boat again!'

Simon shrugged and said nothing.

In her new mood of sympathy for Simon, Joanna attempted to cheer him up. 'She didn't really mean it,' she said when Brenda disappeared. 'She'll forget it once it blows over.'

David's condition was more worrying. He was continually sick, retching on an empty stomach causing further spasms. He had doubled up in pain, unable to move. Joanna tried to force him to eat or drink in order to give him something to be sick with at least. He looked as if he was about to spit his guts out.

'I'll be all right soon, don't fuss,' he kept saying, before another spasm of pain contorted his face and, doubled up, he ran retching

144

over the side. Colin slept fitfully, or perhaps pretended to, whenever she went down to look at him. So, it was up to her and Simon to carry on. She was wet inside the oilskins, her feet were numb, and as the day wore on, her strength was ebbing. All she wanted to do was to lie down and sleep for all eternity. Her mind went into a trance. A dull throb in her brain rendered her incapable of any thought or initiative. Her movements were mechanical like a puppet's. Everything became an effort. The only sensation to penetrate through the fog in her head was the surprise caused by Simon. He didn't look tired, cheerful if anything, as if the whole situation was some kind of a splendid lark, and at last he was enjoying himself. He steered, went down to plot the course humming a tune, took measurements, peered through the binoculars to identify the approaching headland. While Joanna held grimly to vestiges of sanity, he kept up a conversation which, with her lack of response, was essentially a monologue. He talked about what he was going to do, where they were, how many more miles to go, never as voluble as now. It was as if the old Simon, the middle-aged lover, the bored, upper-class gentleman ceased to exist. How was such a complete change in a man possible?

'It might be rather sensible if we had a bite to eat. Could you manage something, do you think?' he said as he turned to Joanna.

It was nearly noon and the wind had abated considerably. There was less noise in the rigging and fewer splashes into the cockpit. The sun managed to penetrate through the clouds, and now looked as if it was about to win the contest over the supremacy of the sky. Joanna lifted her swollen eyelids, pushed the hood of the oilskin off her head and, using her hand, rubbed a layer of powdered salt off her face. Simon's face also showed streaks of white. His blue oilskins were streaked with white patches, and water dripped from the brim of his tweed deerstalker. It must have been heavy and uncomfortable – a more incongruous headgear in this situation was hard to imagine. But then Simon was Simon. *Nothing about him will ever surprise me, not even if he produced an umbrella in the middle of a storm at sea,* Joanna thought.

She went down to the galley and only then realised how ravenously hungry she was. It had been a long time since their last proper meal. It took a fair bit of effort to get at the food as the bread and the tins were strewn all over the cabin.

'Rather good of you not to get seasick,' said Simon, munching a slice of bread on which was balanced a piece of Spam hacked out of a tin. He looked around, surveying the scene. 'It's easing up, almost over, I'd say.'

They were very near the island of Kos which gave them some shelter from the wind. Their course took them round the Turkish coast eastwards, towards Bodrum. Joanna felt much better after the bread and Spam (which in her land life she detested) and took over the steering from Simon. The wind had shifted a little due to the proximity of Kos, so that they had it more on the beam and *Zainda* rode much easier, her pitching and rolling getting to within tolerable limits.

'I think it's a good time to put the jib up,' said Simon and went to the sail locker in a flurry of renewed activity.

David managed to drink the remains of the cocoa from the Thermos flask and looked less limp. It wasn't long before the aft cabin door opened and Brenda came out. Her mood, however, was more than a match for the thunderstorm clouds of the previous night. Simon purposefully ignored her, confining his remarks to Joanna. It was obvious he was going to great lengths to avoid a scene. It nearly made Joanna laugh out aloud.

But apathy, dispelled momentarily by the food, returned, and she could not remember the details of entering Bodrum harbour, or how and when they tied the boat to the pontoon. Her mind registered through a haze the disappearance of Simon followed by his reappearance with two men and a stretcher. Colin was taken away in a car, or was it an ambulance? David was beginning to look more like his old self as they entered the harbour, but was too weak to do more than tie down the sails before flopping on his bunk. Joanna could hardly see her way to the cabin through swollen eyelids. She took off her oilskins and shoes, washed her face, which had been painfully burnt by the wind and the salt, and sunk into oblivion.

When she woke up, it was midday the next day. Her body felt sticky and dirty, her hair stuck to her skull like a tight swimming cap, tongue swollen, and a bitter taste in her mouth. She looked out through the hatch. Outside, the day was sunny and beautiful. The yachts in the harbour swayed gently on their moorings in an almost imperceptible breeze. The air was crystal clear so that the mountains in the distance normally lost in a haze were visible. The harbour water sparkled gold and blue. It was all sunshine and peace, as if the storm had never been. The sea had proved itself to be a temperamental lover, and now it was making amends for its previous outburst. Naturally it was forgiven as Joanna couldn't help smiling with pleasure at the scene around her. David was in the cockpit, mending something.

'Is it all right if I have a shower?' she asked him.

'Go ahead, we've plenty of water. I just filled the whole tank.'

Some time later, she emerged feeling clean and wonderful, tossing her hair loose to dry in the sun. It was as if the shower had washed away all the discomforts of the stormy night. She sang happily to herself while cooking breakfast. On the table was a loaf of delicious Turkish bread and some bunches of radishes, signs of early morning shopping.

'So, how do *you* feel this morning,' asked David. He was mending a rip in the storm jib.

'Wonderful!' she replied, her mouth full of bread. 'And you, are you all right now?'

'I'm fine, thanks. I didn't know I could be that sick. Doesn't happen to me often, but when it does, there's no stopping it,' he said and shrugged apologetically, then eyed her attentively from top to bottom and back to her face. 'You were quite something last night! I suppose you know that?' There was a note of admiration in his voice.

She squirmed, embarrassed. 'Oh, I don't know, I didn't do anything special. You were a great help yourself.'

'Simon was very impressed too. Said you were a great help though, mind you, I don't think he'll tell you to your face. I'm afraid he's a bit like that,' he laughed.

'Simon? Well, I'm glad he noticed me,' she laughed, pleased.

'You mustn't be hard on Simon,' David was suddenly serious. 'He can be a bit offhand. He's had a lot on his plate lately,' he said and gestured vaguely with his hand.

I wonder what, thought Joanna. *Something to do with Brenda, or with being accident prone?* She wanted to press David further, but he had something else on his mind.

'You look wonderful this morning. I like your hair loose like that. Why do you always tie it back? It makes you look like a school teacher,' he laughed.

Joanna went down to the cabin and concentrated on cutting another slice of bread. David dropped the sail and followed. He was now standing close to her, twisting a strand of her hair round his finger. She turned her face away, trying to sip her coffee, sensing full well he wanted to embrace her. She wasn't ready for him, not yet. He let his hand drop reluctantly.

'Where's Brenda?' she asked casually.

'She's left.'

'What do you mean?' Joanna stared at him with surprise. 'What? For good? Here in Bodrum?'

'That's right, she's left. Walked out. Said she'd had enough. Had a bit of a row with Simon. I'm surprised they didn't wake you up – they made quite a racket actually. Simon didn't think he should pay for her ticket home from here. They went into town together. Maybe he managed to persuade her to wait till we get back to Athens, as she could use her ticket there, but I don't know. You can't really blame her. She doesn't enjoy sailing, does she? Got quite sick in the cabin, I believe.'

'But you enjoy sailing even though you get sick.'

'I know,' he admitted ruefully. 'I just like sailing. I'd sail whether I'm sick or not. I must be a masochist, I suppose. Come to think of it, I don't know why I like it. The open air, the freedom of it, I suppose.'

Joanna understood him well. After last night, it would be quite difficult to explain why anyone should enjoy sailing, or the lure of the sea, unless one writes like Conrad.

'She left quite a mess in the cabin, you know. Simon took his sleeping bag and slept on the deck.' He opened the door of the aft cabin and the smell of sick and dampness wafted in. Joanna wrinkled her nose.

'Phew. I suppose he'll want me to clean it up.' The state of her own cleanliness was all too brief.

'It's not really fair on you, is it?' said David looking into the cabin and coming back, holding his nose. 'I don't suppose it was ever cleaned since she came.'

He looked at her again. The intensity in his gaze made Joanna uncomfortably aware they were alone on the boat.

'What happened to Colin?' she asked hastily, trying to put a brake on this silently developing intimacy. She'd rather set her own pace and resented David for rushing her into his arms.

At the mention of Colin, his face darkened a little.

'He was taken to see a doctor.'

'I hope it's a good doctor,' said Joanna anxiously. She remembered having seen doctors' name plates in Turkey in the fly-spattered, rickety doorways of crumbling houses where a hen or two scratched for sustenance in the courtyards. Somehow, they didn't inspire confidence.

'You needn't worry.' David's voice sounded cold, resentful. 'There's a British yacht with a doctor on board. He'll be well looked after.'

'Where? In this harbour?'

'Over there.' David waved his hand vaguely and went up to the cockpit to resume mending the sail.

Joanna screwed her eyes against the sun and saw *Jemima II* on the mooring, on the opposite side of the harbour. She transferred her gaze to David, eyebrows raised, a question forming on her lips. It remained unspoken as David avoided her eye, whether purposefully or not, she could not tell, and bent over the sail.

'I believe I've seen her before,' she tried to keep the sarcasm out of her voice. Maybe she could draw him out on the subject of *Jemima* now they were alone. But David remained laconic. 'Yes,' was all he said and carried on with the stitching. She watched his hand with the leather pad and strap which enabled him to push the needle through the thick canvas, moving in and out, in silence. She almost burst out with *What's going on here, who are they?* but stopped herself and instead asked:

'How long is he going to stay there, do you know?'

'Don't know. Simon said he'll go and see him this afternoon.'

'Does that mean we might be cutting our stay short and sailing back to Athens?'

'I don't know, but I shouldn't think so. Why should we?' he sounded doubtful. 'After all, we haven't finished here,' he added.

'Finished!' exclaimed Joanna. So, there was something going on and David was going to take her into his confidence. 'Finished what?'

'Oh, I meant the holiday. Haven't finished our holiday,' he repeated.

Although disappointed she was at the same time elated for having been given a clue. At least she wasn't going mad, and that meant a lot. So, there *was* something Simon and David had set out to do, and it wasn't finished. She should be grateful to David even for that. In a surge of goodwill, she turned towards him:

'If I help you with the sail, perhaps we could go look at the town later?'

'Good idea. Actually, it's an awfully long tear. I'd like to go out, unless,' he added as an afterthought, 'Simon brings the orders to move on.'

Orders? What orders? Who issues the orders? she wondered silently, trying hard not to look jubilant. 'I hope not,' she said in a casual voice. 'I still feel very stiff after last night. You know, if you hadn't helped me pull in Colin, I don't think I'd have managed on my own. He'd be a goner,' she shuddered at the very thought.

'You almost had him back on deck before I got there,' said David gallantly. She realised what an effort it must have been for him, sick and in pain, to crawl to the fore deck and lift the weight of Colin's body.

'You really were a tremendous help. Thank you.'

David raised his head to look at her. She wished she hadn't said it. *Whatever I say to him he takes it as an invitation to further intimacy.* She hadn't forgotten her resolution to have sex with him for what could be called therapeutic reasons, but this was getting out of hand. It was she who was supposed to be in control, steer the affair on its proper casual course, and instead he was forcing his will on her. Of course, once resolved, she wasn't going to back out, but would see to it that the game was played according to her rules, in her own time.

As Simon did not return to *Zainda* in the afternoon, they felt free to go sightseeing. Their steps took them to the Crusaders' Castle which towered over the town. The Crusaders had no qualms or respect for history, and robbed the ancient monuments as well as the local quarries for building materials. Several of their coat-of-arms were carved on the underside of Ionic capitals from ancient Greek temples fitted into the walls head on. The castle was converted into a museum, the rooms housed various exhibits from Geometric Greek to Byzantine times. They spent some of their time looking at the sea from several vantage points of the castle grounds, only to laugh about it. As if they hadn't had enough of the sea after last night.

If David's comments on history and architecture were not very profound, they didn't obtrude either. He was an attentive and pleasant companion, his mood alternating between pensive and happy. At one point, as they climbed up the twisting stone steps and emerged on top of one of the towers, he took Joanna's hand and pulled her sharply towards him.

'You know, I should be the happiest man alive for being here with you. Thank you.' He bent down and kissed her on the lips. She responded, even though it was rather disappointing not to enjoy that kiss. The wind whipped up her skirt, making her take a step back, holding it down. Although her mind was made up, it felt she was using him by leading him on. Still, once the holiday was over, he was bound to find himself a girl and forget about her. But there was that vulnerability about him, as if he might get hurt and her bit of fun might go beyond the joke. He was looking at her, his eyes searching her face, questioning, but she pretended not to notice. He looked away with a sigh, without letting her go.

'Joanna,' he whispered and buried his face in her hair. 'Joanna.'

She couldn't take it anymore. This was getting beyond a joke.

'Look,' she began firmly, facing him with a newly formed resolution. It weakened when she saw his face.

'Don't say it,' he put his finger on her lips. 'I don't want to hear it.'

She resented his attempts at clairvoyance.

'All I wanted to tell you is … Oh, why don't you find yourself someone your own age,' she burst out exasperated.

He looked at her sadly. 'I've been trying to tell myself hundreds of times.'

She wasn't ready for this profound sadness.

'Oh, come on, cheer up,' she said and kissed him lightly on the cheek and took his arm. 'Let's go and see the rest of the town.'

They went down and walked into town, Joanna talking brightly and inconsequentially. They bought a halva from a tiny shop selling at least a dozen different flavours in as many colours, all kept in large round tins displayed on the tiny window sill. They went further on, bought fruit and a bottle of Turkish wine to celebrate the end of the storm in the evening. She kept up the conversation to calm herself and wipe out the scene in the castle from her mind, wishing it had never taken place. Perhaps David felt the same because he fell easily into her mood as he munched steadily and ate most of the halva.

A stone gate dating from the times of the Crusaders caught their attention. It was built from marble blocks robbed, no doubt, from an ancient site. They went through it. It led to a boatyard, where a pile of huge logs was deposited by the entrance. They watched fascinated as the logs were taken down into the shop and converted into planks using huge, noisy machinery. A man, a foreman perhaps, came up to them and said something in Turkish. They shook their heads, indicating they couldn't understand him, at the same time making gestures asking if they could look around. The man nodded and left them alone. They went into a big shed where three boats were being built at the same time, using the wooden planks converted from the logs by the entrance. They were all of the same pattern, broad, comfortable caiques, characteristic of the Turkish waters. Several were already finished and fitted out, moored on the other side of the harbour, waiting to be hired or sold. They looked very romantic in the glow of their warm wood next to the sleek, stark, fibreglass yachts from foreign lands. Joanna loved them and looked at the three unfinished ones with great interest. Each had a huge blue glass eye hanging from the prow on a piece of string, like a long pendant.

'Look, David, that's for luck, the eye that finds a harbour in the storm. You should've had one of these on *Zainda*! How lovely!' she exclaimed, wondering if this sort of thing was still done anywhere in western boatyards. It was wise to propitiate whatever gods ruled the sea, but she doubted if westerners even recognised their existence.

When they got back to *Zainda*, Simon was waiting for them. He looked cross and out of sorts. There was no sign of Brenda and Joanna didn't dare to ask.

'We sail tomorrow morning,' he said, sounding snappy. 'And I could do with a decent night's sleep.'

'I'll help you with the aft cabin,' offered Joanna and, hoping to mellow him, added: 'Look, we've got a bottle of wine to celebrate our safe arrival in Bodrum.'

Simon grunted in reply.

'How's Colin?' she asked and tried to sound casual.

'Alright, under sedation right now. A dislocated joint and a suspected fracture, I believe. They were trying to take him to an X-ray unit, but I don't know where,' he said, sounding annoyed.

'I suppose he'll be going home now?' said Joanna trying to keep the regret down. It was better for her peace of mind at any rate. What the eye does not see, etcetera.

'It's a bit difficult,' said Simon grimly.

He should know, thought Joanna. I wonder if he spent all day trying to find transport for Brenda? He looked as if he had.

'It's a bit difficult,' repeated Simon vaguely, as he made his way to the aft cabin where he could be heard thrashing about, slamming cupboard doors and drawers. His head appeared in the doorway just as Joanna decided to start cooking.

'I've left some clothing in the cockpit. Needs washing. You might try to find a laundry somewhere.'

'Okay. Will you keep an eye on the pasta please while I go and look for one?' she said to David. She made her way along the pontoons with the bag of clothing until she found a local guard.

'Could you tell me where I can find a laundrette? she asked, but he shook his head. 'Laundrette?' she repeated, this time making gestures as if washing and pointing to the bag. It really was so ridiculous, making those silly gestures. One always felt such a fool waving one's hands about like that. A ray of understanding lit up the man's face.

'Ne, ne, yes, si,' he nodded as she slipped a few coins into his hand. 'Okay, Good. Okay,' he said.

She waved her hand towards *Zainda*. The man picked up the bag and disappeared. Joanna went back to the boat feeling satisfied. It had been easier than expected. Perhaps there was no need to learn Turkish after all.

David was pouring the pasta into the colander, clouds of steam billowing around him. He peered at her through his steamed-up glasses and smiled.

'Done,' she said referring to the laundry and, with a familiarity she wouldn't have believed capable of a few days ago, shouted:

'C'mon, Simon, supper's ready. Who's for some wine, then?'

Simon slid silently into his usual place by the table. She served the pasta with meat sauce, made partly from tins and local vegetables.

'Not bad,' muttered Simon, the nearest she'd ever got to praise.

'I am surprised you like garlic.'

'Garlic, ah, well yes, garlic. No I don't mind it, y'know,' he said, then carried on eating, preoccupied with his thoughts. It was obvious that he didn't mind what was on his plate as long as it was edible.

David was wolfing down his portion without pausing for breath, making up for the enforced fast caused by his sea sickness. He ate without speaking, oblivious to the world, and only looked up once. 'Are there any seconds?' he asked, wiping his steamed-up glasses. Joanna had been prepared for this contingency and loaded his plate again to the brim.

They were interrupted by a noise, as if someone was trying to come on board. Simon, who was nearest to the door, started when Brenda's pale face, lit up by the cabin light, appeared in the doorway.

'Good Lord, Brenda!' he exclaimed. 'What are you doing here? Thought you'd gone to Rhodes on that ferry. Anything wrong?'

'I couldn't leave you. I had to come back.' Brenda's voice sounded plaintive as if she was about to cry. Simon jumped up to the cockpit in a flash.

'Brenda,' he said in a voice that made Joanna blush and wish she could tactfully retreat somewhere. Fortunately, the cockpit was immersed in darkness. Only a murmur of voices, his and hers, reached them, but the words were inaudible. They were followed by silence, presumably because they were kissing. Joanna kept her eyes firmly on her plate, then shifted them onto the food left on Simon's plate. David kept eating, but slowed down, and emptied his glass of wine in one go. He looked at Joanna, then shifted his gaze to a spot on the wall, but his ears were burning.

Joanna had often wondered about Simon's relationship with Brenda. What could that silly girl offer a man almost twice her age, in many ways superior, apart from sex? The sounds coming from the cockpit, the snatched, tearful voice, the sobs interrupted by silences which were probably kisses, only increased her wonder. She shook her head. Obviously, there were many things she'd never understand, though not for lack of trying. It was a pity Brenda couldn't stay faithful to him, but then if Simon would go and involve himself with a young, silly girl, that was his problem.

'Cheers,' she said, turning to David and clinking her glass against his. 'I suppose we might as well finish the bottle, don't you? I don't think Simon's coming back to eat his supper,' she smiled. It dawned on her that as long as Colin was away, they had this half of the boat all to themselves. The sight of Colin's bruised face flashed through her mind. It took an effort to shut it out. As for David, no, not tonight. *I'm not ready for tonight.*

Her head swam slightly from the wine as she washed the dishes. David was helping her in uncomfortable silence. It was more than uncomfortable, it was a taut, quivering silence, imbued with the kind of stillness runners must feel when poised before the start of a race waiting for the signal to go up. There was in his eyes a barely suppressed expectation, while his hands made perfunctory movements with the dish cloth. It got on Joanna's nerves, this silence; it was as if the circumstances were forcing her into David's arms. No, she was going to do it in her own, sweet time.

They finished drying the dishes in silence. Joanna gave another wipe to an already shining sink and was about to go to her cabin when David blocked her way. He stood there, slightly perspiring, drawing the nail of his thumb along his lips as if deep in thought.

'Let me out, David,' she said and tried to slip past him.

He moved away obediently, then, as she came closer, caught her by both arms and started to kiss her. She moved her face away, so that most of the kisses fell on her cheek.

'Come on, Joanna, why not?' He tried to make it sound light and casual, but the little laugh he gave had a rasping tone to it. He propelled her to his bunk. 'You know I'm mad about you,' he mumbled as his lips sought hers. She tried to back away and eventually managed to wriggle enough for him to loosen his grip.

'No, David, please,' she said firmly. He let her go reluctantly. 'I'm tired after last night. I'm going to bed. So should you.' He looked so dejected it almost made her laugh out aloud. She raised her hand to stroke his cheek, kissed him lightly, then turned abruptly and almost ran to her cabin before he had a chance to catch her again. 'Good night, sleep well,' she said and closed the door of her cabin firmly behind her.

Although her body needed rest and sleep, her mind couldn't switch off. She tossed and turned, and in the darkness could hear David do the same. She was never so conscious of the thinness of the partition which separated their cabins as just then. As she closed her eyes, the image of David's face floated in the darkness and she heard his voice, quite near her, full of sadness: 'I've told myself a hundred times I shouldn't have fallen in love with you.' She jumped up, but there was no one in her cabin. It was all a dream. What a fool she was. Now was the time to go back to David, to have it over and done with, instead of letting things drag on and on. After a time, she fell into a heavy sleep and only woke up when the sun was high up in the sky.

All looked tired as they sat round the breakfast table, talking in monosyllables, as if the storm was only now taking its toll. Simon disappeared soon after breakfast and Brenda was uncommunicative. She sipped her coffee, and smoked a cigarette, looking straight ahead. There were dark shadows under her eyes. Her gaze flickered only for an instant on Joanna.

'You're looking very well,' she said, her voice full of acid. 'Storms suit you. Seems only bed bugs make you run.'

Joanna said nothing.

'Why didn't you take your admirer to bed last night?' she added after a pause. 'He looks pretty rough this morning. It would be a mercy if you did; just look at him.' This last was said in a tone of advice as Brenda pointed her chin in David's direction. Fortunately for Joanna he was out of earshot.

It was obvious Brenda considered it her mission in life to get Joanna and David together. Joanna looked up to where Brenda was pointing and saw him through a porthole, walking along the pontoon. Brenda was right, he looked pale, miserable, and in need of a shave. All the same, she glared at Brenda.

'None of your business,' she snapped. *One more word from Brenda and I'll smash a plate on her head, and if Simon comes in to protect his darling, I'll just walk out.* But Brenda seemed to have sensed her breaking point. She got up, wrapping the dressing gown with the tiger on it round her, and walked out without saying another word. Joanna could hear her talking to the man who had brought the laundry back.

Simon returned alone. 'Colin will join us later on. He's better, still a bit groggy after sedation.'

'Is his arm broken?' asked Joanna.

'I believe so. It's been set in plaster. Says it's his left arm, but luckily he's right-handed. Should be alright with a waterproof sleeve over the plaster.'

'Where are we going to next?'

'Well now …' Simon sounded vague as he peered at the chart. 'Down south.'

But Joanna could see he was trying to pinpoint precisely a little bay along the coast on the chart, so he knew *exactly* where they were going. His deliberate vagueness again raised all those fears that had vanished during the storm. She could see a pattern emerging. He must be receiving his orders from somewhere to make the next rendezvous with *Jemima* – that much was becoming clear. But why should the people on *Jemima* be telling him where to sail? What was the reason? What were they supposed to be doing? Try as she might, Joanna had seen no suspicious activity on *Zainda* at all. She wasn't sure if Brenda was in the conspiracy; her behaviour could be construed either way. Either she was remarkably clever or plain dumb, though Joanna was inclined to take the latter view. David, however, knew something, but didn't want to tell her. Well, she might prise some information out of him. Great was the power of a woman in bed, or so it was said. She might try that. But, if there was something going on, what could they be after? Were they looking for ancient statues lying somewhere on the bottom of the sea? Maybe. Apparently, there was a lot of illicit trade in antiques going on in Turkey. But where was the diving gear if they were looking for sunken antiques? They didn't even have as much as a decent snorkel between them. No, that wasn't it. She drew a blank and gave up. Something was bound to come up sooner or later to shed some light on the situation, but right now it was hopeless. Admittedly whatever it was seemed to be worth somebody's while to arrange a couple of accidents. It was sinister and menacing, this unknown something. She wished as never before not to be involved and wondered how best to disengage herself without making too much fuss.

Chapter 13

Their sail out of Bodrum was one that makes people go out to sea again and again and never look back. There was enough wind to fill the sails to give them a good speed of five to six knots. The sun was shining and there was just enough undulation on the water's surface to make the movement of the boat comfortable without that violent, jerky motion that made everything fall on the floor if not secured properly. Their oilskins had been rinsed in fresh water, dried and put away, as were their sleeping bags and other belongings which had been mercilessly tossed about and soaked through. The hatches and portholes were open to let in air, so that the cabin smelled fresh and dry as it hadn't done for some time. David did wonders in repairing the storm jib which was now stored away, hopefully not to be needed again. The barometer reading was high and steady, indicating good weather to come. It was sunny and peaceful, and hard to imagine the storm had ever happened. The world outside smiled and the wavelets sparkled in the sunshine. An occasional brown seagull, or was it a kittiwake, swooped across the sky or took off from the waves on seeing *Zainda* approach. The visibility was good, so that the contours and landmarks were clear and detailed, not lost in the usual heat haze.

They rounded the most easterly part of Kos in practically no time, and sailed due south. Even the mountains of the Turkish mainland, which normally looked rather forbidding, seemed to smile at them. They lunched on fresh bread, butter, delicious salad and fruit. Simon and Brenda were lying on the aft deck in a close embrace. Joanna wished they would confine their petting to the cabin, afraid she might be treated to a show of the real thing, as Brenda's bikini made little difference to total nudity. Their behaviour put a strain on the unspoken and unconsumed state of affairs between her and David. They sat together in the cockpit, David steering, Joanna sitting in the cockpit sunbathing, her eyes closed. There was an uneasiness between them now. Joanna felt it was all her fault for leading him on. It occurred to her she was making too much fuss about a perfectly natural thing. She really ought to let herself go.

David stole a furtive glance at her from time to time, then pretended to be busy with whatever came to hand: controls, binoculars, anything. Joanna, on her part, pretended not to notice and concentrated on sunbathing. But then how was one supposed to switch one's mind off and stop thinking? Their silence was accompanied by grunts, giggles and snatches of endearments from the aft deck. It only helped to deepen the uneasiness in the cockpit.

Zainda sliced through the water with a swish, leaving behind her a hissing wake, the noise similar to that of oil in a frying pan. Looking up from her lying position, Joanna watched the white sails straining with the force of wind against the blue sky, and wondered if there was a more beautiful sight anywhere in the world. This was paradise, and like paradise it was not without its serpent.

'I can see dolphins!' shouted David excitedly. 'Dolphins! Look!'

Joanna jumped up. A whole school was swimming towards them. She ran for her camera and positioned herself on the bow, leaning against the pulpit to watch their antics in the water. She focused her camera on one swimming along the side as if trying to race them, only to dive under the hull and jump up on the other side with a hiss and a sigh, fixing its eye on Joanna as it did so. As the dolphins dived into the blue depths, they made squealing noises. She heard Brenda's excited, 'Oh, oh, oh!' behind her. David was now on the bow, leaning over the pulpit as Joanna followed one of the dolphins with great concentration so she would have it in focus when it jumped. David's arm was around her, pretending to support himself against the pulpit for balance. The dolphin jumped, she pressed the button on the camera and stepped back, excited, bumping against David. As she did the top of her bikini snapped and slid down, revealing her breasts. David's eyes became transfixed and blood rushed to his face. He just gaped at her. It acted like a douche of cold water on Joanna.

'For goodness sake, David, don't just stand there!' she said turning round, holding the two loose ends of the bikini in her hands at the back. 'Do it up for me.'

His fingers fumbled clumsily. 'Anyone would think you haven't seen girls sunbathing in monokinis,' she laughed.

'What's that?' His voice sounded hoarse and he had to clear his throat.

'Topless.'

'Oh.'

He continued to fumble with the bikini top, tickling her back. Suddenly she felt his hot hands pressing her breasts and a hot breath in her ear as he whispered: God, you are beautiful ...' He buried his face in her hair and took a deep breath. 'I love you ... You wouldn't ... I mean ...'

'Why not?' she said casually. 'Why not indeed?' she repeated, as if it was the easiest, most natural thing in the world. 'Some time ...' She let her voice trail, her eyes teasing.

'You would!' he exclaimed, beads of perspiration on his forehead, 'You mean, you would?' He sounded almost incredulous. He put both his arms around her, holding her so close she had to bend back to look at him.

'Hey, break it up you two,' Simon's voice reached them from the aft deck. 'I thought you were steering, David. We're completely off course.'

David let go of Joanna reluctantly, muttering *Look who's talking* under his breath, and went back to the steering wheel. Joanna wriggled her bikini top into its proper place and felt light-headed.

They rounded the headland where the ancient site of Knidos could be recognised from the sea, mainly by the cluster of houses on a stretch of flat land, the hills rising steeply on both sides. From one of the houses flew a large Turkish flag. They stopped at the entrance of a sheltered bay on the southern side. Simon was on the bow, surveying the scene through the binoculars. There were some boats there, mainly small fishing craft, and one or two yachts under anchor. It was on these that Simon trained the binoculars, looking at them carefully. Outside the house with the flag, a number of officials in uniform were sitting on the veranda. There was another house with *Restaurant* painted in big letters on the roof. To either side of the bay were ruins in the shape of open, rectangular boxes with stony, jagged edges. Facing the bay were the outlines of a Greek theatre. Joanna was reminded of the magnificent seated statue of the goddess Demeter of Knidos in the British Museum. So that's where the statue came from – this very place! She looked at the ruins, set out neatly in orderly patterns, with renewed attention. It would be interesting to land and walk among those stones to make more sense out of them. She turned expectantly to Simon, but he was talking to David and shaking his head, as if this place was different to what he had expected, or he hadn't find what he wanted.

'Let's get out of here,' he said. They were circling around and it was evident they were not going to anchor.

'But. … what about all this?' Joanna waved her hand.

'What about what?'

'Aren't we going to visit the ancient site?' she stammered. 'Isn't that what we came to see?'

'We don't have the time,' he said firmly. 'Maybe on the way back. Not that I can see any particular sense in those ruins myself,' he added. 'Not my idea of a holiday, to be honest.'

Joanna sat down with a keen sense of disappointment. She made an attempt to photograph the ruins from a distance, knowing full well it was pointless. There'll only be a heap of stones with lots of the sea in the foreground on the photograph. She glanced at David. He steered as if in a trance, transfixing her with a heavy stare from time to time, so that even Brenda shot a speculative glance at Joanna and whistled through her teeth. Joanna hid her annoyance by finding something to do in the cabin.

They motored along the coast, checking out every bay, every kink in the coastline, every promontory, while Simon continued to scan the land carefully through the binoculars.

'Is Simon looking for anything in particular?' she asked David. His answer was evasive. 'No, not really, I don't think so, a place to stop for the night I suppose ...' Joanna knew he was lying, but gave up pursuing the subject.

They carried on like this all afternoon until the oncoming darkness forced them to anchor in a small, unlit bay. It was open to the north, with a considerable swell rolling in making the boat uncomfortable. Joanna prepared some sandwiches but Brenda didn't want to eat much as the constant movement was. making her queasy. David also wasn't interested in eating. For some reason, Simon had found a lot to say to David on deck, talking to him in a low voice, then making him keep a long watch. At first Joanna thought Simon was protecting him from her, but the idea was ridiculous. No, they were looking for somebody or something. Their suppressed excitement communicated itself to her. On the spur of the moment, she decided to share her thoughts with Brenda.

'What's going on, Brenda? What are they looking for?' she asked when they were alone in the cabin.

'I haven't a clue,' Brenda said and shrugged her shoulders.

'Doesn't it strike you as a bit weird?

'Yeah,' Brenda nodded. She was trying to paint her nails and hold the nail polish pot at the same time which, in the rolling boat, needed all her concentration so that her tongue stuck out in the effort.

'Well, what do you make of it?'

'I don't know.' She looked critically at her nails. Two were already painted a metallic green colour. 'Not bad, is it?' spreading her fingers. 'So, you're having it off with David after all? About time, too. I thought you'd never come round. In fact, Simon and I thought maybe you were frigid, or hung up, or something.'

Joanna decided she was right after all: Brenda thought of nothing but sex. Storms might rage around her, accidents might happen, strange men might be following them in Istanbul, but throughout all this Brenda concentrated only on this one topic, serenely oblivious to everything else.

'Mind you,' Brenda continued in her drawling way, concentrating hard on the nail of her little finger, 'I think Colin will be sorry. I rather think he fancied you himself.'

If a bucket of cold water was poured on Joanna's head, she wouldn't have reacted more strongly than she did just then.

'What did you say?' she blurted out at last.

'Mind you, I might be wrong. I just have that teeny, weeny suspicion. He doesn't show much, our Colin, does he? Quite a cool customer. I know you fancy him too,' she laughed. 'You should have seen your face when you saw him with that woman in that bar in Istanbul. You can't keep things from me, you know,' she waved her painted fingers at Joanna.

'I wish you'd notice a few more things under your nose,' said Joanna through clenched teeth. 'There's nothing between me and Colin, nothing at all.'

'I know, he's holding back, isn't he? I wonder why. It's interesting really. Poor Joanna. Still, David will have to do for the time being. Now, don't look so cross, Joanna,' she glanced up from her painting, then stretched out her hand, fingers apart, to scrutinise her work again. 'If they can't decide where to stay the night,' she said, changing the subject abruptly, 'that's their problem. I never interfere.'

Nothing happened during the night except that they all had an uncomfortable night in the rolling boat. At one point, Joanna heard the subdued crackling of the radio and Simon's voice as he called *Jemima*. At the break of dawn, they were underway. Joanna, dressed in a sweatshirt and jeans and holding a mug of coffee, was sitting on the deck watching the sunrise. It started with a thin strip of yellow which deepened into a golden colour, then in a slow, unfolding motion, changed into orange. The fiery gold disc emerged coyly from behind the horizon like the mischievous face of a child pretending to hide behind a door, peeping out to see if anyone was looking. Then it popped up so quickly she could hardly believe her eyes. In next to no time the whole sky was lit by its golden rays, their warmth already touching her body. An everyday occurrence, yet there was so much magic about it. It didn't matter if it was repeated every day; each time it was like a miracle. The very stuff of poetry. Incredible.

David looked tired as he sunk his teeth into the bread and jam. It was obvious he hadn't had much sleep. Nor for that matter had Simon.

'Where to now?' asked Joanna, breaking the spell. She didn't want to share the magic of the sunrise with anyone, it was hers and hers only. Simon went back to bed to catch a few more winks, as he put it, and Brenda went with him.

'Oh, ahead,' David said and waved his hand vaguely along the coast.

'Maybe I'll steer and look out for whatever it is you're looking for, while you go and rest?'

'No, thanks, I'm alright,' David said but looked a bit unsettled. 'I don't want to sleep, unless,' he added as an afterthought, 'it's with you.'

Joanna laughed. 'We can't now.'

David stretched his hand towards her, letting go of the wheel and making her spill her coffee. *Zainda* gave an unexpected lurch.

'Impossible, see?' she laughed.

David righted the boat grimly. 'How long am I to wait then?'

'It's up to you,' she replied teasing him. 'Or when the opportunity arises.'

David grabbed her hand and held it. 'Do you mean that?' he asked seriously.

'I suppose so. Oh, come on, don't look so serious David. It's meant to be fun.'

'Fun!' he exclaimed bitterly. 'It's been hell.'

'Oh, David,' she said and rubbed her head against his shoulder in a sudden gesture of intimacy. 'What an awful thing to say.'

He turned to look at her, a long penetrating look, slowly taking in the details of her face and her hair, which she had forgotten to twist into the usual pony tail.

'You're so beautiful,' he murmured. 'From the very first time I saw you ...' He plunged his mouth onto hers. She was stunned by the abruptness of his gesture, and could hardly breathe. *Zainda* gave another lurch, her sails flapping. Simon's annoyed voice was heard coming from the aft cabin.

'What's the matter with the boat?'

With a sigh David, righted the steering again. 'Go away, you're distracting me.'

They sailed all day along the coast. Joanna hoped there would be no bad weather which would mean that they wouldn't be able to sail close to the shore. Here the water was deep enough to allow them to see practically all the scrub and bushes growing on the hills. Simon came out and was inspecting every indentation of the land, every bay, however tiny. Joanna and Brenda read and sunbathed, while both men looked strained and anxious as they continued to scan the landscape through the binoculars. There was nothing there. No signs of human habitation.

Once, out at sea they passed the odd cargo boat, a fishing boat, a tanker far away, their barely discernible shapes moving slowly against the lighter background of the sky. At last, they came to a deserted bay. David called out the readings on the depth sounder, to make sure there was sufficient depth to anchor for the night. Unlike the coast they had seen so far, this one was covered with a sparse vegetation – just clumps of yellow-grey bushes the size of footballs scattered among the boulders. As far as the eye could see, there was nothing and nobody around. The sea cut into the undulating brown land, glistening in the harsh sunshine with grey elongated patches of rocky ground, forming a deep, lozenge-shaped bay. It was almost landlocked except for the opening through which they entered. There was practically no movement of air which combined with the heat rising from the land made it almost unbearably hot. A general feeling of emptiness emanated from the hills. It was like a moon landscape, with nothing but rocks and the dry, football-like plants. Joanna, wilting from the heat, looked up, away from the unfriendly land. Somewhere, very high up, an unseen plane trailed a thin stream of white cloud like a wispy ribbon winding across the sky. It only helped to increase the feeling of isolation below. She scanned the shore again and was surprised to spot the remains of a house in one corner of the bay. It had a small, crude landing place in front of it made from stones placed in the water, leading to a strip of flat earth cleared of boulders and bushes. It seemed inconceivable that this land had ever sustained life. Why anyone should want to build and live in a house in this forlorn, barren place was beyond her credulity. As the noise of

Zainda's engine died down, she could now hear in the distance a hollow tinkling of bells. Somewhere in those hills were goats or sheep scratching out a miserable existence. It was a wonder the animals found anything edible in the arid land, but obviously they did.

The heat was oppressive. Simon and David stretched a piece of canvas over the cockpit to provide some shade, while Joanna plunged into the sea with relief. The water felt like warm soup, but it was better than sitting on the deck in full sunshine.

'Hey, come and join me, it's lovely,' she waved.

'Wait for me!' shouted David.

His body executed a not very neat arc as he dived in. They swam round the boat, turning on their backs and bellies, splashing and spluttering like children. The crackling of the radio reached them, with Simon's voice calling *Jemima*. This time Joanna ignored it; she had had her fill of unanswered questions. Brenda's attitude was better than hers, easier on the nerves. She swam with purposeful, easy strokes towards the little landing.

'Where are you going?' shouted David behind her, trying in vain to catch up while she, being the faster swimmer, outdistanced him effortlessly.

'Just to see what it's like,' she shouted back. 'I haven't been on solid ground for the last two days.'

She reached the landing and picked her way gingerly on bare feet along the little path which led to the ruined house. 'It's hot and rough,' she shouted, picking her way along, her wet body – barely covered by the skimpy bikini – glistening in the sunshine. She shook her hair to dry it and it swung round her face and neck in a heavy, blonde mass. David jumped behind her and caught her arm.

'Did you mean … what you said … back on the boat …?' He looked so very young and anxious, his eyes no longer hidden by those rimmed glasses scanning hers.

'Of course,' she said not looking at him, freeing her arm from his grip. She made towards the ruined house where the walls provided some shade. 'Why not?' she continued in a light voice which belied all that had gone on in her mind before. 'You really are making such a fuss, David.'

She sat down in a scrap of shade. David sat next to her, and put his arm round her, pressing her body to his.

'I'm sorry. I didn't mean to upset you, it's just, that, well, I can't believe my luck.'

He began to kiss her face and neck, then moved down to kiss her breasts. His other hand impatiently pulled at the back strap of the bikini top. His body felt hot and sticky as he pressed it hard against hers, so that she was being pushed back on the ground which was strewn with sharp pebbles and broken glass.

'Please, David, not here,' she protested, pulling herself and him up with an effort, pointing to the ground. 'Look.'

He stopped and said, 'I'm sorry,' but his eyes had a glazed look. One of his legs was firmly on top of hers.

'We can't do it here,' she protested. 'I'll be cut to shreds.'

He sighed and said nothing, but the pressure on her legs eased. She wriggled back to the sitting position, brushing off the sand and grit from her body. Now that he was not pressing against her, it was a bit cooler. 'You could brush my back,' she turned round. He did it mechanically, kissing the base of her neck and squeezing her breasts. 'Please, David,' she murmured.

He fell on the ground beside her, kissing her body, his hot lips moving slowly downwards.

'We can't,' she said, shaking him off. 'Not here,' and she shuddered, looking at the uninviting ground. As if to confirm her reluctance, a goat or a sheep bell sounded near to where they were.

'Stop it,' she ordered. 'There's somebody here – a shepherd most probably.'

He looked up obediently and took his finger away from the hip strap of her bikini which he was about to pull down. 'You're right,' he said and sat up, blinking heavily. 'Let's go back to the boat.'

'What about Simon and Brenda?'

'Wouldn't worry about them. Won't notice a thing. Anyway, they don't worry about us.'

They sat for a while in silence until Joanna decided now was the time to ask him a few questions.

'David,' she asked, stroking his hair, 'what's all this about? What are you looking for?'

'Simon's yacht.'

'What yacht? His yacht is *Zainda*, isn't it?'

'No, this one's chartered. His was stolen a few weeks ago and he's trying to find it.'

'And what's *Jemima* got to do with it?'

'They're trying to help us find it,' he replied reluctantly; it was obvious he didn't want to talk about it. 'It's all a bit hush, hush,' he added. 'I shouldn't be telling you this, it's …well … rather involved. Look,' he pointed excitedly. 'They're leaving the boat.'

Joanna looked in the direction of *Zainda* and saw Simon's and Brenda's silhouettes against the sun, climbing down the side steps and into the dinghy. She watched Simon's arm as he wound the rope round the starter of the outboard motor. After several tries, the motor suddenly gave a whirring noise and the dingy moved forward, heading towards the opposite end of the bay.

'Come on, let's go.' David stood up, elated and impatient. 'They'll be away for some time.'

'Oh, look out there!' Joanna pointed her finger in the direction of the entrance to the bay. There, like a graceful swan, sailed a white luxury yacht, none other than the unmistakable *Jemima*! A faint rattle of her anchor chain reached them; she was anchoring not far from *Zainda*. But David was already up and, holding Joanna by the hand, he pulled her along the path and almost pushed her into the water. He swam with hurried strokes while Joanna followed slowly, watching him with amusement. He was already in the cockpit waiting for her, his hand stretched out to help her up. She looked back. *Jemima* was about two, perhaps three hundred yards away from them. On the opposite shore the grey, inflatable dinghy could barely be seen as it bobbed on the water. Simon and Brenda had disappeared from sight.

Joanna went into the main cabin, almost pushed by David's impatient body. He stood over her and with clumsy, hurried gestures began removing her bikini top. His hair was dripping into her face, their wet bodies stuck together with sea water and perspiration. He bent down to kiss her, a deep, wet, sloppy kiss which made her shudder. An image of Brenda sitting by the table near to where she stood now floated before her eyes. She could practically see her looking at her outstretched hand, examining the painted nails, and could practically hear her voice saying: 'Colin will be sorry. I rather think he fancied you for himself.'

David had already pulled down her bikini top and was kissing her breasts. She went stiff and saw, rather than felt, her body being kissed as if from a great distance. Just as he was level with the bunk bed, she raised her hand and pushed him away.

'David,' she said in an unnaturally loud voice, but it made no difference to him. He was moaning softly as he continued to kiss her body. 'David,' she said louder. 'I'm sorry.' She swallowed hard and wriggled out of his damp hot embrace. 'I can't go through with it.'

He shuddered, as if her words struck him a physical blow.

'What?' he reeled back, shaking his head. 'What?' He had difficulty in focusing his eyes on hers.

'I'm sorry, David, I just can't do it,' she said and began to sob. 'I'm awfully sorry.'

'Awfully sorry?' he said, mimicking her, a ghastly grin on his face. He held her by the arms and shook her so hard her teeth chattered. 'Awfully sorry?' he repeated again. He looked terrible with his dark, wet hair plastered to his forehead and his face completely drained of colour. He shook her again and let go so abruptly that she reeled back against the companion steps. 'Oh, that's rich, that's just rich!' he repeated in a daze.

Joanna felt conscious of her practically naked body. She wanted to run to her cabin, but instead stood still, frozen in a kind of horrible fascination. He turned away and flung himself on his bunk, hitting his head against the wall as he did so. There was a gasp as he clutched it, covering his face with his free hand. She could hear him repeat 'That's rich,' to himself as he rolled over and faced the wall.

'Go away,' he said very clearly. 'Go away this minute and leave me alone.' He raised his voice. 'Just get the hell out of here.'

Joanna tiptoed past the motionless figure, snatched her bikini top and ran to her cabin, shutting the door quietly behind her, her mind in tumult. She had surprised even herself. Gasping, she took off the rest of the bikini, changed into dry clothes and lay quietly on the bunk, listening for sounds from the main cabin, overcome by what had happened. There was no sound at all from David's cabin – just a heavy, dreadful silence.

It may have been hours later when a loud rap on the hull registered itself in her consciousness. She must have dozed off.

'Hello, anybody home?' The voice was Colin's.

She looked out through the hatch of her cabin.

'Hello,' she said, for once not glad to see him. 'How did you manage to find us here?' she wriggled through the hatch and walked along the deck, avoiding the main cabin.

Outside in the water was a dingy with a man in white by the outboard. Colin was climbing up. He hovered clumsily over the life lines and stepped into the cockpit. His left hand was wrapped in a band of plaster above the elbow, resting motionlessly in a sling and tied round his neck. Though pale, he had not lost his vaguely military air and, but for the plaster, looked no worse after his ordeal. His tanned, rather severe face covered with short stubble, broke into a smile on seeing Joanna. His eyes lit up with more interest than ever before as she approached him.

'I got a lift on *Jemima*,' he said and pointed with his chin.

'How are you feeling? Here, let me help you,' offered Joanna as he nearly lost his balance in the swaying boat.

'I can manage,' he said curtly, ignoring her outstretched hand. 'Thank you,' he shouted to the man in the dinghy. The man nodded without a word, put the outboard in gear and made his way back to *Jemima*.

'Where is everybody? Are you alone here?' he asked casually as he sat down in the cockpit.

No. David's here … he's … He's not very well and had to lie down,' she blushed furiously at the recollection of the scene, and then blushed even deeper for having blushed. Colin looked at her attentively and raised his eyebrow.

'I see,' he said and sounded reflective. Joanna wondered how she would have reacted if things had turned out differently, and he had discovered her in bed with David. He looked up again. His face now wore the same expression, the slightly mocking smile with which she was familiar. *He thinks we were making love when he arrived*, flashed through her mind. Colin was first to break the silence.

'Where are Simon and Brenda? Gone ashore?'.

'I think so. They took the dinghy. You might just be able to see them, over there,' she pointed.

Colin nodded in silence. Joanna too said nothing and watched him dully as he fumbled in his shirt pocket for a cigarette and a lighter. Having lit it, he exhaled the smoke and looked at Joanna again. Now she was certain he thought he'd interrupted David and her making love. Well, he was wrong, but she had no idea how to tell him. The thought made her angry. *What do I care what he thinks? He didn't care about me when he went off with that woman!* The recollection of the beauty of that body in the pale green bikini still had the power to inflict a pang of something, a sort of feeling of "you've no chance." *I wonder why he left her to come here.* Perhaps the fat man was spoiling their fun.

'Can I get you anything?' she asked in an attempt to dispel the awkward silence.

'I could do with a beer.' His eyes had a rather whimsical expression as he continued to look at her. She descended to the main cabin, making as much noise as she could, hoping to wake up David. He was still in the same position sprawled on the side bed as she left him and seemed hard asleep.

'David, Colin's here,' she called out, but there was no answer.

'I'm afraid David's fast asleep,' she said to Colin, handing him the beer and sipping a lemonade.

'Let him sleep. Anyway, I can see Simon and Brenda coming back.'

He continued to look at her quizzically. Joanna wondered again what to make of his expression.

'How's your arm?' she asked, confused.

'Better, thanks. Should be alright if I don't move it. It's not broken, only fractured. You came to no harm in the storm. I'm glad. Good for you. Looking better, if anything.'

'Thank you.' She was pleased by his attempt at a compliment, then remembered the stunner. He was just being polite and she was rising to the bait like the fool she was, instead of trying to forget him. The whole situation wasn't doing anyone any good, and the scene with David was the last straw. It would be better to cut the holiday short after all. It was the only way to stop seeing either one of them. Added to those riddles and accidents, the whole situation made her tired and fed up.

The idea, once formed, appealed more and more. As a result, there was more warmth in her greeting of Simon and Brenda now that the possibility of saying goodbye to them soon loomed ahead. Brenda's expression stating clearly *I know what you two were up to, aha* changed when she saw Colin. Joanna noted with satisfaction that her powers of adapting to new situations were slow.

She cooked a supper of corned beef hash with potatoes, eggs, tomatoes, peppers and anything else she could lay her hands on. They sat in the cool of the mellow evening, watching the Milky Way grow brighter in the darkening sky. The young Turkish wine soon sent Brenda into Simon's arms. Colin sat in the darkness outside the pool of light cast by the lamp hanging over the table. When he inhaled the cigarette smoke, of which he smoked a considerable number that evening, his face in the red glow was set in a mocking mask. David's eyes were fixed on his plate and he answered Simon in monosyllables. Half-way through the meal, he pushed away his plate with the food hardly touched, and went to sit alone on the fore deck. Brenda and Simon exchanged glances, while Joanna kept her eyes firmly on the plate and concentrated on the possible ways and means of leaving *Zainda* as quickly as possible. The various plans nursed her through the meal which continued in silence.

The sky, however, almost overdid itself in splendid display. The stars shone brightly and the Milky Way glittered silvery white against the background of the indigo sky.

'I suppose that's the Plough,' Joanna said as she turned to Colin, more to dispel the heavy silence than for the need of communication. 'I'm afraid I know nothing about the stars, but the Plough is one I can recognise.'

He took up the cue and looked up.

'Look, there, and there,' he pointed. 'That's the pole star, very bright. And that one over there,' he moved his finger along the Milky Way. 'That must be the Dog Star.'

'I've heard about it,' said Joanna excitedly. 'According to the ancient Greeks, the rise of the Dog Star marked the beginning of the summer time. It was named after a dog whom the gods wanted to reward for its faithful devotion to his master. A kind of medal for bravery, which the gods did in grand style, by setting the name among the stars.'

He smiled. 'Why, what did the dog do?'

'Well, the dog belonged to a man chosen by the god of wine to teach mankind how to make wine. But when he gave it to some shepherds to try, they were not used to the alcoholic drink and thought he was about to poison them. So, they killed him (as one does), buried him and fled. The man's dog was watching all this from a safe distance and once they had disappeared, he led the man's daughter to the place where his master was buried.'

'What happened to the daughter?'

'She couldn't handle it and hanged herself. The dog was left all alone in the big, wide world so the gods decided to set his name, Sirius, among the stars.

'An interesting story. I've never heard it before. All I know is the Dog Star appears in the summer and sets when it ends.'

They looked at the sky again and saw a star moving.

'What's that, the moving one?' pointed Joanna.

'That must be a satellite. Lots of them about.'

'You know,' said Joanna dreamily, 'if you see a star fall and make a wish, it'll come true.'

'What, every time, every wish?' There was mockery in his voice.

She found the proximity of his body unsettling. 'Every time,' she nodded in mock solemnity. The other two joined in. 'I could do with that,' drawled Simon.

'Me too.' Brenda's fingers were entwined with his.

'Let's watch out for one, then,' said Joanna.

They sat in an expectant silence like children in a theatre.

'Here's one!' Brenda jumped up excitedly. They could clearly see one small, glittering fragment detach itself from the twinkling firmament as it made a swift arc across the sky.

'Quick, let's make a wish!'

They sat in hushed silence. *Please*, said Joanna to herself quickly, *please make Colin fall in love with me*. She saw him looking at her, heard him clear his throat, before he lifted his eyes back to the sky. Surely her thoughts didn't actually show?

'Of course, you mustn't tell anyone of your wish, or the charm will be ruined,' she said.

'There's a saying,' Simon's voice drawled in the darkness. 'If the gods wish to punish us, they listen to our prayers. You may have read that in one of your books, Joanna.'

'No, I haven't,' sighed Joanna with disappointment. 'I hope you're wrong. It's nice to have a wish granted.'

There was a movement on the deck and David appeared in the circle of light.

'You just missed a falling star and a chance of a wish come true,' said Joana in a light voice, belying her guilty conscience. Perhaps she was to blame for leading him on, but it irked her that he was taking the whole incident so badly. That's what happens when one gets mixed up with a kid fresh out of school, or was it college? She moved up the seat to make room next to her in an attempt to make amends. 'You had better sit with us and wait for another.'

But he only shrugged his shoulders and went back down to the cabin. Brenda and Simon again exchanged glances. Another short, uncomfortable silence was followed by a strained, inconsequential conversation.

Chapter 14

The following morning, they left the bay and once more continued to sail slowly along the coast. *Jemima* was still there on anchor as they motored past her.

'What are they doing?' Joanna asked Colin casually.

'Fishing,' he replied, equally casually. 'The fishing grounds are excellent here. There's quite a party on there, keen on fishing.'

'I see.' She could not get any more out of him.

Still, David had given her a clue. They were looking for Simon's yacht which had been stolen, and Simon had chartered *Zainda* to look for it. *Jemima* was capable of greater speed than *Zainda*, and with her superior equipment could relay any information to them. Simon and David were probably the only people able to identify the stolen yacht. Still, it was a bit odd to look for a boat in a chartered one and have a big motor cruiser involved as well. Surely there were better methods, such as using police patrols, checking ports and harbours by the port authorities, that kind of thing. On the other hand, there was a lot of coastline in Turkey and Greece, full of bays and little harbours, and it could take a long time to flush out the thieves from their hiding places.

But why should Simon bother to bring a girl like Brenda and herself along with them? It didn't make sense. But then, why not? Somebody had to cook, and Simon wanted his girlfriend to be with him. What was Colin's role in all this? Simon said they were good friends, they'd known each other for years. Supposing he too had been asked to join in and have a holiday at the same time? What about those supposed accidents, which she simply did not believe were accidents? How could that incident in Marmara be an accident?

No way. Or that stone that nearly killed her in Kusadasi? She shuddered involuntarily. That was a near miss. If that was no accident, then the thieves were well organised, and what's more, they meant business. It was frightening just to think about it.

She remembered having heard about pirates operating on the seas. They stole boats and yachts, drowned the owners, repainted the boats and sold them where no questions were likely to be asked. The whole operation was made to look like an accident, a yacht lost in a storm, that kind of thing. But surely this could not apply in their case? There were no pirates here. There was bound to be an easy explanation; it was just a question of patience, no need to panic. Her mind, however, was made up; she had had enough. As soon as they reach Rhodes, a convenient town with a good ferry and air connection to Athens from where she could catch a plane home, she was leaving.

There was one more reason for her decision and that involved David. He continued to sulk and had not spoken to her at all since that fateful incident. His silence and manner only succeeded in drawing attention to him, making it clear to everybody that things had gone wrong between them. Joanna was mortified. His silence couldn't be louder than words if he had shouted them from the top of the mast. Admittedly, having led him on, she was partly to blame, but the way he carried on was ridiculous.

Colin's presence only helped to increase her irritability. She sensed a change of attitude towards her. He seemed less indifferent to her than he pretended to be, which buoyed her hopes in spite of all those resolutions. Maybe she was right about that, but then, maybe not. One thing was certain – the existence of that other woman. Altogether, the sooner she could get him out of her mind, the better. The best course of action was to cut the holiday short and leave. As soon as they reached Rhodes, she repeated to herself, that was what she'd do. It might be better to say nothing of her plans beforehand, not to make fuss. Simon would have no difficulty in finding somebody in Rhodes to replace her; there'd be lots of people there willing to crew. Anyway, it wouldn't hurt Brenda to do a bit of cooking for a change.

She spent the day on the fore deck, making new plans. Simon was on the deck now all the time, scanning the coastline through the binoculars, changing over with David, so that when one watched, the other steered. Colin spent most of his time at the chart table, taking measurements, plotting their position on the chart, or trying to establish radio contact. Brenda stayed on the aft deck. It was plain she felt neglected by Simon, and her pout deepened as the days wore on.

The sun was well past its zenith when Colin came up from the main cabinet and said to Joanna:

'How would you like to be on Greek soil again?'

He was the only one who spoke to Joanna now. Simon had lapsed into his old self again, as if the one revealed by the storm never existed. His energies were concentrated on scanning the shore and on Brenda, leaving no room for conversation, which he confined purely to giving instructions. Brenda was uncommunicative. Joanna's own mood was beginning to pall, now that she had finished reading all the books on the boat. Colin's question put her in a good mood; any diversion was better than the present monotony.

'Sounds lovely. Where are we going?

Perhaps they were going to Rhodes. That would mean she'd be able to carry out her new resolution pretty soon, and realised with a pang it would be a pity to leave the sailing life and join the landlubbers. Still, it was the best way for all concerned.

'We might be sailing to Symi, just for one night. If we go to Panormitis, we won't meet any officials to check on us, so we'll miss all that paper work.'

'What a good idea. We have no more wine or fresh provisions. Maybe we could stock up with Greek retsina.'

'I doubt if there are any shops there. But I take your point about the retsina. I quite like it myself.'

Zainda was now in a long, open bay and Simon relaxed his vigil. The sun was getting behind the mountain and the contours on land were already blurred. When Simon came back into the cockpit, Joanna realised how much that continuous watching of his was getting on her nerves. Why had they started on this now and not at the beginning of their trip, anyway? They must be acting on instructions or a tip-off from somewhere. And how did Colin fit into all this? Was he just a friend of Simon's, invited to spend a holiday with him? There seemed to be more to him. Could he be his bodyguard? There was an air of military standing about him; he must have been in the army judging by the way he carried himself. He was athletic and he moved with the springiness of a jungle cat. In spite of his warm smile, there was a cold detachment in his eyes. Joanna could well imagine that if he chose to be ruthless, he'd be very ruthless indeed. A bodyguard? No, that's a ridiculous idea. And yet a good and useful friend to have, especially if you're chasing thieves who have stolen your yacht, she concluded. It puzzled her too as to why he had come back so soon after his accident; surely it must be pretty uncomfortable on the boat with an arm in a plaster and sling. Could it be that he was determined to see the whole thing through? What thing? She realised she had made a complete circle and her head was spinning. Meanwhile, Simon started the engine.

They motored almost to the end of the bay before a break in the solid mass of land appeared. Joanna decided to stop thinking about all those riddles which pressed on her mind during the enforced idleness of motoring and concentrated on looking around her. They steered into a patch of pale green indicating shallow water, and found themselves in a big, almost landlocked bay. On the other side, almost opposite the entrance, was a big monastery with a bell tower and steps leading to the water's edge. On either side of the monastery were houses scattered along the water front. On the promontory, up on the hill by the entrance to the bay, stood a windmill. As they entered the bay, the bell on the tower rang out. It had a melodious tone which carried clearly along the water. It was all so lovely and peaceful that Joanna stood there enchanted, and only the rattle of their anchor chain interrupted her reverie.

Once they had anchored, they took the dinghy to the shore and explored the hamlet. A monk in black, flowing robes and a tall, black, rimless hat, hair pulled tight into a knot at the back, came down the steps to meet them. A few words were exchanged with Simon, while the rest of the party stood by. Simon came back to join them a few moments later.

'The monk wanted to show us round the church, but it's too dark now. If we like he might take us round tomorrow morning. Apparently, the bell was rung for our benefit. It's their custom to welcome visiting yachts in this way.'

They waved goodbye to the monk and walked along the edge. Not far from the monastery was a monument to a monk shot by the Germans during the last war. Next to it was a restaurant. They sat at the table under a tree from which hung coloured electric bulbs. Soon the food arrived, brought by a man and his son. There was meat on skewers which was delicious, and a huge plate of salad studded with crumbled white goat cheese. There was also some Greek retsina which they all drunk with the exception of Brenda who wrinkled her nose after one sip and exclaimed:

'Ugh! What on earth is this?'

'Divine turpentine,' said Joanna and giggled.

After a whole day of wind, sun and sailing, the meal gave them a feeling of drowsy satiety. Joanna stood up.

'Phew. Who's for a short walk then? I can't go back to the boat feeling as full as this.'

Nobody stirred. Simon and Brenda sat close together, holding hands. Colin, nursing his bad arm, continued to smoke in silence. David looked away.

The sky was indigo-blue against the solid blackness of the surrounding mountains. Several small open boats were coming into the bay, their motors making slow, regular beats. They died down as soon as they reached the monastery steps. The silence which followed was overwhelming. Then, somebody switched on the radio and the bay was filled with strange sounds of a bouzouki which harmonised gently with the surroundings. The moon hung above the top of the mountains and lit up a little path along the water's edge. It shone like a silver thread.

'I'm only going as far as the windmill,' Joanna said over her shoulder, pointing in its direction. 'If you want to go back to the boat, please don't wait for me. I'll give you a shout when I need the dinghy.'

She got up and made her way slowly up the hill towards the windmill, suddenly aware of her wobbly "sea legs" and the effects of the potent retsina. She felt ridiculously happy for no reason, or rather, for one reason – too much wine. Slowly she went round the windmill, singing to herself. One of its paddles was broken. She was still humming when it occurred to her that some of that feeling of well-being could be due to a sense of security, as if the unknown thieves couldn't reach them here in Greece to stage yet another so-called accident. She heard footsteps behind her which turned out to be Colin's.

'Why, hello. Out on your constitutional like me?'

'Something like that.' He leaned against the wall of the windmill, took out a cigarette which he lit clumsily with one hand. In the flicker of the light, Joanna saw that he was looking at her. Was he going to kiss her? But he stood motionless, then looked away as if he had changed his mind.

186

'How is your arm?' she said to try to break the silence.

'Much better, thanks. Doesn't bother me so much now.' He sounded impatient, as if didn't like to be reminded of his accident.

They continued to sit in silence watching the moon. Joanna was imbibing with her whole body the warm darkness, the murmur of voices and the music wafting from below. It was a moment she had longed for, to be alone with Colin. Now that it was happening, she didn't know what to do with it. Here was the man she fancied, here was the opportunity to build up a connection, to get to know each other, to see if her feelings for him might be reciprocated. Instead – no reaction. It was like a useless gift from the gods, like a cupful of water poured into a hand seeping into the desert sand. She sighed and looked down. Below, the reflections of the moon broke into patterns on the rippling surface of the sea. *'Though the night was made for loving, and the day returns too soon, yet we'll go no more a-roving by the light of the moon.'*

'I've always wondered,' Colin's voice cut through the darkness, 'what Byron meant by "a-roving".'

She started, unaware that she had spoken out loud.

'I don't know, a multitude of sins, I guess,' she said, laughing, and got up. 'We'd better be going. Shouldn't we call out for the dinghy?'

'I brought it back; the others are on board.'

'What, with one hand?'

'It can be done, but you'd better row back.'

She wondered why he came to join her. He certainly made no attempts at any intimacy, but continued to smoke in silence. Most likely he had come for whatever they were all looking for, as the windmill offered a good vantage point from which to see the entrance to the bay. She got back to the boat nursing a sense of disappointment. Fancy knowing Byron, though; he didn't look the type who read poetry in his spare time.

Chapter 15

Zainda was anchored in a bay on the Turkish coast, from which the outlines of the island of Rhodes could be barely distinguished, blurred by the heat haze. The entrance to the bay was guarded on one side by Hellenistic fortifications, its ruins clearly visible against the sky. Once they sailed through a narrow entrance into the bay, an expanse of water opened up to reveal another bay, almost landlocked, as if nature had taken two scoops out of the mountains and filled the hollows with water. The land was a grey mass of small and large rocks heaped on top of each other, overgrown with sparse bushes and gnarled trees. On the other side of the bay, the rocks cascaded straight down to the sea. Again, it was a kind of a moonscape, grey rocks spilling in and out of each other, the dirty yellow tufts of vegetation struggling in the cruel sun, interspersed with the green of mastic and strawberry trees. As far as the eye could see, there was nothing that had any connection with the work of human hands, except for those ancient walls which stood out in a symmetrical outline against the sky. Were they a monument to human defiance and endeavour, a testimony to the superiority of ancient man over modern man? Joanna was fascinated by that lonely outpost and its forlorn, neglected appearance, so unlike the manicured ancient sites of Britain and Northern Europe. As far as she was concerned, this was the most romantic place, apart from that ancient site on the island of Marmara.

There were only four of them now on *Zainda*. *Jemima* had reappeared on the horizon as they were leaving Symi, shortly after a radio conversation, the words of which Joanna couldn't quite make out. Colin left them after a perfunctory goodbye. Joanna wondered if she would see him again, but pride prevented her from asking and Colin said nothing. It was just as well. If only they might reach Rhodes soon, then her little holiday interlude would be over. She'd just pack her bag, say goodbye and slip away, just like Colin, with as little fuss as possible. She had rehearsed the final farewell many times in her mind, and now looked forward to sailing into Rhodes. It worried her somewhat that Rhodes was not mentioned on their itinerary, but then nobody bothered to inform her much in advance of any plans. Most likely Simon would announce it by breakfast time, and then she'd have to be ready.

There was one more reason for concentrating on ancient sites and forgetting the present. The atmosphere on board, more specifically at her end, was one it was better to ignore, especially after Colin's departure. David made a point of avoiding her and never spoke unless he had to. His face had acquired a haggard look. He looked unwell, his movements became slow and deliberate like those of a much older man. More visibly, he lost his appetite. When not doing anything about the boat, he spent his time lying huddled on his bunk, facing the wall. Everything about him was a constant reproach, and only helped to make her resolution to leave more firm.

They anchored in the inner bay. Simon stood on the fore deck, holding the binoculars which by now seemed to have become a part of his body. Both he and David took the dinghy and went to reconnoitre the shore. They went behind the corner of the nearest headland and were soon out of sight, although the sound of the outboard motor on the dinghy could be heard for some time reverberating against the mountain opposite. Joanna decided to have a closer look at the ancient ruins and suggested to Brenda to join her. But Brenda was not a good swimmer and didn't want to go unless in the dinghy. She excused herself by saying she preferred to sunbathe anyway. To prove her point, she rolled on to her stomach, took out a paperback romance from her bag and with a sigh of contentment and a *this is the life*, ignored Joanna's presence completely.

Joanna rolled up her T-shirt and sandals and put them in a plastic bag, lowered herself carefully into the water holding the bag above her head to keep it dry, and swam slowly towards the shore. The piled rocks which looked so formidable from the sea made good stepping stones. The sun dried her quickly as she made her way towards the ancient fortifications. The ground was uneven, full of unexpected little hollows and mounds covered with all kinds of weeds, shrubs and trees. The strawberry tree caught her attention with its extraordinary fruits which, at that time of the year, looked a bit like horny, withered strawberries. She remembered having read somewhere that the fruit was not very good to eat, one was enough according to a Greek saying. She spotted some mastic trees and scraggy oaks with tiny acorns and leaves like miniature holly.

Having reached the top of the hill, she walked along the ancient walls built from huge, regular stones, in some places well preserved. The stones had to fit into each other perfectly as the ancient Greeks had not used cement. Each stone had a smoothed edge round it, while the rest was left rough and convex so that it looked like a stone cushion.

This was an ancient military fortified outpost, with various barracks, stables and rooms barely discernible now. Where it faced the sea, the walls rose even higher due to the hilly nature of the ground, so that the ground level on one side of the hill meant a drop of two floors on the other. She stood still in the middle, trying to imagine life as it might have been two or three thousand years ago. At her age she would have been a mother of at least a dozen children, only some of whom would have survived, and very likely a grandmother, too. She tried to visualise the soldiers in their leather-and-linen garments stationed in this place, the creaking carts, the muleteers with their mules, the stone masons working on those stone walls. She pretended to be a sentry standing watch on the tower where she now stood. What would it have been like for him, standing there, watching, listening for the sounds issuing out of the dark wilderness around him? He would have been young, probably sixteen. What would life have been for a boy/man like that in this place, and for others of his age? She tried to imagine the camaraderie, the crude food, the camp fires. Outside there would always have been the possibility of an enemy lurking in the bushes, and wild animals ready to pounce on the unaware. Standing on the watch tower, always on the look-out, day and night – what did a man feel after hours and hours? Fatigue? Excitement? Boredom? Most likely boredom.

She jumped up. Something snake-like slid between the stones and disappeared in the cracks. On closer inspection, it was a large lizard. But there could be snakes here, so better not to take any chances. Snakes were positively creepy. Slowly she made her way down and heard a rhythmic put-put in the distance. Below, out in the bay, was a small open boat with two men. They were going towards *Zainda* from the direction of the mountain on the opposite side of the bay. There, against the background of the rocks, Joanna could just distinguish the outline of a yacht with a dark hull which almost blended into the background. The little boat must belong to it. In fact, it would have been difficult to notice the yacht if the boat was not pointing the way to it. Joanna also saw a tiny figure of a man below, facing the open sea. That must be either Simon or David, still searching for whatever it was. Oh well, let them get on with it, it was none of her business any more. Rhodes was not far away. One day, in a month or two, she'd phone Simon and find out what it had all been about.

Joanna decided it was a bit of luck to have seen the ancient military fort before going home. She thought it would be a good idea to come back again in the morning with the camera if time permitted. She climbed down the big boulders strewn along the slope and came down to a hollow surrounded by strawberry trees. It was a small patch of flat ground. On it, lying flat on his stomach, was David, looking through the binoculars. He was looking at the sea and didn't notice her. She nearly stepped on him, hidden as he was by the trees and the rocks. It was impossible to avoid him now. Joanna braced herself against the inevitability of a confrontation. It had to come; the unspoken words lay heavily between them. But what was there to be said? She had surprised herself by her reaction after all those inner resolutions. The whole thing had just got out of hand. It was all so confusing, and he was being absurd and childish.

On hearing her footsteps, David looked up, and, having seen her, seemed willing to back away before realising the futility of his wish. They were trapped in that hollow and faced each other with resentment at not being able to escape.

Joanna was mortified. There in front of her sat a very unhappy young man, with a drawn face, pale in spite of the suntan, and deep shadows under his eyes. It was her fault; she shouldn't have led him on.

'Oh, it's you,' he said and changed to a sitting position to face her. Joanna sat on a rock opposite him and lowered her head, wondering what to say. Her long legs brushed against David's who drew himself away as if the touch might burn him. She drew her legs back under her chin and looked down on the ground, making patterns with her toe. When she looked up again, he was staring at her intently as if contemplating her appearance for the first time. His scrutiny made her uncomfortable and confused her further. They sat like this in silence for some time. She was the first to break it.

'Look, David,' she said with her head down, still making patterns on the ground. 'Can't we forget what happened? Look, I am sorry, okay? I really am. Couldn't we be friends again?'

David put down the binoculars he was holding with slow deliberation and placed them on a rock next to him.

'Friends!' he exclaimed. His sneer deepened. 'Friends!' he almost shouted. 'Never!'

She was taken aback by the force of his reply. It had not occurred to her he had built so much hate.

'I said I'm sorry,' she said in a conciliatory tone. 'I mean it. I see you can't forgive me. Well, that's all right, I suppose it's understandable. If it's of any help,' she continued, uncomfortable under his unflinching gaze, 'I might as well tell you I've decided to leave as soon as we reach Rhodes. You won't have to see me ever again.'

She raised her head and saw David's expression flicker and the sneer gone. Only that intense scrutiny remained as he sat perfectly still. He was so young, so absurdly young. She continued in a patient voice, as if talking to a child.

'It wouldn't have worked anyway, between us, I mean. Once the holiday was over, we'd all have gone our different ways.'

Still, he said nothing.

'You're eight years younger than me.' There was exasperation in her voice now. 'It wouldn't have worked, surely you can see that, can't you?'

But he sat silent and aloof, as if it were he who had all the right reasons on his side, and it was she who was in the wrong. She had to admit, he had unsettled her. There was nothing more she could think of to say to him.

'I'll soon be out of your way,' she said at last. 'Can't you be reasonable for the remaining few days and stop sulking like this?'

But Davis sat motionless and said nothing. Wearily, she got up to step past him and was almost on the other side of the hollow when her movement seemed to put life into him. He grabbed her hand. The sneer and the bright, blazing intensity were gone. Instead, she saw a face of a defenceless child trying not to cry. A hot flush of embarrassment went through her. He looked away with an effort to compose his features sufficiently to formulate words, while still gripping and pulling at her hands so that she was forced to sit down beside him. Eventually, he managed to stammer: 'But why? Why?'

'David, please.' She managed to free her hand from his grasp and stroked his hair. 'Please don't look like this, please.'

She kissed him lightly, drawing him closer. A shudder went through his body. Suddenly, he knelt beside her and put his arms around her in an embrace so tight she could hardly breathe. A shower of kisses descended on her face, lips, hair while he kept repeating, 'I love you! I've loved you, ever since I first saw you!' It seemed to her she had unleashed a force like the gush of a damned up river finding an outlet, over which she had neither control nor the will to fight. This was no time to analyse her feelings or where she stood in relation to him, or what *she* wanted. She let herself go limp in his embrace and vaguely felt herself being pushed back on the ground by the weight of his body.

Some time must have elapsed before they became aware of noises almost next to them. Two men were talking in low voices. There was a crunch of footsteps followed by the sound of a heavy load being dragged along the rocks. A loosened stone tumbled down the slope and dropped into the water with a splash. They drew apart and looked at each other with surprise.

'I'll go and see who it is,' said David gruffly and jumped over the rocks to the other side of the hollow. Joanna was left alone, still in a daze, hugging her knees, trying to collect her thoughts. She was too absorbed in her own emotional turmoil to notice the noises were getting louder and more agitated, and only penetrated her consciousness after some delay. She heard David's voice asking loudly, 'What are you doing there?', then the rasping voice of a man answering in a language Joanna didn't understand, followed by running footsteps slapping on the rocks and a cascade of stones splashing into the waters below. The men's voices grew more and more excited as they dragged something obviously heavy and cumbersome. They were passing very near her. She fell flat on the ground and grabbed the binoculars David had left behind. Everything was out of focus.

Suddenly there was a loud thump, voices grew louder accompanied by running feet. Then more shouting, followed by David's excited: 'I say, stop there, leave the dinghy alone.' Then another noise, as if a car had backfired, and men's voices calling to each other with unmistakable urgency. She looked out from the edge of her hiding place and peered through the binoculars again. This time she managed to focus on the running figure of a man who turned round to help his stumbling companion. A round, bullet head with hair cropped close to the skull, heavy features and a thick moustache filled the lenses. With a shock she realised she'd seen that face before. But the man turned away quickly so that she could only see his back and then he was hidden by the other man who followed him, stumbling as he ran. They both wore dark shorts and no shirts, the first man tucking a small black object into his waistband as he ran. The other man stumbled again and nearly fell under the water as they waded in. The first man helped him up and both jumped into the boat. For an agonising short moment, she had another glimpse of his face as he was starting the outboard motor. The other man untied the painter, then jumped into the boat and quickly moved towards the opposite end of the bay, trailing a grey object in the water. Joanna followed the departing boat for as long as she could, trying to focus the binoculars on their faces until the distance was too great and everything got blurred. She tried to make out what the object was they were trailing behind, and realised with horror that it was their dinghy, with most of the air let out so that it was half submerged in the water.

Where was David? She got up quickly and looked around. He was nowhere to be seen.

'David!' she shouted. 'David1'

She descended as fast as she could down the slope towards the place where their dinghy had been tied. It was a shock to realise the whole incident could not have taken more than a couple of minutes.

'David!' she shouted desperately. 'Where are you?'

She reached the edge of the water where, on a patch of sand, were signs of several footprints. A slight sound by the side caught her attention. She turned back and walked slowly along the water's edge. Suddenly, she saw him. He was lying, as if thrown across the stones, about twenty yards from her, partly hidden by a big, thorny bush.

'David!' she said and ran towards him, fear gripping her throat. 'Are you alright?'

He was lying with his eyes closed, his face very white. She knelt by him.

'I think they hit me,' he whispered, his body at an uncomfortable angle. 'I fell.'

'Can't you get up? I'll give you a hand,' said Joanna trying to lift his head. If she didn't control the fear rising inside her, it would engulf her. She must stay calm; she mustn't let it swamp her. 'Try to sit up, you must be terribly uncomfortable like this. You've probably hit your head on the rocks,' she said and tried to sound almost matter of fact.

David allowed himself to be half-lifted when Joanna's eyes fell on his T-shirt. There was a red stain on his chest which was getting larger. She blinked, horrified, and looked away.

'You can't lie here, come on, there's a nice, flat piece of ground where you can rest while I ...' *What?* she asked herself. She must get help quickly. Where, for God's sake, was Simon? And what was Brenda doing all this time? She put her hands under David's arms and dragged him through the loose stones while he lay limp, not making any effort to get up. Neither did he seem to be in pain. Did that mean he'd been paralysed? She dropped him by the edge of the water on a tiny piece of flat ground and noticed the stain grow bigger until it almost covered his chest. She took off her T-shirt and stuffed it under his.

'You've been hit. Now lie still while I swim to the boat and get help.'

'They were sinking our dinghy,' he mumbled. 'I wanted to stop them and I must've slipped. When they saw me ... he took a gun and ...'

His head rolled to the side as if he was about to fall asleep. He hadn't noticed the blood. Joanna looked helplessly around. There was nobody in sight, even the two men in the boat were no longer visible.

'David,' she shook him gently, 'we must get a doctor. How do you contact *Jemima*?

He had fallen asleep and she had to shake him again. After a while, he opened his eyes with an effort.

'You mustn't. Only Simon and Colin.'

'David, I must get help for you!'

The urgency in her voice conveyed itself to him. He made another effort to speak.

'You've got to dial a number, then you tune in,' his voice was very weak.

'What number, David? What number? Tell me the number!' she had to shake him again.

'It's sixteen point three, eight three point seven,' he said, sounding utterly exhausted. She repeated the number several times and wrote it on the sand, then ran into the water and swam as never before towards *Zainda*. Brenda was lying on the aft deck, sunbathing.

'Brenda, quick, for God's sake!' Joanna swam round the slippery hull, unable to find the steps. Brenda must have pulled them up. 'Give me a hand, quick.'

No reaction from Brenda. With great effort, Joanna managed to haul herself on board, panting and wheezing. Brenda was asleep, her face buried in *Today's Romances*.

'Brenda!' she shouted and shook her, perhaps more strongly than intended. 'I need your help. David's been shot!'

'Shot!' exclaimed Brenda jumping up. 'What do you mean, shot! Shot where? What are you talking about?' Her voice rose to a high pitch.

'Shot and wounded. We've no time, it looks pretty serious. We must get help for him. Where's Simon?'

'I don't know, he didn't say.' Brenda was shaking like a leaf.

'Find a fog horn and keep blowing until he turns up.'

She rummaged in the main cabin and found the fog horn – a small aerosol tin with a little tube stuck on it. 'Here, press this button while I try and figure out how the radio works.'

'We're not supposed to touch it.' Joanna made no reply. 'Where is David? Where did you leave him? Is he very bad?' She kept asking questions while pressing the button of the fog horn. The contraption gave off a fairly loud hoot which echoed around the mountains. At least it was loud.

'There, by the water's edge, on that tiny beach.'

'I think I can see something,' Brenda screwed up her eyes, peering in the direction pointed by Joanna. 'Oh my God, he's there! What happened?. Who was it? Where are they?'

'Tell you later. They're gone. Didn't you hear or see anything? The two men who came in that small boat?'

'I didn't hear a thing. I must've dropped off.'

Joanna sat down by the chart table, facing the ship-to-shore radio. The instrument faced her back with all its array of push buttons and dials with cryptic letters and numbers. She had never operated a radio like this before, never even watched the others doing it, either. They were always so secretive it would have been like prying. And now? Would it work for her? She switched it on and dialled a number, turning the knob facing her. What was it now? *Sixteen point three eight three point seven.* Had she remembered it right? Or had she managed to get it wrong? *If I've got the wrong number, I've had it!* With shaking hands, she took out the microphone from its little nest on the side. Her hand trembled so much she had to press it hard against the table in an effort to steady it. Nothing happened. It should be emitting crackling noises. What was wrong? She looked at the radio again, then to either side of it. I mustn't panic, I must concentrate, there must be a logical way to go about it. By the side of the radio was a plastic sheet stuck to the wall, a list of instructions for transmission of the Mayday call. She didn't want to do that yet, but at least it was there as the last resort. Surely Simon should turn up any moment now? He couldn't have gone very far.

Brenda was dutifully blowing the horn, but there was no sign of him. *Let's try again. Please God let it work, please. Now, keep calm and start from the beginning.* Surely there must be an operating instruction manual somewhere? She rummaged through the pile of charts under the chart table and found it hidden between them. That was better. She switched on the radio and pressed the little button on the side. The radio sprang to life and began wheezing and crackling. The interference was very loud. Their range couldn't be very big either as they were surrounded by hills. She pressed another button by the side of the microphone. The crackling almost ceased and a whine took over like the moan of a strong wind. She spoke into the microphone.

'*Jemima II*, this is *Zainda*. We need medical help immediately!

Jemima II, we need help. Please, do you hear me? We need a doctor urgently! This is *Zainda*.' Her voice was unsteady, tears were running down her cheeks, unchecked. It took an effort to pull herself together and repeat the message.

There was no response. The radio was silent. Perspiration and tears were trickling down her face. Her hand slipped as she wiped her face. Suddenly the radio came to life. There were many voices speaking at once, then one came through very clearly.

'*Zainda*, this is *Jemima*. State your exact position, please.'

So that's how it worked. Her fingers slipped off the button on the microphone. You had to release it to hear them answer you. Their position, of course! How silly of me, of course I should've thought of that. But where exactly were they? She looked helplessly at the chart. Oh, where was Simon?

'I think we are … She read the numbers of longitude and latitude off the chart. 'I am not sure. It's a little bay, two bays really, with a Hellenistic ruin to port as you enter.' That must've sounded idiotic. Colour rose to her cheeks. She let the finger release the button.

'Roger. We've located you,' said the voice through the crackling. Joanna felt weak with relief.

'Come quickly, please, come quickly. He looks pretty bad,' she sobbed. The radio whined and moaned in response. Wearily she switched it off.

Brenda was standing on the deck pressing the button on the fog horn. Simon was still nowhere in sight. Joanna blew her nose and looked through the First Aid box. Everything in it looked ridiculous. There were plasters the size of thumb nails, a roll of bandage like a reel of cotton thread, aspirins, sea sickness tablets and a small bottle of disinfectant. The huge, red stain swam before her eyes as she looked helplessly at them. Eventually, she grabbed another T-shirt, a towel and a small cushion, wrapped them in a plastic bag and lowered herself into the water.

'I'm going to stay with David,' she said to Brenda and pointed to the shore. 'There. Keep signalling for Simon. *Jemima* said they were coming.'

'Okay. God, this is awful. Where's Simon? You don't think he is there, too? Oh, I wish he'd come back. What can I do?' She peered anxiously over the side.

'Just hand me the parcel.' Joanna was already in the water. 'And pray,' she added, swimming swiftly towards the shore.

David had not moved and was lying in the same position as she had left him. He seemed to be sleeping.

'David,' she said as she bent anxiously over him. 'How are you doing, are you alright?' She lifted his head up and put the cushion under him. His head rolled to the side but he opened his eyes and focused on her. 'I've contacted *Jemima*. They're coming to pick you up. They've got a doctor on board. You'll be alright. Are you in pain?'

He didn't answer and closed his eyes again. She took his hand in hers. It was limp and damp. Her eyes moved to his chest but the stain seemed about the same size as before. Thank goodness, maybe it's only a superficial wound. She re-arranged the T-shirt covering the wound but when she tried to move him into a more comfortable position, he moaned in protest. There was nothing more to do but wait. Wait for the doctor, wait for *Jemima*, wait for Simon, wait, wait.

The sun had moved behind the hill and they were now in shadow. She began to shiver in her wet swim suit. David lay motionless, keeping his hand in hers. His eyes flickered open from time to time as if making sure she was still there. She sat still while in her anxiety every minute stretched into infinity. If only they would come quickly, if only they were here now! After a time, her legs developed a cramp, but when she tried to move, David opened his eyes and said, 'Don't leave me,' and continued to keep his hand in hers. So she tried to sit still so as not to disturb him. Her eyes wandered from his face, then out to the bay to the direction from which *Jemima* should be coming, then shifted up to the sky, to the odd cloud as it moved slowly above the mountains, utterly indifferent to the events below. Where is Simon? She gritted her teeth. Where is the help that's supposed to be coming from *Jemima*? A feeble hoot of the fog horn reached her: Brenda was doing her best.

David stirred and closed his eyes again. She gazed at the ground on which he lay, so that every detail was imprinted in her memory, seemingly for ever. She could tell with her eyes closed the position of every pebble, every little piece of dry grass, every impression on the sand. Occasionally she would look, almost reluctantly at David. Will he be alright? Why wasn't he in pain? Did that mean he'd be paralysed? Paralysed at twenty for life? His stillness frightened her. She shifted her gaze to the blades of grass and the pebbles. At last, the cramp in her legs gave way to a merciful numbness, and her mind followed.

She was woken up from this state of complete inertia by shouts and footsteps. It was Simon. She got up stiffly.

'Here, Simon, we're here!' she waved.

For the first time in their acquaintance, Simon was actually showing signs of animation.

'I believe we're on the right track at last,' he panted from a distance. 'Look, see that yacht over there?'

She followed the direction of his outstretched hand. There, a long way away, in the distance was the yacht with the dark hull, the one moored on the opposite entrance to the bay from where the two men had come. A hoot from the fog horn rang through the air.

'What's Brenda up to?' he asked impatiently, drawing nearer. 'She's been doing that for the last half hour. I need to find David. You haven't seen him by any chance, have you?'

'Simon, I asked Brenda to call you! It's about David! I'm afraid he's been shot!'

'What's that?' he turned round abruptly and faced her for the first time since he spoke. 'What d'you mean, shot? What are you talking about? Where is he?'

Joanna pointed in silence. Simon was by David's side in a flash.

'David, David!' he said, slapping David's hands and face. He turned to Joanna. 'What happened here, who's done this?' His eyes focused on the red stain. 'We must get help. I'll go and …'

David's head slumped to the side and his hands made searching movements. Joanna sat by him and put his hand into hers. Her gesture seemed to calm him. He closed his eyes again.

'Better not move him,' she said. 'Anyway, I called *Jemima* on the radio, to get a doctor,' she said, looking at Simon. 'They said they were on the way,'

'You *what*?' his eyes widened in surprise. 'How did you do that?'

'David told me the number and I managed to get through.'

He stared blankly at her, making her feel like she should apologise. 'Well, I'm sorry, but you weren't here and I had no time to lose.'

'All right, all right,' he waved impatiently. 'What happened?'

Joanna told him all she had seen, omitting her suspicion that she had seen one of the men before. It was not important right now, and she still couldn't place the man. Simon kept looking at her in a funny way and then at David. Was he still cross with her for using the radio? To hell with Simon! She just hoped David was going to be alright. They sat in silence. Nothing stirred. A hoot came from *Zainda*.

'That's Brenda again,' she said. 'Maybe you could let her know you're here.'

'Brenda!' shouted Simon. 'It's all right! You can stop now!' he shouted then waved.

In response, another hoot reached them. Brenda didn't or couldn't hear him. Joanna said nothing as precious minutes trickled slowly. David lay motionless, seemingly asleep.

Finally, there was a noise of engines reverberating against the rocks. It came almost like an anticlimax. Joanna looked up. Out there was *Jemima*. Two men in white jumped quickly into a dinghy even before the anchor was dropped, and started the outboard engine. They went straight to *Zainda* where she could see Brenda's excited gesturing pointing in their direction. They reached them very quickly and jumped out as soon as the dinghy touched the shore. Simon met them and led the way to David. The men looked at him, their faces expressionless, exuding efficiency. One took out a walkie-talkie and barked into it.

'Come on, old chap,' said the other gently, bending over David. 'We must take you to the doctor.' He lifted David, holding him under the arms, while the other lifted his legs. David's chest sagged. Simon stepped in to help and hold him up. Joanna stood up, looking at the place where he had been lying. Her eyes widened with horror. A big pool of blood was seeping into the sand, leaving a dark brown stain. She ran towards David as the men carried him to the dinghy.

'Hang on, David,' she called. 'It's going to be alright.' It sounded hollow, verging on hopeless. There must be something she could do for him, there wasn't a moment to lose. His eyes flickered and focused on her.

'David!' she repeated and blushed, aware of the presence of the three men who had stopped. He hadn't much time left; it was obvious to her now. She caught his hand as the men moved forward impatiently. 'I love you, David. Just hang on,' she repeated.

He turned his head towards her and tried to smile. 'I hoped you would,' he said with great effort and coughed. A pink foam appeared round his mouth. The men moved again, brushing past her as they carried him into the dinghy and out of her sight. Joanna's legs gave under her. She sat down on the ground, wearily watching them make their way towards *Jemima*. It was the right thing to say to David, of that she was convinced, nevertheless her face was burning. Wiping away her tears, utterly exhausted, she made her way slowly back to *Zainda*.

Brenda, for once, rose to the occasion and kept silent. The two girls sat huddled in the darkness when a dinghy pulled up alongside and Simon and Colin came on board. Joanna sat with her knees pulled up to her chin and didn't bother to look up. It was Brenda who asked how David was. Simon's face moved in and out of the light of the cabin lamp lit by Colin.

'He's gone,' he said curtly and went down to the main cabin. There was a clutter as he rummaged noisily in the semi-darkness, before reappearing into the cockpit with a drink in his hand. Joanna went down, poured herself a brandy and brought the bottle into the cockpit. Simon had just finished his drink. Without speaking, she pointed to the bottle. He nodded. She poured him another drink and swallowed hers in one go. The warm liquid constricted her throat and made her gasp for breath. Still, it was better than crying. She saw Colin pour himself a tumblerful, and offer a drink to Brenda. Without a word, Joanna finished her drink, still felt awful, and stretched out her hand holding her empty cup.

'Joanna, I'm sorry.' Colin's voice sounded hesitant while he ignored her gesture to refill the glass. 'But I think all of us would like to hear from you what happened this afternoon. Could you come to *Jemima,* if that's alright with you?'

She winced and said in a thick voice: 'What, now? I'd rather go to bed if you don't mind. I'm whacked.'

'I'm sorry,' his voice was firm and at the same time genuine. 'It would be better if you came now. You'd be a great help to us in tracking these men.'

All eyes were on her, even Simon's.

'All right. I'll go and change.'

They all piled into the dinghy that Simon had come in, presumably a spare one from *Jemima*, now that their own was gone. Once on board, Colin led the way as they walked the length of the cockpit with its big, comfortable armchairs and coffee tables. They went into the main saloon which with its mahogany wall panelling, shiny brass fittings and beautifully polished table in the middle. Round the table were leather-covered settees actually smelling of leather.

The contrast between this luxury and the lack of any on *Zainda* was too obvious to even comment on. No wonder Colin tried to stay here as often as he could.

Two men stood up as they came in. They wore casual clothes but there was something in their expressions and in the way they moved, a certain alertness and neatness, which gave them a military bearing. With a start, Joanna recognised one of the men. He was the man who had followed them in Canakkale and in Istanbul. Now he gave her a small bow.

'Yes, we have met before. Tarabya, wasn't it?'

She nearly laughed aloud for having ever imagined he could have been Brenda's possible lover. Then it dawned on her that Colin's manner matched theirs – the same precise movements, the same alertness. Birds of a feather – she could see it now. Who were they?

There were no introductions. The two men behaved as if they knew them well, at the same time maintaining their own anonymity. Joanna's head was heavy and her mind wandered as she looked wearily at them.

'You must have had a hard day,' one of them was saying. There was sympathy in his eyes, but also cool detachment as he looked at Joanna. She felt almost X-rayed by his look. 'We should all be most grateful if you could tell us what happened today. You may not know it but we've been helping Simon here trace the men who stole his yacht. So far, we have managed to avoid trouble. This is certainly the most unfortunate incident. It would be of great assistance to us to bring those men to justice. Are you alright? A small drink perhaps?'

She nodded. 'A brandy, please.' It burned her throat but at the same time cleared her mind.

She recounted the whole story starting from the noises the two men made near the place where she had been with David, leaving out what happened between them. Their feelings for each other were surely of no relevance. When she came to describe the men, she was suddenly struck with a clarity which had eluded her so far.

'I realised I'd seen one of the men before, but I couldn't place him at the time. I remember now. He was the taxi driver in Canakkale who took Brenda and me to Troy.'

From the way they nodded, it was clear her remark made an impression. She turned to look at Brenda and was startled by the change in her appearance. Brenda's face was drained of colour and she swallowed hard. Nobody else seemed to have taken any notice. Simon was staring at his feet, too preoccupied with his own thoughts, while the others were waiting for her to go on. They asked more questions, but her mind was going numb. Mercifully they finally released her. Colin took her and Brenda back to the boat, and returned to *Jemima*.

Joanna was too full of the events of the afternoon, and all that brandy, to be able to take in much more. There was something she had to tell Simon, something very important. What was it? Ah, yes, of course. That she was leaving tomorrow when they got to Rhodes.

She woke up in the middle of the night and the events of the previous day hit her with renewed clarity, like a replay of a tape. She cried as if not only her heart but her whole body would break. The sound of her sobs seemed to resound through the cabin, and she tried to stifle them with a pillow. Nobody could hear her now; David was no more, there was only Simon and Brenda at the other end in the aft cabin, separated by the main cabin and the cockpit.

She could hear soft footsteps on the deck which stopped half way to her cabin, then silence. Maybe Colin had come back, or maybe Simon couldn't sleep either. What did it matter? She continued to cry well into the night before finally falling asleep. On waking up, her pillow was soaking wet.

Chapter 16

She did not go home as planned after all. *Zainda* did sail to Rhodes way behind the *Jemima* which, thanks to her powerful engines, disappeared into the distance before they even managed to put up the sails. Once at their destination, all kinds of bureaucratic formalities awaited them in connection with the despatch of David's body to England. It was devastating to think of David in terms of a body to be dealt with, and reconcile oneself to the finality of his going out of their lives. She caught herself expecting David to come on board any minute, demanding food.

They were moored next to *Jemima*, the pretence of having nothing to do with each other now finally dropped. Simon spent most of his time there, as did Colin. Simon began to rely more and more on Joanna to keep them ready for sailing. He was admittedly easier to get on with now, and did not quibble about the money Joanna spent on housekeeping. Brenda kept in the background because, to use her own words, the recent events had shaken her, sailing bored her, and she couldn't be bothered. She was strictly a passenger and a bed companion and never ventured beyond those self-imposed limits. Joanna was at first mad at her for not helping, but changed her mind after Brenda produced a meal. It was simply awful, and she left such a mess in the galley it took longer to clear up after her than if she had cooked the meal herself.

'I'm not at all keen on cooking, and definitely not on boats,' declared Brenda, looking at Joanna with those wide, made-up eyes. 'If it wasn't for Simon, you wouldn't see me for dust.'

On the first evening when they sailed into Rhodes, the day after

David's death, the two girls were left alone. Simon, his face drawn and haggard, had gone to see the officials and start the formalities rolling.

'Don't wait for me. I might be quite late,' he said heavily and disappeared.

Joanna went to the harbourmaster's office to see if there was any mail waiting for her. While sifting through the letters, she noticed several addressed to Simon. There was an official looking envelope which had *Hon.* typed in front of his name. Did that mean Simon was the younger son of an earl? Or the son of a baron? Or a viscount? That would account for his drawn, nasal accent and his general air of languid aloofness. He probably couldn't help putting some distance between himself and the rest of the humanity if he was one of the privileged classes.

She strolled back to *Zainda*, looking through her mail. There was a letter from her parents and a postcard from her girlfriend, Marjorie. Marjorie was on holiday in Majorca having a lovely time with a lovely chap called Geoff she had met in the same hotel. The hotel was just lovely with a fabulous, open-air swimming pool. She said she hoped Joanna was enjoying her holiday and had found a handsome sailor for herself. Joanna sighed. There was also a letter from her solicitor, informing her of the progress of her divorce proceedings. They were going smoothly and the documents would be ready to sign on her return. She'd be a free woman soon.

Joanna made her way slowly past a big, yellow building which separated the market from the quay. There was a proliferation of tables and chairs on the pavement, with waiters in white coats, balancing trays in one hand and weaving their way with expert adroitness. The boats, yachts, luxury cruisers and ferries bobbed and swayed whenever a new arrival stirred the muddy waters of the harbour. Occasionally a loose halyard, brought to life by a breeze, clanged as it hit a metal mast. The sun shone, bringing the windmills on the opposite side of the quay into a dark relief while at the same time allowing the construction works to melt into a shadow. Up on the hill above the harbour flickered red and yellow lights illuminating the Crusaders' castle in preparation for the evening's display of the *Son-et-Lumiere*.

Brenda was waiting for her in the cockpit, nervously smoking a cigarette. Joanna interpreted her behaviour as not wanting to be alone rather than a sudden surge of affection. Sometimes death affected people that way. 'Let's go eat outside,' Joanna suggested. 'I spotted a cheap restaurant over there, and the food's bound to be okay.'

'I don't want to go out,' said Brenda impatiently. 'I want to talk to you.'

'Okay.' Joanna sat down, surprised.

Once she faced her, Brenda seemed to be at a loss of words. She inhaled the cigarette smoke deeply, looked at the glowing tip, then crushed it with impatience although she'd only just lit it.

'I don't want you to think …' she started haltingly. 'I'm not asking you to do anything wrong, or anything like that.' She paused. Joanna waited in silence.

'I don't know how to put it,' she lit another cigarette. 'You said there, in *Jemima* …' She waved her hand vaguely in the direction of the boat.

Joanna continued to watch Brenda in silence, noticing the green lacquer on her nails had been replaced by red. Her hand looked as if she had crushed it in the doorway.

Brenda took another deep breath and continued haltingly.

'It was what you said about the man … who … killed David. The taxi driver.' Joanna nodded. *So that's what was bothering her.*

'I just want you to know I didn't know anything about him. I mean, he was just a stranger. When we met that time … you know … back … wherever … Troy, it was just … a bit of fun really … with a stranger. Yes, I know, Simon invited me to spend this holiday with him, but it was kind of loose, not really committed. I never promised him anything … I mean … it wasn't that serious or anything between us … until after the storm, you know, when I left when we got to Bodrum. That sort of changed everything … I mean … between us.' She swallowed hard, threw the cigarette into the water and lit another one. 'It just seemed like fun at the time, the taxi driver, I mean, you know, sort of different.'

Joanna nodded. Brenda was right there; the two men were as different as a tiger was to a domestic cat. 'My shrink,' continued Brenda, 'he said, why don't you let yourself go, you're too inhibited, enjoy yourself.' By now Brenda was sobbing. 'How was I to know it would turn out like that? It was meant to be fun. I didn't expect to see him ever again.'

'Did that man,' asked Joanna, 'that taxi driver, ever ask you anything, or tell you anything for that matter?'

'No. We didn't talk much; it was all a bit of a giggle. Anyway, once we started petting, he came very quickly, know what I mean? He didn't waste time talking. Struck me as if he was in a hurry, left soon afterwards, said he had to see his cousin about something. We didn't spend much time together.' She sounded almost wistful, as if that little interlude held more promise than was subsequently fulfilled.

'But surely he must've said something, or asked you something, perhaps when you were driving back?'

'Oh no, nothing much. He kept trying to … well, we just talked as you do … like, where are you going, how do you like sailing, what do you do on your holiday, how do you like visiting places. That kind of thing. I told him we just sort of wandered around. I said we might go to Kusadasi and then along the coast, and there was a big luxury cruiser following us and how I'd like to be on it and not be cooped up on ours, you know, that kind of thing.'

'Did he know we were going to stay the night in Istanbul?'

'Why? What's on your mind? No, of course not. I didn't know myself, did I?'

'He might've followed you!' Joanna said as she sat up, horrified. So, the thieves had known all along about their route. Somehow, they must've learned about their hotel in Istanbul. It was they who had staged that accident in Kusadasi; they had been prepared for them and had expected their arrival. And now they had shown their true colours – they would stop at nothing. Already one person had been killed. Who was to be the next one on their list? She looked grimly at Brenda who was sobbing loudly. It was no good blaming her now that they were armed with hindsight. Brenda was talking, leaning her forehead on her arm which was resting on the side of the cockpit. She was mumbling and her words were further muffled by sobs.

'After I came back, in Bodrum, Simon suggested we might go into a more committed relationship, maybe even get married.'

Joanna stared at her in disbelief. Good Lord, the man was twice her age at least. Still, an 'Hon.' could be quite a catch. But what did he see in Brenda, with her wispy looks and slovenly ways?

'... and now he'll never want to marry me if he hears what happened with the taxi driver, will he?'

Joanna sat deep in thought. What purpose would it serve if she told on Brenda? Perhaps none, but the men on *Jemima* should at least know Brenda had told the crooks of their sailing plans. Did her little love-making have to be turned into public knowledge at the same time? There was another possibility, of course: Brenda was at times a pretty clever girl and could be acting on their side. She could be using her, Joanna, to cover up for her and that gang. But Brenda's sobs were so genuine, she couldn't believe it of her. She was too simple, too transparently stupid. Joanna decided to risk it.

'We'll have to tell the men on *Jemima* what you told the taxi driver

213

about our sailing plans. I think it's important they should know about it. But we don't have to tell them about your ... er ... little affair. Simon needn't know.'

She patted Brenda's hands, inwardly shaken. 'I certainly won't tell them or him.'

She went down and fetched a bottle of whisky. It was warm and they had run out of the ice again. 'Let's have a drink and go out to dinner. I'm famished,'

'Thanks,' Brenda said and smiled through her tears before blowing her nose loudly on the handkerchief which she had screwed into a ball while talking to Joanna. It was by then very dirty.

The effect of the conversation on Joanna only confirmed her resolution to leave. She had had enough of other people's problems. What about her own? Her chief reason, she didn't mind admitting, was fear. Did those men know about her? Had they see her with David? They had already followed her and Brenda once in Istanbul; they might also turn up in Rhodes. She was the only witness who had practically seen David killed, and the only person who might identify them. She walked in fear all the time now, at night half-awake listening for unfamiliar sounds, in daytime forever watchful, wondering if she was being followed. This was no way to spend a holiday. She was a nervous wreck.

The feeling of gloom and despondency had deepened, if that was possible, when Colin had moved onto *Jemima*. His presence had given her a certain amount of reassurance, and now even that was gone.

Something was going on aboard *Jemima*, preparations were afoot. She remembered Simon's excited remarks just after David's attack: that the yacht in which the killers came was very similar to his. She overheard him saying to the two men on *Jemima*: 'I'm ninety five percent sure. They've repainted the hull and changed the name of course. I'd have been one hundred percent certain if I hadn't left the binoculars with David.'

Joanna saw her chance when Simon came up unexpectedly, as was his habit of late, and sat down in the cockpit holding a can of beer. He looked so haggard and tired it needed all her courage, now sadly lacking, to broach the subject of her leaving. She felt even worse about it, being aware that now, without David, Simon was depending a lot more on her to do things around the boat.

'Look, Simon,' she began, staring at her feet. 'I've given this a lot of thought, and I hope you don't mind, but I'd like to go home. What with Colin and the two of you, you'd be able to cope; you don't need me,' she finished lamely.

Simon listened to her in silence. He must have been sent to a good public school because his face registered nothing but indifference, only a twitch of an eyebrow betraying any sign of emotion. When he finally spoke, his voice retained his usual casual note.

'You want to leave? Now? My dear girl, what an incredible idea! I'm sure I didn't hear you right.' He sounded so pompous it made it easier for her to continue.

'Well, yes, I should like to,' she persisted, feeling rotten. On the other hand, she hated to be called "my dear girl".

'My dear girl, now? When we need you most?'

'Why, what do you need me for? You two can cope and three's a crowd.' No need to tell him about her fears, her pride wouldn't let her. Simon drew his hand wearily across his brow.

'Of course, it was selfish of me to expect you to stay after all that's happened. It's just that you are the only person who can identify the killers. You know how much you meant to David, and frankly, from what you said to him there, if I heard you correctly, I gather my nephew was not entirely indifferent to you.' Joanna blushed furiously. 'I thought we could count on you. I suppose it's all been a bit of a strain lately, but to leave now – ' He broke off and looked at the sky, not at her. Seeing him in the sunlight for the first time since David had died, she noticed how much he'd aged. Her resolve was melting away. She tried her last argument.

'Brenda can identify one of the men for you ... when you catch them, that is.'

'I admire your confidence,' he interrupted with sarcasm.

'I'm sure it was the taxi driver who took us to Troy from Canakkale.'

'And suppose it wasn't, only looked like him?' he asked with unaccustomed sharpness. '*You* saw him clearly through the binoculars, nobody else. You also saw the other man you could identify, didn't you? Only two people saw them – you and David.'

Joanna gave an involuntary shudder. That must have occurred to the killers, too. Had they seen her watching them through the binoculars, or sitting by David's side?

'Well, I can't keep you against your will, of course,' he continued in his lazy drawl, 'but if you leave, our chances of success will be considerably diminished.'

He glared at her with a cold, unfriendly look, as if disgusted with the whole conversation and with her in particular. Joanna felt thoroughly chastised. 'I hadn't thought about it that way. I'm sorry. Of course, I'll stay.'

He got up stiffly and moved towards the gangplank. 'We're counting on you, Joanna. For David's sake,' he added and made a small movement as if to touch her, then thought better of it and walked out.

That same day, Joanna nearly changed her mind again. As she walked past *Jemima* a big limousine pulled up. There was a lot of commotion, several pieces of luggage were being carried out by the crew, and a chauffeur stood stiffly by the open door. From the car emerged a woman – the stunner from the Tarabya bar. She was greeted by the men Joanna had met on the day David died. The rest of the party was already assembled on the deck, Colin among them. Joanna's heart froze. That was too much: she was going to pack her bags and go home. On top of everything, she would have to put up with Colin and that woman together having a great time on that luxury cruiser, right under her nose. Dear, useful Joanna, creating wonders with the tinned food, good for keeping a watch during a storm. Oh yes, she was good enough for that, but when it came to … Words failed her, tears welled up in her eyes. Nevertheless, she remained standing in the crowd, fascinated in spite of herself. The woman wore a creamy dress which clung to her superb figure, revealing long, brown legs through the slits in the skirt. A blind person would have been aware of the electrifying effect she had on the men around her!

Then a bald head, glistening in the crowd, caught Joanna's attention. She recognised the face. It was the man who had spoken to Colin on *Jemima* when she was anchored off Kusadasi, centuries ago it seemed to her now. That arrogant air of self-assurance, the tuft of black hair above each ear, the white shorts and the unbuttoned shirt, completed with a cigar which seemed to be an integral part of his body. He was met by everybody with great deference as he waddled towards the gangplank.

What a lot of fuss about that right so-and-so, thought Joanna, watching the woman disappear slowly from view. I bet she's making a bee-line for Colin. Joanna wasn't wrong. Colin looked very smart dressed in casual holiday clothes he had never worn on *Zainda*. He had taken off his arm sling but had kept the thumb of his left hand tucked into the hook of his belt. As he exchanged a smile and a bow with the woman, the fat man caught up with her. He was greeted by Colin with an almost exaggerated politeness. The smile on the woman's face faded and she was about to move on when the fat man restrained her by putting out his hand, forcing her to stay by his side.

'So, that's the set-up,' Joanna laughed inwardly. 'She belongs to him. A wife? A mistress? Poor Colin. I shouldn't wish to take on a man like that; he wouldn't give way easily to being a cuckold. I'd say he looks positively dangerous.'

That seemed true enough. Unlike most fat men who tend to exude bonhomie, this one, in spite of an overall appearance of cordiality, had a sinister, heavy air about him. It would take a brave man to cross him. And here was Colin with designs on his woman! Well! Some people *will* thrive on danger!

By now, the big shiny limousine was gone, but the crowd still lingered on the quay. Joanna went back to *Zainda* and sat in the cockpit from where she could see events unfolding on *Jemima*. There was a party in progress on the huge upper deck. The crew had been transformed into waiters and were circulating among the guests, serving drinks from trays. One of them, wearing white gloves, was opening bottles of champagne with a loud pop. Joanna had another look at the owner of the mass of dark hair and lovely face. She had somehow managed to leave the fat man and was standing next to Colin, holding a champagne glass and smiling at him, a slow, sensual smile. Joanna could take it no more and burst into tears. Her heart contracted at the memory of David. She badly needed to be told that she, too, was desirable.

Chapter 17

A few days later, *Zainda* left Rhodes harbour and sailed towards the Kekova Roads. As soon as they turned the corner, they lost sight of *Jemima* rising above the anchored boats like a swan among the minnows, and headed eastwards. Joanna had not enquired where they were going, by now she knew better than to ask Simon questions. It probably never occurred to him to inform her of his plans anyway. He had changed considerably since David's death. Now he was pale, haggard and withdrawn. Gone were the days of heavy petting with Brenda on the aft deck. Joanna managed to buy a supply of books in Rhodes and spent most of the day sunbathing and reading when not helping with the sailing.

Sixty miles east of Rhodes, they stopped at the tiny island of Kastellorizo. Though only a few miles off the Turkish coast, it was Greek, a fact which the inhabitants, reputedly a couple of hundred of them if that, went into great lengths to proclaim. Three huge flags were placed in strategic places, flowing in the wind and visible from afar.

They arrived in the evening, just as the lights went up on the magnificent, crescent-shaped quay. Along it stood three-storey-high houses in mellow colours of yellow and white. Joanna had a glimpse of cobbled streets, arched passages and a tiny square with an octagonal-shaped fountain. At one end of the crescent stood a modern hotel, the other end was tipped with a white mosque and a minaret. Sounds of Greek music greeted them as they approached. Dusk descended quickly, replacing the sun which was sinking behind the bare, treeless mountain overlooking the harbour. Inside the harbour, tied to the quay, was a grey patrol boat, a few pleasure boats and several small open fishing boats bobbing in the swell.

Zainda was greeted by the harbourmaster who, as it turned out, also carried out the duties of policeman, mayor and midwife on the island. Joanna longed to be alone and left Simon and Brenda on board as soon as she could. Once on land, she found herself in a huge open-air theatre surrounded by stage props. Out of all the houses lining the quay, which from a distance gave the impression of a substantial town, only a few were inhabited. The others were mere shells, their painted fronts hiding the ruins behind. The windows behind the pretty shutters had no glass panes. Through the cracks in the doors, she could see the hollow interiors, without floors or ceilings. In some there were even trees growing inside, filling the empty shells with their branches.

She wandered into the square. It would not surprise her to see Montagues and Capulets or a *corps de ballet* come out from behind the little side streets to start a performance. The fountain was dry – the harbourmaster had stressed the acute shortage of fresh water on the island which was why so few people lived there. She walked on, past a big white and blue church and a gaily painted school as deserted as the houses, their colours already changing to grey in the gently falling dusk. A rusty metal swing moved by the wind was making an eerie sound.

After a while, she had the feeling she was being followed, a creepy sensation between her shoulder blades. She looked back, but there was nobody about. Nevertheless, her pace quickened. The soft footsteps behind her also quickened. They stopped when she stopped. She hurried on and the footsteps followed as soon as she moved. The memory of the two men and what happened to David was too fresh; she began to run, gripped by an overwhelming panic. The footsteps followed. There was nothing for it but to face her unknown pursuer. Heart in mouth, she peered cautiously from behind the corner of a deserted house. The sight which presented itself made her laugh aloud with relief: there stood a dozen or so sheep! Seeing her turn around to face them, they ran to the nearest empty house through a doorless opening, wagging their long, yellow tails in panic. It was their feet which made the soft patter on the cobbles. Nevertheless, her imagination had stirred enough memories to rejoin Simon and Brenda quickly.

The three of them dined in a little restaurant facing the harbour whose owner was a local fisherman. They ordered fish which the owner's wife weighed before cooking it, calculating the price not on quality or kind but in terms of grams and kilos. It was delicious. They ate in silence. The recent tragedy had united them enough to dispose with the need to keep up a conversation. Their table was surrounded by a motionless circle of at least a dozen lean cats, each watching intently their every single move, patiently waiting for scraps from their plates.

The following morning there was still enough time before their departure to wander about on the island. Joanna found those ruined, deserted houses, so incongruously large for such a small community, curiously soothing as she walked slowly along the strip of the road. It led to a walled cemetery. Inside were rows of rectangular stone chests painted white. Obviously, the earth was too stony for the coffins to be dug into the ground, so instead they were placed inside the stone and plaster box-like structures on top. Above the graves were stone crosses, some of which carried sepia photographs next to the engraved names and dates of birth and death of the occupiers. Joanna looked at the faded peasant faces who had come to their end in this forlorn corner of the world. Outside the cemetery the sea licked gently at the grey and brown rocks. A breeze stirred the warm, spicy smell of the cypress trees which grew by the wall. She stood absorbing the peace and the sadness. A place, perhaps like this but far away, in a different land would be David's permanent home now. He was too young to die. No, she was not going to cry.

They continued to sail to the Kekova Roads – a stretch of water sheltered by a string of small islands from the open sea. Having reached them, they had to manoeuvre through a rather tricky entrance. It was crucial to get their bearings right so as not to get stuck in the shallows or get impaled on a rock. Joanna had to move double quick, tacking, winching and taking readings on the depth sounder. Once inside, there was a lovely calm stretch of water of sufficient depth to sail in and anchor. In the distance was a small hamlet huddled at the foot of a hill, topped with walls with crenulated outlines – the well-preserved ruins of a Venetian fort. At least, that's what it said in her book on Turkey.

The water's edge was fringed with lots of rectangular, ruined buildings, much overgrown with bushes and small trees. Some of these ruins were submerged a foot or so under water and rose straight from the sea, only to be hidden by bushes and rocks. To Joanna, they were a tantalising mystery – what were they? She did not remember having read about them. Were they Roman granaries, houses of merchants, ancient temples? A delightful cove opened up on one of the islands facing the mainland. The entrance was narrow, edged with ruined walls, its floors partly submerged. At the far end of the cove was a piece of flat land from which rose the sweeping, graceful arch of a ruined Byzantine church. Simon steered them towards this cove where they anchored. Joanna gratefully dipped her hot body in the turquoise waters. She was not left alone for long, though. Two men and a woman came from behind the promontory in an open boat, one man rowing, the other waving a big fish. As they came nearer, the woman lifted a shawl covering the basket by which she sat, pointing to the tomatoes and fruit inside. Joanna swam towards them and bargained with them, treading water. The men seemingly thought this was the most natural thing to do, to bargain for the price of fish with a woman in a bikini encountered in the middle of the sea! It annoyed Joanna to think the same men would not let their women sunbathe on the beaches or mix freely in public places. What an amazing attitude! Either they had a double morality code, one for themselves and the other for the rest of the world, or they didn't consider tourists to be human. She bargained furiously and managed to whittle the price down to half of what was originally asked. With the fish out of the way, as it were, she asked the woman if she had any fresh bread. The woman, dressed in baggy trousers and a pink blouse, face half-covered by a scarf, sitting motionless in the boat, smiled shyly at Joanna, not understanding a word. Once Joanna's request was translated by one of the men, she nodded and produced a bundle wrapped in calico cotton hidden by the tomatoes. She untied a knot and unfolded a cloth revealing a stack of thin, brown pancakes.

'Bread?' queried Joanna. Was this bread?

'Bread like this is normal,' said the man.

Well, why not try their normal bread? 'How much do you want for it?' The whole rigmarole of bargaining had to start again.

'What you will?'

'Ten liras.'

'No, twenty cigarettes.'

'You mean one packet?'

'No, twenty packet.'

That was another thing one learned quickly in Turkey. They asked ridiculously high prices for low-price commodities. Ignorance surely, or insolence? By now she knew better than be indignant. She kept on bargaining until all eventually agreed on a price which had a bearing on the value of the article and she brought her purchases to *Zainda*. Joanna felt she had done a good day's work even though it was no later than eleven in the morning.

As she got up to the fore deck to sunbathe, she saw *Jemima* in the distance as she sailed past their cove and disappeared behind the promontory. After a while a Turkish caique appeared, of the kind she and David saw built in Bodrum, blaring loud music in its wake. To

Joanna's dismay, it turned towards "her" cove, nearly ramming into them as they anchored. The charm and the silence of the little cove was completely shattered. The caique was full of tourists who in no time at all had jumped into the water to splash, swim and generally fool around. Some were being carted in dinghies with loud outboard motors to the shore and back, to view the Byzantine ruins. Joanna saw a couple of men trying to windsurf, wobbling precariously on the narrow boards, hanging tightly to the handle of the sail, only to fall into the water sooner or later. A voice was heard above the din:

'I say, have you sailed all the way from England?'

Simon disappeared into the cabin and Joanna tried to make herself invisible by pressing hard against the deck. Brenda waved gaily.

'Yes, actually we did.'

'Gosh!' there was admiration in the voice now. 'How long did it take you?'

'Oh, a couple of weeks, you know.'

Joanna looked through the hatch at Simon and winked.

Someone in the caique emptied a bucket of slops into the sea. Joanna watched fruit rinds, chopped tomatoes and other debris float slowly towards the shore. That took care of her swimming. She didn't dare ask herself about their toilet facilities, preferring to stay on the deck and read. They stayed for the rest of the day and did not sail away in the evening as she had fervently hoped.

In the evening, a huge moon rose early and was reflected in the water when Joanna joined Simon and Brenda in the cockpit. The tourists were now having a party and were dancing on the decks to the music which continued to blare through the loudspeakers. Joanna wondered if she was the only one who preferred peace as she watched them dance and enjoy themselves. Simon was his usual uncommunicative self, but Brenda longed to join the party. She went as far as to ask if Simon might take her, but was stopped by Joanna.

It would have been in bad taste to suggest it so soon after David's death. So, the three of them sat in the cockpit in silence, forced to listen to the sounds imposed on them. Brenda nodded and swayed her body to the beat of the music. After midnight, the western music stopped and was replaced by the twang of Turkish melodies. Two of the crew who, until then, had been busy serving drinks and food, now stood in the middle while the tourists made a circle around them, clapping rhythmically. At first, they stood still, their arms on each other's shoulders, then suddenly they crouched, swaying in time with the music, then hopped on one leg, then on the other. To Joanna, it looked like a re-enactment of bird courtship, but it had another meaning to the rest of the Turkish crew who grew excited watching the two perform, clapping as if unable to contain themselves any longer, then jumping into the ring to join them, hopping and crouching. The guests swayed and clapped more or less in time, politeness taking the upper hand over the alcoholic haze.

Joanna went to bed but couldn't sleep, disturbed as she was by the noise. When eventually she did, it seemed only minutes before a hand shook her. It was Simon.

'Joanna, wake up. I think there's something going on,' he whispered. She sat up with a start.

'What d'you mean?' she asked, shivers going down her spine.

'That yacht I saw before, the one I saw the day David was attacked. I think it's here. I need to investigate. Now, don't do anything, and don't wake Brenda. I shan't be long. Just be on the lookout. Whatever happens,' he added with emphasis, 'do not use the radio. Anyway, I'm sure nothing's going to happen.'

Joanna rubbed her eyes which were heavy with sleep.

'I'm taking the dinghy,' said Simon, already in the cockpit.

'Wait,' she called. 'Where are you going? What do you intend to do?' she wrapped her naked body in a towel and followed Simon.

'There,' he whispered. She followed the direction of his finger with difficulty. The night was pitch-black, the moon was gone. All was silent on the Turkish caique. Only a tiny anchor light, like a pin prick in the dark sky, illuminated the tip of the mast. Further out was the barely distinguishable outline of another yacht. It had no lights, not even an anchor light. Joanna thought she could detect a tiny scraping sound, possibly an oar in a rowlock.

'You think that's your yacht over there? I can barely see it.'

'It could be,' he whispered. 'I need a closer look to make sure.' He was already standing in the dinghy, picking up the paddles from the deck. 'Untie the painter for me, will you please.'

'If something should happen, what do you want me to do?' she couldn't help sounding fearful, suddenly conscious of being left alone in this darkness.

'Nothing will happen,' Simon stressed impatiently. 'I should be back in ten, twenty minutes at most. You'll be all right. Just don't use the radio, that's all.'

'Where is *Jemima*? she whispered. Simon had already cast off and was paddling away from the boat. 'There,' he said as his chin moved to the right. 'About a mile or so further down the coast.' He was already a blur in the darkness and disappeared quickly from sight.

Joanna shivered with fright. The presence of the caique with the tourists restored some of her confidence; at least it made her feel she was not utterly alone. Nobody would start any funny business with so many people around. If it came to the worst, she could always shout for help. There was no point in waking up Brenda just yet. Simon would be furious, particularly as he had asked her not to bother her. Of course, he was right: Brenda was bound to make a lot of noise and ask unnecessary questions.

She went back to her cabin and dressed in her jeans and sweat shirt. Her head half-way through the hatch, she scanned the darkness anxiously, listening for the reassuring sounds of Simon coming back.

Suddenly there was a flurry of activity on the caique. Dark figures appeared on the deck, talking in low voices, followed by the unmistakable rattle of the anchor chain on the winch. They were getting ready to leave, she realised with dismay. While the tourists slept, the crew were making ready to sail to the next destination on their itinerary.

The figures moved efficiently. A torch flickered here and there, the anchor chain rattled, followed by the sound of an engine in low revs. The caique began to move in reverse, going backwards out of the cove, changed gear to move forward and disappeared behind the promontory. It happened very quickly. Her view no longer obstructed, Joanna detected the outline of the other yacht at the entrance to the cove. In the deserted darkness it had a sinister air. She heard the crunch of footsteps from the direction of the land and voices, kept deliberately low, but too faint to recognise the words. It couldn't be Simon, could it? Who could he be talking to? He said he was only going to have a quick look round the yacht. She glanced at her watch. He had already been gone three quarters of an hour. How long did he say he'd be away for? Ten to twenty minutes, so say half an hour tops. She tried to keep her panic down. What was fifteen minutes either way? *If he doesn't come in the next five minutes I'll go and wake up Brenda. Then again, what good will that do? She'll only make a noise.* What could be detaining Simon? It shouldn't take three quarters of an hour to paddle round that yacht and back. Where had he gone to? Why would he have gone on land? A faint noise at the bow interrupted her thoughts and relief flooded her mind. How silly of her to worry so. She jumped through the hatch and leaned over to give him a hand with the dinghy painter. There was nobody there, just a piece of wood bumping against the hull, now slowly floating away. Another noise alerted her, at the stern this time. She turned to look and froze in horror. Two men jumped from the aft deck into the cockpit. Neither of them was Simon. The men crouched in the cockpit, then one pulled open the door to the aft cabin while the other sprung forward to the main. Without stopping to think what she was doing, Joanna crawled through the hatch, slipped under the pulpit, down the anchor chain into the water, swimming away as quickly as she could.

While she tried to swim making as little noise as possible, her wet jeans weighing her down, Brenda's voice rang out for a moment and then was silent. Joanna shuddered and tried to put some distance between herself and *Zainda*. The hull of the dark yacht loomed ahead. She swam towards it, hoping to meet Simon in the dinghy. A light was shining in one of the cabins, but the window was too high to see the interior from the water level. The yacht was similar to *Zainda*, about the same length and beam. It was a yawl with an aft cockpit, and a dark-coloured hull. On the stern someone had painted the name in crude, red letters – *Ali Baba*. The ensign was Turkish. Shadowy figures were moving in and out of the cockpit and there was a murmur of low voices. None of them she recognised as Simon's. She kept a discreet distance, looking around to see if Simon was somewhere about in the new dinghy they had to buy in Rhodes. There was a chance he might be hiding behind the nearest headland. The voices on *Ali Baba* grew more agitated. Judging by the shadows against the light of the cabin, there was increased activity inside. All kinds of noises reached her now. There was a hollow sound like thumping, followed by groans, then something like an 'ouch' followed by a stifled cry, then a crash and a thud. The light went out suddenly, and two men came out into the cockpit, wiping their faces.

Joanna was almost paralysed with fear. She only now noticed that she had drifted too close. Any moment now someone in the cockpit was bound to see her. Those sounds put fresh terror into her. Someone in there had been beaten. It could have been Simon. As if to confirm her suspicion, she thought she could detect the blurred outline of a dinghy tied to the yacht. Now she knew what to expect if she too was caught. Could it be that the caique with the tourists had arrived to create a diversion while the thieves who had stolen Simon's yacht were out to catch them? Now they've got Simon, and Brenda, and most likely would be looking for her too. She must get away quickly before they realised she was not on board of *Zainda*. Her mind cleared instantly now that the realisation hit her that she had to fight for her life. It was no good trying to get to the dinghy and paddle away. They were bound to notice its absence and that would give her away. It was better to swim quietly and find *Jemima*.' What was it Simon had said? He had pointed to the right and said she was anchored a mile or so away. Joanna kicked off her jeans and took off her sweat shirt, thankful for her swimsuit underneath which she wore almost by habit now. The water was warm, the sea calm, almost flat. So far, it appeared nobody was looking for her. That was some respite. Maybe the men who boarded *Zainda* didn't know how many people to look for, or they would have raised an alarm by now. There was no sound from either of the yachts as she swam away and, with slow, measured strokes, made towards the middle of the Kekova Roads. *What's a mile, as long as I don't panic? All I have to do is not to flap, just keep going.* What was that Chinese saying? *The hundred-mile march starts with but one step, or, in this case, stroke.*

She kept swimming. Soon her arms and legs began to ache and her head felt very heavy. After only a couple of hours sleep, it was now beginning to tell. She allowed herself to tread water before resuming swimming. Just concentrate on one stroke at a time, she told herself, and keep going. Don't let your mind drift, don't let the temptation to let go and go to sleep gain the upper hand.

How long she kept going like that became a blur. The coast line, once so enchanting when seen from the deck of a yacht, was now dark and hostile. Behind every rock there could be armed men, ready to shoot. She had to keep going and get help. No radio contact, said

Simon. He obviously did not want to let them know of the link between *Zainda* and *Jemima*. It was all so unfair. Nobody ever told her anything, and now she was as involved as they were. Beastly unfair. Well, she was in it now, fighting for her life. Somehow the thought was not frightening any more. If only she was less tired. All she had to do was to keep going, that's what it boiled down to. Keep going. Tread water. They'd got to Simon all right, they must have. What had they done to him? It had sounded as if it had been a major fight. No, better not to think about that. Think of something else. Keep counting: one, two, three ... fifty-seven, fifty-eight, fifty-nine. Would he be still alive when she finally got help? Surely she must have swum more than a mile! Where was *Jemima*? She should be able to see her soon!

There was nothing as far as she could see: no fishing boats, no anchor lights, no *Jemima*. Perhaps they had sailed away? What would she do, alone in this wilderness? They'd kill her, just as they had David. The darkness gradually changed to greyness, and again the golden strip in the east heralded the re-enactment of the arrival of a new day. She wasn't looking forward to it. Daylight meant possible detection, and though the sea was empty right now they might sail past her any time. Her eyes felt sore, her eyelids caked with the salt water, and there was bitter taste in her mouth. Each stroke became more of an effort and she allowed herself to drift and tread water more and more often. Thank goodness it was summer and the sea was warm and flat, otherwise she'd have gone numb by now, maybe even have drowned. Her mind began to wander. She saw Colin and the stunner looking at each other over the champagne glasses on the deck of *Jemima*. There was music and the woman suddenly laughed, looking not at Colin but at her, Joanna, sitting alone on *Zainda*. She shook her head and the faces disappeared. From the grey mist David emerged. He was bending over, his lips on her face. 'I love you, Joanna,' he was saying. 'I've been trying to tell myself hundreds of times to find someone my own age. You didn't have to tell me that.' Then Brenda's tear-stained face appeared. 'He'll never marry me when he hears of it, never,' she was saying.

Twice her head went under and she had to shake off the increasing stupor. As it went down for the third time, something slimy and horrid hit her on the back. It was a piece of drifting sea weed but it made her raise her head and look up. Way, way ahead in the distance was *Jemima*, the unmistakable line of her bow, the two-tier decks. It was far but it was there. What a relief! However, Joanna realised with dismay that her strength was failing her. It was too far. Without a rest she'd never make it. The sun was high up now, and she was very thirsty. There was a small, sandy beach much nearer and she made towards it. There was no other way. She simply had to lie down and regain her strength. Perhaps she could send a signal to draw their attention. She simply had to rest.

It took a long, indeterminably long time, before she felt solid ground under her feet. The water was up to her waist and when she tried to walk, a wave would push her so that she fell forward. She got up, coughing and retching. More waves washed over her as she reached the beach on all fours. Finally, she wriggled up on to solid ground, panting and racked with thirst. In the last moment of consciousness, she was reminded of Odysseus who had also been wrecked on an island and found the princess Nausicaa to rescue him. Lucky Odysseus.

'Joanna! Joanna!' Someone was shaking her by the arms. 'For God's sake, Joanna, what are you doing here? Are you alright?'

She started and blinked, barely able to open her eyes through the swollen eyelids. She tried to get up on all fours and failed. 'Water,' she croaked. 'Water.'

'Joanna!' A man's voice was in her ear. She was lifted up. gently. She blinked again and couldn't believe her eyes. It simply couldn't be true – she was dreaming. It couldn't be – Colin!

'Water … I…' but no further sound came through her parched

lips. Colin's worried face floated in and out of her vision. He pressed a bottle to her lips and she drank greedily then spluttered. He poured more water on his handkerchief and wiped her face and eyes with it.

'What are you doing here? What's going on?' His voice, agitated and distressed, pierced through her numbed brain.

'I swam from *Zainda*. Two men came on board but I got away. They've got Simon on their yacht, but Brenda's still on *Zainda*.' Her mind went blank again. She shook herself, prompted by a nagging thought.

'They need help. Simon said no radio contact so I swam. They beat him … I am sure of it. I heard them as I swam past. He screamed. I'm sure it was him. Must get help…'

'There, there, take it easy, everything's going to be all right.'

He was holding her in his arms. It was marvellous to lean against his body and sleep. Everything's going to be all right now, she had made it. It was all right to sleep now. Another man's voice drifted into her consciousness, 'She must've swum more than a mile.' She jerked her head up again; the thought that had kept her going would not be assuaged.

'They need help. You must go and help!' She made an attempt to stand up. There were several men on the beach. Colin was there, and he'd get help, he said so. He put her down gently on a blanket and she drifted again into a deep sleep.

Someone was shaking her by the arm again. The sound of men talking through a walkie-talkie droned as if from a great distance. There was Colin's voice, giving instructions. She opened her eyes and found herself lying on a small indentation of the beach on soft, blissfully soft sand. Colin was bending over her.

'You can't stay here anymore. You must wake up and come with us.'

Deathly tired, she tried to get up and failed. Colin lifted her up and carried her to a motor boat. It started with a tremendous roar of the engine. The bow rose instantly as the boat planed along the water. There was a rhythmic thud, thud, thud, above the regular noise of the engine as the bow rose and fell. She clung to Colin who took off his shirt and put it round her shoulders. She noticed a thick leather strap lying diagonally across his chests ending in a holster. He was wearing a gun. What was it Simon had said when he had introduced him? A car salesman? What would a car salesman be doing with a gun on a deserted beach off the Turkish coast? She looked around her now that the wind and the spray were reviving her. There were three men besides Colin, crouching rather than sitting in the boat. It was a proper speedboat, not a dinghy. They were all carrying guns, she noticed, one also carried a walkie-talkie. The guns were like those small submachine guns used by the Israeli army. What did they call them? Uzis? What were these armed men doing here? Her head was in a daze, but at least she was no longer sleepy. Was this a preparation for a showdown with the men in the dark yacht? The speedboat slowed down to cruising speed as they followed the shore, past the Venetian castle, past the little hamlet, and turned round the corner. The engine stopped and one of the men jumped into the water and tied the painter to a rock. It wasn't really a rock when she looked at it closely, but a half-submerged rock tomb.

'You'd better have this.' Colin thrust a piece of chocolate into her hand. 'Better than nothing.'

She took a bite and only then realised she had had nothing to eat since the previous evening. 'We've got to go up this hill. Do you think you'll make it?'

'I think so. I feel better now. Where are we going?'

'Up,' he said curtly, pre-occupied.

Joanna looked around her and saw they were in the cove where

Zainda was still under anchor. So was *Ali Baba*. That tortuous journey which had taken her so many hours to swim had now been achieved in what seemed a matter of minutes. She turned to Colin who was walking ahead of her.

'I'll slow you down. I've no shoes.'

'Come with me. I'll help you.'

He picked her up and half-carried her as she stumbled on the rocks, still weak from the long swim. He turned back and said something to the men walking behind them. They nodded, fanned out along the side of the hill and were soon hidden by the rocks and the bushes. Joanna and Colin made their way slowly up, stepping from rock to rock until they reached a cleared footpath. Colin was holding her by the waist with one hand, his other tucked into the belt of his shorts while she picked her way carefully to avoid the dry, prickly thistles. They were startled by the sudden sound of a shot.

'We must hurry,' said Colin grimly, lifting her up. Two more shots rang through the air.

'What's that? Where are they?' she panted. Colin didn't answer, just dragged her along as she tried to keep up with him. In this way they ran past ruined houses and found themselves inside the walls of the Venetian castle. She had a brief glimpse of a tiny Greek theatre within the medieval battlements when a bullet whizzed past no more than two yards away. She had a prickly sensation of someone following them pretty closely. It put new strength into her as they ran through an opening in the wall and into an open field on which were scattered large stone sarcophagi among the olive and carob trees. They found themselves in an ancient necropolis. Another shot rang through the air, and this time there was no doubt their adversary was very close indeed. They ran for the nearest cover behind a rectangular sarcophagus mounted on a high plinth, and fell on the ground. Colin gripped his bad arm, his face white with pain. Joanna gasped for air while her heart beat fast with effort and fear. She saw Colin crouch behind the corner, looking in the direction from which the shots came. The gun was in his hand now. He took careful aim, pulled the trigger and instantly turned back flat against the side of the sarcophagus. A shot rang through the air in response, hitting the lid lying askew on top of its rectangular base behind which they were hiding. It made a loud twang, and a chipped piece of stone fell near Joanna. Colin aimed and pulled the trigger again and again. Joanna lay on the ground, conscious of the inadequate protection the sarcophagus afforded them. She pressed her body flat, hands on her ears, face on the ground.

The air was then filled with a whole volley of shots. She lifted her head long enough to watch Colin as he raised himself slightly, slowly took aim, pulled the trigger and rolled quickly back for cover. Another shot hit the sarcophagus, and a piece of flying stone grazed her leg. Her head covered by her arms, her whole body quivering, all she could think of was to pray for the shooting to stop. She lay like this for ages, or maybe it was only seconds, when she felt an ant crawling on her face. Colin was taking careful aim again. His jaws were clenched, his eyes almost like slits while he steadied the gun with both hands in absolute concentration. There was something in his face that made her realise this was not the first time he had had a man at the end of his gun. She peeped out from behind the corner of the sarcophagus. There was a movement behind the gnarled, twisted trunk of an olive tree about twenty yards from them, a tuft of hair or a hand perhaps, and a flash of steel in the sunlight. A shout followed a shot in quick succession. She turned to look at Colin. The deadly glint still lingered in his eyes. If this was the end, she was dammed if she was going to meet it lying down with ants crawling all over her face! Carefully she raised herself and peeped above the stone plinth which gave her cover. Nearby, a rifle was lying by the side of the tree not far from the figure of a man sprawled in its shade. More shots could be heard in the distance, coming nearer. She looked again at the lying, motionless figure, her mind made up. Once she was sure there was no movement from him, she began to crawl slowly in the direction of the rifle. She crept forward, close to the ground, her eye fixed on the rifle. Colin only now noticed her.

'What the f…k are you doing?' he shouted. 'Come back, you fool, get back at once!'

Swiftly, she grabbed the rifle and cast a quick glance at the slumped man to see if there was any reaction. He continued to stare motionless at the sunny sky. Her eyes focused on his face, she crawled towards him and jerked at the ammunition belt. It made him tip to one side and a mouthful of blood ran down his chin. She pulled again and the belt opened loose. That was a piece of luck; she didn't think she'd have the courage to undo the fastening. Another shot whizzed past; someone must have spotted her. Crouching, she ran back to Colin, trailing the belt on the ground. He was beside himself with rage.

'You stupid bitch!' he grabbed her, looked as if he was about to slap her, then shook her so violently that her teeth chattered. 'He could've been alive! You could have got yourself killed! Jesus!'

'Leave me alone!' She shook herself free from his grip as a shot hit the sarcophagus with a whine. With her back against the wall, she loaded the rifle with the cartridges from the belt, grateful to her cousin who had taught her to shoot, then very slowly and carefully peered to survey the scene before her. Another shot was fired – it must have come from Colin. Then she saw her adversary. A man was leaping towards them between the ruined tombs. She fired and missed. 'Shit!' she swore aloud. Now that she had something positive to do, her fears and prayers were forgotten. Colin fired again. She saw one of their men standing by a hole in the wall which surrounded the necropolis; she watched him take aim, fire and hide instantly behind the wall. Another series of shots followed. There was a movement to her right. She took aim, fired and watched closely for further movement by the sarcophagus nearest to theirs. Instead, there was a shout. Something did move – a dirty shirt wrapped on the barrel of a rifle appeared above the sarcophagus nearest to theirs. Someone was waving frantically and shouting 'Stop!' She looked at Colin.

'Is he surrendering? I'll cover you.'

Colin was already up, moving slowly in the direction of the shirt, gun at the ready. She too kept her rifle aimed at it. A dark, swarthy man stood, half hidden by the wall of the sarcophagus, waving the shirt. He shouted something which sounded like 'No shoot!'

'Come out!' shouted Colin. 'Hands up, nice and easy.'

Hesitantly, a dishevelled man with a grazed forehead, dripping with blood, moved into the clearing between the sarcophagi which was now in full sunlight, hands raised above his head, one of which was still holding the rifle with the shirt.

'Drop it!'

Whether the man understood English or not, Colin's gesture was unmistakable. The rifle was dropped with a clatter on the stony ground.

'Here,' Colin gestured to one of his men standing by. 'Take him down.'

He stooped to pick up the rifle when a bullet whizzed by. If he had remaining standing, it would have gone right through him. The two men, the guard and the prisoner fell to the ground instantly and tried to hide behind the sarcophagus. Colin ran for cover crouching and reached Joanna just as another bullet hit the sarcophagus with a wham. She took aim and fired in the direction of the shot, but it was a token gesture and she couldn't see anyone being hit. The quality of silence which followed was as tense as a tightly coiled spring kept immovable only by the pressure of a thumb. Joanna had her finger on the trigger, perspiration pouring over her face in the now oppressive heat. Her feet, now out of the shade, were painfully sunburnt. Above and around them, cicadas droned steadily, oblivious to the events around them, steadily pursuing their own lives on the nearest carob tree.

There was a sudden movement and, in that instant, she saw a man crouching behind a sarcophagus. She gasped.

'Colin,' she whispered, 'it's him. The man who killed David! The taxi driver.'

Colin shifted his position and looked in the direction pointed by Joanna, trying to pick out the man between the sarcophagi and the pattern of shade and light thrown by the carob trees. There was a tick in his jaw.

'Just leave it to me,' he said tensely, carefully taking aim.

There was a shot, but not from Colin. It came from the man who was guarding the prisoner. Joanna saw the taxi driver run towards the hole in the wall. Colin fired and missed. She ignored Colin and fired. The bullet must have missed him again. The man ran through the hole and disappeared. Colin ran after him. Joanna also got up and tried to run, but her bare feet and a general feeling of weakness delayed her considerably. She saw the taxi driver plunge rather than run downhill towards the water's edge like a mountain goat. Colin kept shooting, obviously missing because the man never stopped. Joanna climbed down enough to see him wade into the water towards a small boat tied to a rock. Out in the bay, sailing towards them, was *Jemima*. The man continued to fire sporadically with one hand while he tried to untie the boat with the other. Joanna opened fire from her vantage point. Suddenly he doubled up. He was hit at last but recovered himself sufficiently to look up. Whatever he saw made him stop, as if he couldn't believe his eyes. Then, very slowly he raised his arm in a gesture which could be accusing or asking for help. She followed his gaze. It stopped at *Jemima* which was by now very near the shore. There, on the bridge, she could see the fat man watching the proceedings. He was alone, leaning on the balustrade, smoking the ubiquitous cigar. Once aware of the taxi driver's gesture, he shook his head as if disowning the man. The taxi driver shouted hoarsely in a language she couldn't understand, but this much she realised – they knew each other, though the fat man was trying to appear as if he didn't, and the taxi driver was accusing him of something. She was about to fire again when she saw Colin, who had wasted no time and was already by the water's edge. He came in to full view, holding the gun with both hands. A volley of shots followed. Then events moved so quickly that it seemed to Joanna that they happened in two blinks of an eye. The taxi driver lurched forward, grabbed the gunwale of the little boat and fell into it head first. His legs continued to move as if he tried to get into it, then his hands slipped and his head slid back into the water as if bowing in prayer. The boat, released from his grip, swung away like a tethered animal.

At the same time, more shots were fired, in the direction of the *Jemima*, hitting the fishing rods on the bridge. One of them broke, hitting the fat man on the head as he was leaning over the pulpit to get a better view. He lost his balance and fell overboard, his hands slipping down the side of the hull before he hit the water. He sank like a stone without making a sound. Joanna waited with baited breath for him to reappear on the surface, but there was no sign of him anywhere. The decks of the boat were curiously deserted. There was no one about to raise the alarm. The man disappeared – just like that. Joanna sat down on a warm rock, holding her rifle. Nobody noticed him going overboard and she was too far away to raise the alarm. All the men were busy on the shore. She saw several of *Jemima*'s crew, guns in hand, heading towards the taxi driver. His body was clearly visible in the shallow water, and if there was any movement now it was due to the gentle swell of the sea. Joanna looked out further to sea to mark the spot again where the fat man had fallen in. Already she had difficulty in finding it, as if nature was trying to obliterate all traces of him as quickly as possible.

She had no time, however, to ponder at the swiftness and loneliness of his end. Her attention was diverted by the sound of more shots being fired in the distance. The commotion was now centred around the dark-hulled yacht, *Ali Baba*. Two speedboats from *Jemima* were circling round her as shots were fired. After a while, yells of 'No shoot!' and 'Stop shoot!' carried across the water. Joanna wondered what had brought about the quick surrender and looked around. From the eastern end of the Kekova Roads, a grey patrol boat was coming towards them at great speed, white foam at her bow, two diagonal lines of wake at her beam. There were men at the guns and men in uniform lined up on the deck. So that was that: the rest was just a mopping up operation.

Joanna now became aware of having sat on the hot rock in full sunshine for some time. Her head was throbbing. She put the rifle and the ammunition belt by her side, wrapped Colin's shirt tightly round her and wondered where to lie down without getting scratched by the thistles. Listlessly, she watched the men with whom she had come in the speedboat bring two bodies and place them in the boat. Two more men came along the footpath. She recognised one, having seen him in the necropolis, now escorting a handcuffed prisoner. He pushed him to the water's edge and into the speedboat. The crew started the engine and motored towards *Jemima*. Then more footsteps, this time behind her. It was Colin.

'Joanna,' he whispered. She looked straight into his eyes. They were no longer steely blue but a sort of liquid gold. She remembered they had turned that colour when she had nursed him after his injury in the storm. 'You are quite a girl, you know! Where did you learn to shoot?' His voice was unnatural, as if something was constricting his throat.

'My cousin taught me. He was quite keen on shooting, clay pigeons, that kind of thing. I'm not very good, I'm afraid, never kept it up. Still, I did manage to hit the taxi driver, didn't I?' She couldn't help sounding pleased. But Colin wasn't listening. Before she realised what was happening, he had gathered her in his arms and was kissing her fiercely. She gasped, but made no movement as the celestial choir filled her whole being, singing 'He cares, he cares!'

'Oh Colin,' she sighed after a time, at a loss for words. Should she tell him she had loved him for as long as she had known him? Should she ask why it took him so long to fall in love with her? What did it matter? In spite of her exhaustion, she was kissing him back and he laughed at the warmth of her response. She was aware of his body pressing against hers, and nearly cried with pain as the belt of the gun holster cut into her. He let her go. Together they hailed the speedboat which was just starting in the direction of *Jemima*. Colin, however, had a different idea.

'I need to go to the yacht over there,' he said and pointed to *Ali Baba*. The man obediently changed course. As they climbed on board, they were met by two men from *Jemima* in the cockpit.

'Everything okay here?' asked Colin.

One man, obviously in charge, nodded. 'Just waiting for the patrol boat to take them away, sir,' he said, pointing towards the men in the cabin with his chin. He took Colin to the side, lowering his voice so that Joanna could only catch '... in pretty bad shape, if you get my meaning, sir.' Could he be talking about Simon? she wondered, stricken.

She went down to the main cabin. Two Turks were sitting listlessly by the table, resting their foreheads on their handcuffed hands. Clasped in this way, they looked as if they were praying. As she entered the cabin, only one of them looked up. She recognised him with a start – the stone mason from the island of Marmara who had showed her and David the marble washbasins for the Turkish baths. That explained a lot about *that* so-called accident, when they were set adrift outside the harbour. They were all in on it. Past history now. Whether the man recognised her or not she could not tell; his face was impassive.

Simon worried her more. She went forward to the fore cabin. The door was slightly ajar and she could see a V-shaped bed where Simon was lying on one of its "arms". His face was one huge, purple bruise, his eyes closed, though he probably couldn't open them anyway they were so dreadfully swollen and black. Her gaze fell on his hands. They must have tied him up tightly and now his wrists were swollen in huge wields like bicycle tyres. He was snoring loudly. As she pushed the door further, she bumped into a doctor who was standing over him, preparing a dressing.

'Excuse me,' said Joanna.

The doctor made a sign, asking her to leave. She could see there was no room for her in that tiny cabin.

'Will he be all right?' she whispered, horrified at the sight of the frightful mess that was once the languid, unruffled Simon.

'I think so, given time. Right now, he's under sedation. He's been …' he said, looking for a word to describe the dreadful beating which had reduced Simon to his present state, '… badly treated.'

By now there was a commotion in the cockpit. They both looked up when Brenda's shrill voice reached them.

'Where is he? I want to see him!'

'That must be the other girl' murmured the doctor to no one in particular.

'That's right. That's his girlfriend.'

'Keep her away, will you? He must be kept quiet at all costs.'

Joanna went to the cockpit, feeling very tired. Would this day never end?

'Hello, Brenda. How are you?'

'Where is he?' Brenda was dishevelled, no make- up, hair hanging limply, but not visibly harmed. Joanna didn't dare to think what picture she herself presented in Colin's dirty shirt.

'He's in the fore cabin and the doctor is with him. He's alright, but he mustn't be disturbed.'

'Why, what's happened to him?' her voice was unnaturally high and loud. She stared wildly into the cabin.

Joanna nearly told her, but bit her tongue just in time.

'Well, he's alive, and that's the main thing. He'll be alright. Right now, he's been sedated, he's sleeping it off. Why don't you stay here with me here? He mustn't be disturbed.'

But Brenda pushed past her and managed to look over the doctor's shoulder. She drew back, screaming. 'Oh my God, what have they done to him!'

She rushed towards the handcuffed men and dug her nails into the face of the one sitting nearest. He raised his handcuffed hands in an attempt to shield himself. She tore at his hair as Joanna grabbed her by the arm and called out to Colin for help. They both dragged her back into the cockpit.

'Murderers, bastards, swine!' She struggled with them, screaming hysterically.

The doctor rushed out, holding a syringe while they tried to hold her as she made another lunge towards the men in the cabin, crying and laughing hysterically. While Colin and Joanna were making superhuman efforts to keep her still, the doctor managed to give her an injection. After a while, the medicine began to work, and her screams subsided to hoarse whimpers.

'You'd better stay with her, Joanna,' said Colin. 'I need to go see to things.' He stepped into the speedboat waiting for him, gripping his bad arm again.

Joanna sat by Brenda, saying 'There, there!' mechanically in a calm voice, deathly tired and exhausted. Her mind was in a thick haze in which nothing, but nothing mattered any more. Through this fog she registered the stretcher party taking Simon away with the doctor in tow. Another speedboat, or maybe the same but now empty, came to pick up the prisoners. By this time Brenda was asleep, her head in Joanna's lap, snoring slightly. She wasn't comfortable nursing her, but it didn't matter, not in the least; nothing mattered as long as nobody disturbed the fog and nobody asked questions.

They were helped to the waiting speedboat. The man who was steering looked familiar. Ah yes, he had been guarding the prisoners when she and Colin had arrived and then spoke to Colin. As the speedboat made its way towards *Jemima*, clouds gathered, hiding the sun. Joanna shivered, wrapping Colin's shirt tightly around her. The man noticed her gesture and nodded towards the clouds.

'Weather's breaking up,' he said. 'Summer here always ends like this – suddenly, like.'

Chapter 18

Since the eventful day of the shooting, Joanna and Colin were never alone. They and two men from the crew of *Jemima* volunteered to sail *Zainda* back to the charterers in Athens, taking the shortest route. Simon and Brenda remained in Rhodes, installed in his yacht which she knew only as *Ali Baba*. It had been returned to Simon after many formalities, but by the time Joanna left, he hadn't got round to painting out the name and replacing it with his own.

After that, it was simple. Together they checked into a hotel Colin knew in Athens on Omonoia Square. It felt like the most natural thing to do. By that time, she managed to get some information about him, such as the fact he clearly wasn't a car salesman as Simon had said but an officer in a special detective branch of the police force. He told her in a joking way, but she could tell he was serious, that she mustn't ask too many questions about his job, that he wasn't able to discuss it with other people, but he'd tell her all he could in his own time.

'I lead a very unsettled life. Here today, there tomorrow. I can't tell a soul where I'm going, don't know myself half the time. Now you know why I don't want us to get too involved. You deserve a better man. Well, I held out for as long as I could, trying not to fall under your spell and now look at us. It's not fair on any girl. You don't deserve the only life I could offer you.'

'As long as you come back to me, it wouldn't matter. Weren't you ever serious about anyone?'

He drew away from her, lit a cigarette and glanced at his watch. He was not looking at her when he spoke. 'I was married once. It didn't work.'

'I see.' She knew from the experience of her own marriage how it felt. At the same time, she was reminded of her wish back in Turkey when they watched the falling stars. Perhaps the gods were out to punish her after all. This involvement with Colin wasn't going to be easy. Her love for him seemed so hopeless, so insignificant.

'Let's take each day as it comes,' she suggested shyly. He was still withdrawn, looking not at her but at the ceiling, saying nothing. 'So, you don't want us to get too involved,' she said, stressing the phrase he used. 'Is that right?'

'You might put it that way.'

Was he going to disappear from her life for good after all? Well, she wasn't going to push him into anything he might regret. That way it just wouldn't work at all. 'I'm going home tomorrow,' she said wearily. 'Will I see you in London?'

She tried to make the question sound casual and got up to turn the shower on, not waiting for an answer. Her tears mingled with the water in the shower. That was it then, she'd just have to live with it. Trust her to pick a man who thought love would only fetter him and was about to bolt at the very thought of serious involvement.

She came back to the room, shaking her hair and rubbing herself with a towel. He was still lying in bed. He stretched out his hand, held her by the waist, playfully traced the outline of the bikini on her tanned body and made her kneel beside him. His hands cupped her face and he kissed her gently on the eyelids.

'You have beautiful eyes,' he murmured. His hands slid down her body and he kissed her breasts. 'You are beautiful.' He pushed her away abruptly, almost angrily, and got up quickly. 'I just wish you weren't. Well, I must be going. I'm late already.'

So that was it. Not much of a goodbye.

'But you promised to tell me more about those men in the Kekova Roads,' she protested, not wanting him to go, trying to detain him a bit longer, her curiosity aroused, so many questions still unanswered. 'What was it all about?'

'Why, drugs basically. We were trying to break up a drugs smuggling syndicate.'

'So, they were smuggling drugs? Is that all you can say?' She noticed he was using his left arm more freely.

'How is your arm now?' she asked, watching him dress in silence.

'Fine,' he said curtly, and his face darkened. 'You don't have to remind me what a bloody fool I've been ...' he broke off. 'I'm sorry, darling. You were terrific, I must be going now.' He kissed her lightly on the forehead. 'So long,' he murmured as he opened the door.

'Bye,' she whispered, raising her hand to wave, watching him disappear down the corridor. Slowly she closed the door and only then realised she had nothing on. The empty room stared back, matching her mood. She sat down on the unmade bed and let her mind drift to those last days of the holiday.

She remembered getting to *Jemima* shortly after Simon was carried in on a stretcher. Brenda was taken to the cabin below to sleep off the drug the doctor had given her. The men put down Simon on the floor of the deck to prepare a bed for him. As Joanna moved towards him, Simon woke up and appeared to look through his swollen eyelids past her, at the door leading from the deck to the saloon. Joanna followed his gaze. There, in the doorway, stood the stunner, but this time there was none of the careful poise and self-assurance. Her face was contorted in a grimace, her eyes darted from side to side as she watched the comings and goings of the crew. She looked scared, scared out of her wits. That expression summed her up, thought Joanna. The woman cast a furtive glance at Simon's prostrate figure and was about to move away when a movement from him arrested her. He raised his head and pointed at her with his horribly swollen hand, at the same time trying to say something. The sound was inarticulate and he fell back, exhausted. The woman looked closely at him, then took a step back, her eyes wide with horror.

'No, Simon, no … I didn't know… I never intended …' She shook her head violently, turned around abruptly, and disappeared into the saloon.

At that moment, the doctor reappeared, followed by Colin, and bent down over Simon who lay seemingly lifeless.

'What is it? What's worrying him? How come she knows him?' Joanna asked Colin, puzzled.

'She was married to him once,' he whispered in her ear.

Joanna tried to work out the implications of this information. So what, she asked herself. So now he's got Brenda and she had the fat man with his cruiser and the luxury life that went with it. 'Have they found the fat man yet?' she asked aloud. 'I saw him fall into the water and disappear.'

'You saw that, did you?' Colin's interest was aroused. 'It very much looks he has drowned. They're looking for him now.'

'But what has Simon against her?' she persisted. 'He looked as if he was accusing her of something.'

'Can't you see?' he sounded impatient. 'She was involved with a man who ran a drugs syndicate. It kind of rubs off. Oh, never mind, Joanna, let me take you back to your cabin, you need a rest.'

Joanna badly wanted to know how he had become involved with her, too. Was she looking for a break from the fat man's attention, a lover on the side? But she thought better than to ask. From that moment, however, her attitude to Simon had changed. That cold man deserved her sympathy in spite of his supercilious manner.

Simon's recovery was slow, but he refused to stay in the hospital once pronounced out of danger. Joanna and Brenda were already on *Ali Baba* which was now moored in Rhodes harbour, next to *Jemima* and *Zainda*.

Once out of hospital, Simon insisted he was perfectly alright and able to look after himself, though it was plain he could hardly walk on his swollen feet and was still in pain. From time to time, his face would set in a grimace he tried to control but not very successfully. Also, he had to be fed as his fingers were stiff and swollen and he could not grip a knife or a fork. Brenda insisted it was her job, crooning and talking as if to a baby. Joanna could hardly tolerate those scenes and cringed at the thought of meals together. She gave up trying to understand what Simon saw in Brenda in the first place. Perhaps it was the complete contrast between her and his first wife? Joanna heard all the emotional outbursts from Brenda, ranging from 'If only I could lay my hands on the bastards who did this!' to 'Oh my poor darling!' From time to time, Simon showed signs of exasperation. He would then send Brenda on an errand and call in Joanna, asking her to rub his wrists and ankles with an ointment left by the doctor. His face bore a deep wound hidden by the dressing. Once the stitches were out, he left it uncovered. Joanna thought this most inconsiderate of him as she could not help being drawn in a kind of compulsive revulsion to the red, unhealed gash, while dutifully rubbing his wrists and ankles. Although he always lay still and silent, staring at the ceiling and never at her, it was obvious it was giving him some relief.

'I owe you thanks,' he said one day, breaking the long, habitual silence, his eyes never leaving the ceiling. Brenda had been sent away to do the shopping and they were alone in the cabin. 'They told me you were very brave.'

'Not really,' Joanna muttered, confused. 'I did what anyone would do in my place.'

He nodded in agreement, as if it was all part of the job he had advertised. But Joanna felt there was some sympathy between them now, an understanding (friendship would have been too big word) which flourished on silence, as if words might dispel its timid appearance. They never spoke of the recent events though Joanna wondered what had happened the night they caught him. David was never mentioned either.

'You know,' Simon was speaking, still looking at the ceiling while Joanna continued to rub in the ointment. It took a moment to realise there was something on his mind. 'They hit me in … my private parts. I wonder if they've injured me for life.'

So that's what was worrying him. She shifted her activity to the other foot.

'Don't worry,' she said as she tried to find words of comfort. 'It's never permanent.' She had no idea if it was true or not, but there was no point in keeping him worried.

'Hope you're right. Always wanted a son, y'know.'

A scraping sound announced the arrival of Brenda making her way along the gangplank. 'Don't tell Brenda,' he said in the same even voice, not shifting his gaze.

Two days later, Joanna boarded *Zainda*, ready to sail back to the charterers in Athens. When she said goodbye to Simon, he responded with an air of the usual polite boredom. Only when she picked up her kitbag and was about to walk away did he give her a hug, kissed her on both cheeks, then turned abruptly away and hobbled back to the cabin before she could see his face. Brenda blew her nose and said something about keeping in touch. 'I might phone you when I get back; I never write,' she said. Joanna saw her standing forlornly in the cockpit, waving as *Zainda* sailed past the column with the deer which marked the entrance to Rhodes harbour.

*

After her return from Athens, it was time to pick up the pieces. She finally managed to find a small flat in Ealing at a reasonable rent, mainly due to its bad state of repairs. All those rolls of wallpaper, the pots of paint and their pervading smell urged her to finish decorating as soon as possible.

The telephone had only just been installed when she had a call from her friend Marjorie who was full of gossip. Majorca had been ever so lovely, so was the hotel, just lovely. She hinted at the possibility of getting engaged to Geoff, the lovely guy she had spent the holiday with.

Apparently, Joanna's old job was hers if she wanted it. They never found a permanent replacement for her after all. That was alright then. There wasn't much money left in the kitty once she had bought things for the flat and paid the solicitor's expenses. She was a free woman again.

The thought of freedom reverberated in her head like hollow laughter. Now was the time to pull herself together, go out and mix with people again. It wouldn't do to be on her own; too many thoughts pressing heavily in her mind. She had to build a new life for herself. Perhaps join a gym, get fit and healthy, especially as she had recently felt her body was changing, which left her puzzled.

The telephone rang. It was Colin.

'Joanna, is that you? How are you? When can I see you?'

If she had entertained any thoughts of playing hard to get, they evaporated quickly.

'How did you find my telephone number?' To her great annoyance, her heart was beating fast. She was supposed to keep her distance.

Colin laughed. 'I have my ways and means. You haven't answered my question. 'When and where?'

'We could meet in town, I suppose. I'm afraid my flat is full of paint pots, rubbish and no furniture.' She rummaged through her brain thinking of any nearby pubs and drew a blank. 'How about Harrods?

We could meet in one of the cafeterias. The parking's good, and I could buy a few things there.' *If I can afford them,* she added silently.

'OK. Meet you in an hour. Second floor.'

She sat holding the receiver, now dead, staring at it reflectively. *So that's how things are going to be with Colin from now on.* A hurried goodbye, no word from him for weeks, then 'meet you in an hour'. She looked at her paint-stained hands and wondered if it would be difficult to put him out of her mind and her life for good. This state of affairs wasn't going to get her anywhere, this wondering whether he cares, whether he'll keep in touch, constantly hoping to hear from him again. Hope could be a killer. Better stand on your own two feet, my girl, depend on no one.

Nevertheless, she changed into a blue dress which matched her eyes and was nibbling a salad in the cafeteria when she saw him. Colin. Her heart missed a beat, her new-formed resolution melting away as if it had never been. He looked tanned and handsome and slightly out of place in these tame surroundings as he moved between the tables with the agility of a jungle cat. His face broke into a smile the moment he spotted her.

'Joanna!' He sat beside her, took her in his arms and kissed her, a long, deep kiss which took her breath away. He drew back and looked at her for a long time without speaking. 'God, I've missed you,' he said at last. 'Promise you won't stir while I get myself something to eat. I only had a drink on the plane.'

'When did you arrive?'

'A couple of hours ago. I rang from the airport.'

She smiled. This was not the Colin she knew till now, the one who acted as if he hated finding himself attracted to her.

He was back with a tray. 'I got thinking,' he said, stirring his coffee. 'After you left Athens. What a fool I've been to let you go. I suppose it was a question of pride, stupid pride. You see, I couldn't forgive myself for that accident in the storm. Me, me, rescued by a mere slip of a girl! It was hard to take. I was furious with myself and I suppose I took it out on you. Will I be forgiven?' He cast a long, apologetic look.

Joanna shook herself with disbelief. This simply wasn't the Colin she knew. This one was much nicer. Colin continued as if he had rehearsed his speech and was going to say what he wanted to say without interruptions. 'And then I knew, after that shooting in Kekova, what I suppose I had thought for a long time – that you were the girl for me. But I had to fight the feeling, I couldn't forget my wounded pride, it sort of stood in the way. Then, one night, after you'd left, I thought of you alone in London. Maybe there was somebody else in your life now? When I thought of that boy David, the way he fell for you. God! He caused me some jealous moments, I can tell you.'

Joanna opened her eyes wide. Colin jealous! And all that time he had acted as if he never noticed anything. *Now* he tells me.

'I wouldn't have been surprised if there was somebody in your life now – a girl like you. I couldn't bear the thought I'd lost you, though I dare say it would've served me right. I took the next available plane to London. There isn't anyone, is there? I don't have to tell you how much you mean to me.'

Joanna looked at him, so changed, so different. Any thoughts of playing hard to get evaporated. 'No, there isn't.'

'Then you feel the same way about me as you did in Athens?'

'I suppose so. I mean, I do.'

'That's alright then.' His confession out of the way, he was looking more like his old self again. She could see it was not in his nature to apologise, or express emotions such as "I love you". That wouldn't be his style.

'What have you been doing with yourself?' he asked, eating quickly as though he had only just noticed his heaped plate.

Joanna told him about the flat and her job. 'And you, how long are you here for?'

'Don't know. Few weeks maybe, until something crops up.'

Was the "something" a euphemism for another assignment like the one she had witnessed? Presumably it was – that was his job. His hand strayed and held hers while he ate, as if to make sure she wouldn't run away.

'Have you come straight from Rhodes? How are Simon and Brenda, and things generally?' she asked.

'Simon and Brenda are still together. They send their regards.'

'What happened to the others?'

'The others? You mean the men we caught? They're awaiting trial for drug smuggling. Mind you, the sentences for that are pretty stiff in Turkey, so we shan't be seeing them for some time.'

'How did you know about them in the first place? Why did you need us girls to sail on *Zainda*? Were we some kind of a decoy, pretending we were just a couple of tourists who had hired a yacht for a holiday?' Questions were pouring out of her now.

'Well, we knew there was a drug smuggling ring operating through stolen yachts. So, when Simon reported the theft of his yacht, we decided to stay with him, keep a careful watch. We didn't think it would go so drastically awry until David got killed. We thought we'd be there first. Anyway, to go back to your question. Yes, a decoy, I suppose. Everything had to be as normal as possible not to arouse suspicions. That's why we wanted girls in the party and we got you and Brenda to join in.'

Joanna repressed a feeling of resentment for having been used as a prop to create the impression of normality on a cruising yacht. Now she knew why the terms were so generous.

'So, Simon and David knew all the time?' she said aloud.

'David knew a little, but Simon was in on it, yes. Anyway, we also wanted to draw in Michaelis, the fat man as you call him. We knew he was involved in drugs, he was the head of the syndicate, in fact. What better way to do it than through a woman. You saw her on *Jemima*, you know, Simon's ex. Not a bad looking woman, quite striking in a way,' he added, too casually for Joanna's liking. She cast him a long, searching look.

'It was my job to lure Michaelis to *Jemima* which was controlled by us,' Colin continued. 'He was fond of deep-sea fishing. Fortunately, the engine on *his* cruiser had to be repaired. You may have seen her; she was moored in Istanbul.'

Joanna nodded. That must have been the cruiser with the Panamanian flag, emitting those horrid fumes.

'A piece of luck, those engines breaking down,' continued Colin, a note in his voice betraying an implication that luck played a small part in that incident. 'We were able to invite them both to *Jemima*, and keep a watch on him, to see if he might slip up, incriminate himself. Until now, we had nothing on him, you see. Quite a clever chap, always managed to keep clear of trouble. We had our suspicions, of course, but that's all they were – suspicions, nothing tangible. The woman was a great help ...'

At the mention of the woman, Joanna's eyes hardened involuntarily. Colin grinned, and patted her hand. 'Don't look like that. It wasn't all roses. Still ...' A smile lingered round his lips at the memory while he pressed Joanna closer to him. 'All in a day's work, as they say. Anyway, as it turned out, the gang knew about us, took us by surprise. We didn't expect our cover to be blown so soon. But we managed to find their drop points for drugs and money. We were about to warn David and Simon but came too late. David discovered them in Loryma Bay, had caught them in the act. They were either picking up drugs or money or both from their drop point when he saw them.'

'David never said anything to me,' interrupted Joanna.

'No, that was the irony of it, he didn't know what they were up to. He thought they were after the dinghy. You were with him practically to the end, weren't you? He died soon after we got him to *Jemima*. Poor kid, he was very much in love with you, kept asking for you, I've been told.' He glanced at her, but Joanna kept her head low. She didn't want to speak about David with anyone. Colin continued.

'By that time, we had found out there was another drop point in Xera Cove, you know, the place where *Zainda* was anchored.'

'Oh, where were the drop points?' she asked eagerly, the events of that night coming to her with fresh force.

'Why, in the ruins, further up, past that ruined church. There was a dry cistern there, rather obvious really once you knew where to look. We were busy pretending we were cruising for pleasure and what with Michaelis around we couldn't maintain radio contact. That man was everywhere. We didn't expect his boys to come out that night. Thought it might be the one after. They caught Simon as he paddled around their boat. There was no need to beat him up, he wasn't armed or anything. Rather primitive, those people, a bit on edge by that time. The taxi driver gave Michaelis away. His fatal accident was very fortunate,' he added in a lightly mocking voice. Joanna wondered if it was a real accident. She remembered thinking at the time it was an extraordinary way that fishing rod had hit him on the head, uncanny really, and the curious absence of people when he drowned. No attempt of search or rescue. It certainly was fortunate – that "accident" had saved everybody enormous trouble.

'Colin …' she sounded anxious, 'that taxi driver, when he took us to Troy …' She wondered how to phrase the question without giving Brenda away. He nodded with understanding.

'If it's about him and Brenda, I can tell you we kept a watch on them. Actually, we were worried about Brenda, kept her under surveillance. She didn't give anything away, just acted stupid. Simon doesn't know about it.'

Joanna was relieved.

'Where is the Michaelis woman now?' she asked, not looking at Colin.

'Don't know. She wasn't implicated in his business, simply there for his money and a good time, happy to have found herself a sugar daddy. I don't doubt for a moment she'll find another rich man soon enough, that is, if she hasn't done so already.'

He put his arm around her, then let go abruptly and started playing with the fork.

'Do you think we … that is … you and me … seeing as I'm not able to stay away from you … could get together?'

Joanna marvelled at the transformation. She had never seen him like this, almost humble in his uncertainty. Forget the hard-to-get bit.

'We could give it a try.'

He pressed her hard and kissed her, a long kiss that made her toes melt.

They were so absorbed in each other they hardly noticed the cafeteria had slowly filled with customers. An elderly woman made her way toward their table. She put the tray down and looked with dismay at the tea spilled in the saucer. Her expression deepened when she looked up, her eyes resting on the embracing couple. Joanna caught her look of disapproval. She disengaged herself gently from Colin's embrace, took his hand, placed it carefully on his knee and put on a posh accent: 'There. This won't do, da-h-ling. Not in Harrods.'

*

They continued to meet whenever Colin was in town. Finally, Joanna, her suspicions confirmed, decided it was time to take the bull by the horns next time they met.

'Colin, I need to tell you something.' Deep breath. 'I'm going to have David's baby.'

'What!' followed by a long silence. Colin lit a cigarette. Joanna kept biting her lip. Finally: 'Are you sure it's not mine?'

'I am. We took precautions. That was unplanned.'

Another long silence. 'So. You'd been at it all that time on the boat?

'No, of course not!' said Joanna, adamant. 'It was a spur of the moment thing, just before he was shot.'

'What just once? And now this?'

Her recent conversation with Brenda flashed through Joanna's mind. Brenda had had a lot to say on the subject when they spoke on the phone. 'Didn't you take any precautions then?'

'It was all rather sudden. Spur of the moment thing.'

'Jesus, it just shows you,' she sighed. 'Just one night stand and bang. How's Colin taken it? Have you told him yet?'

Well, she was telling him now.

'It does happen. Has happened.'

Silence continued. He lit another cigarette from the stub of the previous one. Joanna was torn between defiance, the protective instinct coming to the fore, and the yawning gap of losing Colin. Finally, he stirred himself.

'Come here.' He took her in his arms and kissed her, a long, tender kiss. 'You mean too much to me,' he murmured. 'I'll take care of you.'

What followed, however, was not much taking care. Good intentions were one thing, reality another. Colin was posted abroad. He kept in touch by phone and several postcards bearing exotic postage stamps were dropped on her doormat.

Finally, Joanna was delivered of a baby girl, with David's pensive eyes and a radiant smile. She left a message on Colin's phone, telling